He

"*Heart Strings* is poignant, punny, and preciously sweet. Fairbanks effortlessly tells a story of love and loss that makes you believe in the power of second chances."

—**Lana Ferguson,** *USA Today* **bestselling author of** *The Nanny*

"Second chance always gets me right in the feels, but add to that a lush Irish setting, an independent woman who thinks she doesn't need love, and a hot, sweet musician who still writes every song for her? I MEAN. Ivy Fairbanks has done it again—I'll travel to Galway with her for as many books as she'll let me!"

—**Alicia Thompson,** *USA Today* **bestselling author of** *Love in the Time of Serial Killers*

"Ivy Fairbank's *Heart Strings* is for all of us who adore second-chance romance books filled with yearning, tenderness, and sizzling chemistry. Cielo and Aidan's love story is one that will stay with me for a long, long time."

—**Hannah Bonam-Young,** *USA Today* **bestselling author of** *Out on a Limb*

"*Heart Strings* has a gorgeous setting, second-chance angst, complicated family dynamics, and at the center of it all, a beautiful love story. I loved watching Cielo let her walls down for Aidan—who is a TOP-TIER romance hero—and learn to lean on others. Cielo's fear of opening her heart again and letting people into it, not just in the good times but in times of uncertainty as well, is deftly written and deeply relatable. I was rooting hard for Lo and Aidan with every page."

—**Sarah Hogle, author of** *You Deserve Each Other*

Praise for *Morbidly Yours*

"Sweet and spicy and fabulous . . . Ivy Fairbanks is a terrific addition to the romance genre!"

—**Abby Jimenez, #1** *New York Times* **bestselling author of** *Just for the Summer*

"Fans of Abby Jimenez will love this fresh, tender, and deliciously spicy romance."

—**Paige Toon, international bestselling author of** *Seven Summers*

"[A] charming romance . . . Poignant and heartwarming, this is a quirky love story you won't forget."

—*Kirkus Reviews* **(starred review)**

"A delightful, wonderfully disastrous romp through love. Fans of the marriage-of-convenience trope will swoon—as did I!"

—**Ashley Herring Blake,** *USA Today* **bestselling author of** ***Delilah Green Doesn't Care***

"Adorable! *Morbidly Yours* is equal parts playful and poignant, as satisfyingly spicy as it is sweet. I dare you not to fall in love with Lark and Callum, an endearing, quirky grumpy/sunshine pairing who couldn't be cuter."

—**Chloe Liese,** *USA Today* **bestselling author of** *Only When It's Us*

"The setting is unique, and Fairbanks is admirably frank about death and grieving. . . . Callum himself is an admirable hero, with impressive depths. . . . This will appeal to readers who don't mind some death in their 'til death do us part.'"

—*Publishers Weekly*

"With *Morbidly Yours*, debut author Ivy Fairbanks delivers an enchanting friends-to-lovers romantic dramedy. . . . Lark's and Callum's grief and reticence to fall in love anchor this lively first novel. Gaelic charm and a sweet, simmering romance, coupled with tender plot dilemmas driven by a well-drawn, small-town cast, lend hopeful buoyancy to the novel's more serious themes."

—*Shelf Awareness*

"With a fantastic Irish setting; sensitive portrayals of demisexuality, grief, and workplace misogyny; and a sexy friends-to-lovers romance, Fairbanks makes an excellent debut."

—*Library Journal*

"Offbeat and atmospheric, *Morbidly Yours* is the perfect escape for anyone who likes their romances to feature multidimensional characters, a cozy plot, and quick wit. It's utterly unique and I adored it."

—**Tarah DeWitt, author of** ***Funny Feelings***

"If lighter scares are your thing, then *Morbidly Yours* will tickle your skeleton bones. . . . Readers will feel the color returning to Callum's pale life as he gets to know Lark searching for his dream woman. The fact that she's an animator and he's well, not, further illustrates their differences. This sweet, fun read should become a classic."

—*Pittsburgh Post-Gazette*

"Kudos to Fairbanks for creating a world where heartache and romance can coexist. I laughed, I cried, I definitely swooned. Emotionally complex, wholly unique, and absolutely wonderful—if you haven't discovered Ivy Fairbanks already, you're in for a treat!"

—**Marissa Stapley,** *New York Times* **bestselling author of** *Lucky*

Heart Strings

ALSO BY IVY FAIRBANKS

Morbidly Yours

Heart Strings

IVY FAIRBANKS

G. P. PUTNAM'S SONS
New York

PUTNAM

— EST. 1838 —

G. P. Putnam's Sons

Publishers Since 1838

An imprint of Penguin Random House LLC

1745 Broadway, New York, NY 10019

penguinrandomhouse.com

Book design by Patrice Sheridan

Title Page image: Shutterstock

Library of Congress Cataloging-in-Publication Data

Names: Fairbanks, Ivy, author.

Title: Heart strings / Ivy Fairbanks.

Description: New York : G. P. Putnam's Sons, 2025.

Identifiers: LCCN 2025002155 (print) | LCCN 2025002156 (ebook) |

ISBN 9780593851883 (trade paperback) | ISBN 9780593851890 (ebook)

Subjects: LCGFT: Romance fiction. | Novels.

Classification: LCC PS3606.A348 H43 2025 (print) |

LCC PS3606.A348 (ebook) | DDC 813/.6—dc23/eng/20250117

LC record available at https://lccn.loc.gov/2025002155

LC ebook record available at https://lccn.loc.gov/2025002156

Printed in the United States of America

1st Printing

The authorized representative in the EU for product safety and compliance is Penguin Random House Ireland, Morrison Chambers, 32 Nassau Street, Dublin D02 YH68, Ireland. https://eu-contact.penguin.ie.

For Bobbie

Heart
Strings

PROLOGUE

Lo

MARCH

"IF YOU'RE BRINGING me out to the middle of nowhere to kill me, can you please hurry it up? I have study group at six." I shout to be heard over the wind and the rumble of the old scooter's engine.

My arms cinch around my cousin's waist as she leans the Lambretta into a sharp turn. The tiny woman has a death wish driving around on this thing.

"We're almost there," Lark says with a laugh.

The quaint, bunting-lined cobblestone streets of Galway's city center gave way to gentle hills and bright clusters of hawthorns twenty minutes ago, as her vintage scooter sped deeper into the Irish countryside. Spring is beautiful in Ireland, but when Lark asked me to hop on the back of her scooter to check out her wedding venue, I didn't expect it to be quite so far. I'd only allocated an hour and a half for the errand, marking it in my calendar app between the cadaver lab and study group.

"Besides," she adds in a light Texan drawl that reminds me of home, "if I wanted to get rid of you, Callum could make your body disappear way easier than I could."

I will never get over the fact that my bubbly, blonde cousin is engaged to an undertaker. A fantastic guy, if a bit on the quiet side. The last person you'd picture with someone who enthusiastically sings along to the *Beauty and the Beast* soundtrack. Proof that sometimes opposites do attract.

A dense row of birch trees has lined the last few miles of the road, and then it breaks. Sunlight warms my bronze skin as we turn at the gap between the trees and pass under an arch emblazoned with CASTLE TEACHAN.

"You'll lose your mind when you see this place." Lark's eyes bounce to mine from behind her helmet's visor.

A massive, multistory castle comes into view. Granite parapets and a pair of towers frame a huge carved wooden door. Wrought-iron lanterns line either side of a winding driveway and dozens of windows glint in the afternoon light. How many rooms does this place have?

Lark kills the engine and smacks a pink cowboy boot into the kickstand. I shake out my thick brunette bob. We crane our necks, following the rise of the building against the cloud-scattered sky. Okay, color me impressed.

"Really taking this whole Disney princess thing to the max, huh?" I ask with a wry smile.

"Maybe it's a little over the top." Lark's cowboy boots skip along the cobblestone drive. She circles a topiary by the fortified front door, seconds away from spontaneously breaking into song. I half-expect the china and furniture inside to pour out the double doors and join her in a musical number about the wonder of love. Chipper under normal circumstances, Lark's basically been on good-mood steroids since getting engaged. "But look how pretty it is! Imagine an autumn wedding here."

"Oh, it's beautiful. Just surprised me. I thought you were bringing me to some cottage or farmhouse converted into a rustic banquet hall. Something more Pinterest and less *Game of Thrones*. But this suits you."

"Castles are surprisingly affordable to rent for events here. Callum and I figured the wedding party and out-of-town guests could stay there together for the weekend of the ceremony."

I freeze. The best man's been living in London since he scored a record contract and unceremoniously left me behind two years ago.

"Aidan, too?" I ask, voice neutral as possible. It's been a while since the last time I said his name. Usually, if he must be mentioned, I refer to him as a charming anatomical euphemism.

"He is Cal's closest male friend," Lark reminds me. "Well, he's kind of his only male friend."

Aidan and I haven't set foot in the same room since the breakup, but I was prepared to deal with being in close proximity to him for a few hours. With all the dancing, toasting, and crisis-averting expected of me as the maid of honor, along with the presence of my mom and extended family, there would be plenty of distractions to get me through the night. I'd even hoped that I might be able to forget my ex was there at all, so long as he didn't grab a microphone and make a spectacle of himself. But I hadn't counted on having to endure a whole weekend together, staying in the same beautiful castle.

Lark halts her twirling to stare up at me with apologetic eyes. I can do this. For Lark. I have six months to build defenses around my heart before her wedding. Enough time to dig out a moat and stock it with hungry crocodiles, metaphorically speaking.

"A whole weekend with my ex? No problem." I stretch my mouth into a smile.

She grimaces. "Lo, I know this is asking a lot. You have veto power if it'll be too awkward. Family comes first, of course."

It's no secret that I feel some lingering bitterness toward my ex, the ostensibly romantic man who gave up the woman he supposedly loved without a fight.

Lark and Callum watched the romance blossom between me and Aidan. Thanks to all the time the four of us spent together, I know what Aidan means to Lark's introverted fiancé. The two are different in countless ways, but a shared love of trad music cemented their unlikely bond. Aidan might've destroyed my belief in him at the very end of our relationship, but he has always been a solid friend to them. And I'm not about to dictate whom Callum can and cannot invite to be part of his own wedding.

Lark's brows pinch together as she watches me mentally revisit the relationship we tiptoe around in conversation. She's worried about me, but I'm fine. Better than fine. The attending physician actually remembered my name yesterday during rounds *and* I found the perfect bridesmaid dress on sale that hugs my body in all the right places and loves my curves as much as I do. She doesn't have to worry about me. Fine is what I do.

"You can bring a plus-one, if you want."

"Eh." There have been hookups since Aidan. No relationships, or even situationships.

"What about that guy from your class? The one you said looks like Dev Patel."

"I was ovulating when I said that. He's nice, but I'd prefer not to make things weird by sleeping with anyone in my study group. And I don't want to bring some random dude to your wedding."

"Suit yourself," Lark says.

"I'll be too busy doing maid of honor duties, anyway. You'll have activities to keep everyone busy over this weekend, right?" I ask. With enough distractions, I can get through this.

"Of course. The castle has all kinds of stuff. Local whisky tastings and yoga classes and even falconry! Ain't that wild?"

Think I could train a bird to peck Aidan's eyes out? I don't say.

I love Lark, but we're at different places in our lives. Though we probably always have been, given our six-year age difference. When we were younger and my mom was reinforcing the protective bubble around me, Lark took me under her wing. She listened to my restless teenage rants, and when I was healthy enough, she indulged me in a few harmless adventures to keep me sane. When Lark suddenly lost her husband about four years ago, I repaid the favor as best I could. It wasn't good for her to stay in that newly hollow house, so I invited her to crash at my off-campus apartment in Austin until she managed to sell her home and move to Galway for a fresh start. Not long afterward, I followed her abroad to attend medical school. I'd been the unofficial maid of honor at her first marriage's impulsive courthouse ceremony. This time around, she wants the fairy tale. God knows she deserves her happily ever after. Even if I have to walk down the aisle with the frog I used to believe was a prince, I want to be a part of it.

With a fortifying breath, I sling an arm around her shoulders. "All right, a weekend with Aidan, then. No big deal."

CHAPTER 1

Aidan

SEPTEMBER

"YOU'RE LISTENING TO Today's Top Forty live from London. This morning, we are joined in the studio by breakout Irish singer-songwriter Aidan O'Toole. You might know him from the summer smash 'Come Here to Me,' which hit number three on the Irish charts and number twenty on UK Billboard. Welcome to the show, Aidan."

Adjusting my headphones, I lean close to the mic. "Thanks for having me. I've been a longtime fan."

"Please tell our listeners a bit about yourself. You were raised in County Cork, adopted by Galway."

"Yes! I'm sure they're happy to claim you," her co-host interjects with a hand on my arm. Her cheeks pinken when I flash a smile.

"I live here in London now. Galway is where my family is, though, and I'm heading back there for a month. Leaving London tomorrow, actually."

"We hate to see you go . . ."

Don't worry, I think, *it won't be permanent.*

"Let's talk about *Heaven-Bound,*" the main host says. "It's been nominated for the RTÉ Choice Music Prize."

"And well-deserved! It's so heartfelt."

"Thank you. It still hasn't sunk in, really, but it's such an honor."

I adjust the collar of the designer button-down the label's stylist asked me to wear today. Being dressed by someone else makes me feel like a paper doll.

"On the album, there's an arc of hope, of ecstasy, of loss," the host opines. "Honestly, I can't listen to that last song without getting a little lump in my throat."

"Tell me about it!" the other host jumps in. "The first time I listened, I ruined the eye makeup I was trying to apply because I couldn't stop crying but I didn't want to turn it off. Which gave me flashbacks of my Sufjan Stevens phase."

They share a quick chuckle.

"You're too kind," I say. "To even be mentioned in the same breath as an artist like Sufjan . . ."

"Really, it captured heartbreak so vividly," the first one adds. "And now the whole music world wants to know, who is this Irishman and who did he write these songs about?"

"Yes, are they all about the same muse? The songs seem too personal to simply be about character archetypes. You write about the different facets of love so well."

"I fall in love all the time," I lie. "I've fallen in love hundreds of times. Lyrics come easier when I have the right inspiration."

In the past, I'd fall fast, although admittedly, never deep.

Not until Cielo. She made me realize those passing fascinations and lust hadn't been love at all. Two years after our separation, I still catch myself looking for glimmers of her in strangers. Sometimes I even realize I've been subconsciously scanning the front row, seeking her smoky hazel eyes so I can sing directly to her.

I haven't been truly in love with anyone before or since Lo.

"Your lyrics have been described as 'poignantly provocative.' How does it feel to hear that about your songwriting?" The interviewer keeps a straight face, but she's slowly crossing her legs while she stares at me.

"It's certainly flattering." Regardless of how the journalists and DJs goad me, I've no literary degree, and no interest in academically dissecting the sexual themes of my own songs during an interview. The music speaks for itself.

"Well, I'm sure your latest muse is very lucky."

I fidget with the spiral cord of the headphones. We're broadcasting live across the UK right now, and they want to bring up my ex-girlfriend, approaching the taboo subject deliberately because that's what listeners theorize about.

"I appreciate that, but I'm afraid a lad's got to keep some things to himself," I answer with a wink.

According to my manager, Martin, keeping tight-lipped will add to my "mystique." The label wants me to cultivate a slightly edgy image. More important, without details on my past relationship, fans can imagine themselves in my songs. A woman all but worshipped by a man, but the two destined to permanently part ways before the last reprise. In some songs, he is a warrior fighting for her. A fool. A lover. In my latest single, he is a marionette, strings pulled in every direction until he is drawn and quartered. But in every song, she is a goddess. Every woman, Martin argues, wants to be loved like that. Loved so hard that her memory alone will drive a man to rip himself apart.

And that's what I've done for the past year while touring for *Heaven-Bound*. Night after night, city after city: I tear myself open for an audience and enjoy a collective catharsis as we share in that emotion four minutes at a time. And I wonder if Cielo is listening.

"CHRIST! YOU'RE PURE style," I say when Fionn answers the front door of our parents' house wearing a Fair Isle jumper in red and white, Cork's colors, with Gaelic footballs knit across his chest. He refuses to adopt the Galway jersey.

"Why are you knocking? It's weird and you'll offend Mam."

Although I bought this house, I've never lived here. Entering without knocking wouldn't feel right. Everyone else insists it's weirder that I don't simply let myself in through the back door.

"What is that abomination you're wearing?" I ask.

"Mam has gotten into patterns lately."

Garish but well-made knitwear is nothing compared to our seventeen-year-old sister's hobby of ventriloquism. Nine months ago, when I'd last visited, Marie brought out two horrific dummies while my da silently begged me not to say anything negative. Their wooden grins made my skin crawl. So of course, Fionn and Marie teamed up to place them in unexpected spots during my visit. I nearly soiled myself stumbling to the bathroom on Christmas morning half-asleep, only to come face-to-face with the soulless eyes of one perched on the toilet. Marie, with her angelic smile that has Mam and Da fooled, was the mastermind behind that prank.

My family's new place is two stories tall and a short walk from a waterfront park. A far cry from the peeling paint and leaking roof of the cottage I was raised in back in Cork, and an even larger departure from the dodgy council flat my family had squeezed into when they first moved to Galway to be closer to Marie's specialist. After signing with the record label two years ago, one of my first orders of personal business was moving my parents out of that moldering flat. Even after selling our old house and with Da working two jobs, they could barely afford to rent in Galway, with Mam staying home to care for Marie. I'd put my musical ambitions on the back burner then, in favor of a more stable job as a solicitor so I could help out. It feels good to provide for my family.

Mam wordlessly wraps her arms tight around me and gives me a good shake.

Still in his work clothes from the warehouse where he drives a forklift, Da rises from the battered old recliner he's had since I was a boy and claps me on the back. "Good to have you home."

"Aye. Missed you, Da."

Marie bolts down the stairs, prompting Ma to shout, "No running!"

She tackles me with surprising strength for a teenage girl.

"Well, then. Nice to see you, too." I muss her pixie cut and take a step back to observe the subtle changes since I was here for Christmas. She'd started the new year by chopping seven inches of hair, pleased that it was finally long enough to donate to a wig-making charity. "The jumper's lovely, too."

Bright purple knitwear adorned with clowns and elephants swallows up her torso. Marie lost interest in elephants back in third grade and has never shown an affinity for the circus. "Oh, just you wait."

"I've got a surprise for you!" Mam says. "Fionn, will you be a dear and go fetch your brother's gift from my room?"

The sparkle in Marie's eyes makes me uneasy as Fionn ascends the stairs and returns with a box. Mam eagerly gestures for me to open it. Music notes, harps, and guitars undulate in alternating stripes across the handmade jumper. It's the most hideous garment I've ever seen—except for Marie's.

"I made one for everyone," Mam says proudly.

"What about Da?" Fionn asks. "He didn't get a jumper."

"Ach! You're absolutely right. James, I'll get started on one for you straightaway."

Da shakes his head at Fionn. Marie bites the inside of her cheek, trying not to laugh.

"Look at this! It's lovely." I lift my jumper out of the box. If I make eye contact with Fionn, he's going to lose it and hurt Mam's feelings. She obviously spent loads of time on each one.

"I thought you could wear it onstage. You won't find quality like this on those high streets in London." She tugs at the Thom Browne cardigan the label's stylist sent to my flat a week ago. Other than surprise at its price tag, I don't have any strong feelings about it. "They couldn't even be bothered to put stripes on both arms."

Fionn laughs then stifles it with a cough. Da shoots him a death glare.

"Thank you, Mam." I slip off the cardigan and pull the

jumper over my head. It fits well, and the craftsmanship is impeccable, but I've never owned a piece of clothing so ugly. "I love it."

Herding us in front of the fireplace, Mam raises her phone. "Now, I want a photo of all of you in your matching jumpers!"

CHAPTER 2

Lo

A FLYING BEDPAN narrowly misses my head, striking the wall behind me with a clatter and a splatter.

"Get fucked by a fish!" the ancient patient shouts in Spanish from her hospital bed. Well, that's an insult I haven't heard before. Instead of the Irish lilt belonging to most of the staff and patients here, I recognize her lispy accent as Castilian. "I told you I never want to see you again."

The nurse pulls me into the hallway. "I have four other patients to tend and it's going to take ages to calm her down."

"I'll clean it up," I offer. Environmental Services isn't permitted to actually clean hazardous waste at our teaching hospital. Unfortunately, that means the worst of it falls on the already overextended nursing staff or students like me. "Really. I've got this."

"Your funeral."

A nasty fall explains why Mrs. Serrano is in the Accident & Emergency department; dementia explains her explosive reaction to a nurse coming in for vitals. Breathing through my mouth, I reenter her room with absorbent pads and sanitizer. Medicine isn't for the faint of heart. People have been telling me that since the day I announced I was becoming a doctor at seven years old.

"Good morning, Mrs. Serrano. I'm going to take your blood pressure now," I tell her in Spanish. Bilingual people with memory issues often revert to their first language and lose everything else.

She examines me with filmy, cataract-covered eyes. "Where are you from?"

"I'm American, but my dad is from Oaxaca, Mexico." Although it's a different dialect, the familiarity of Spanish seems to soothe her as I'd hoped. She offers me her arm and I slip the cuff on quickly while she's agreeable.

"She thinks she can just walk in here?" She goes back to muttering about the nurse she confused for her sister. "I'd rather rot than accept her help."

Contradicting a memory care patient only makes them more agitated, so I nod empathetically.

"And I don't like people bothering with me. I can take care of myself," she adds, sounding a little more lucid.

Looking at this woman feels like getting a peek at a possible future version of myself: a fierce sense of independence, colorful use of insults, the ability to hold a grudge for decades. Maybe that's why I didn't leave the room immediately after cleaning up. Combativeness is common, and there are plenty of other patients to see as I shadow the attending physician, but something about her flash of anger made me approach her instead of moving on.

"I understand it's frustrating to be here," I tell her with a soft smile. "We're doing our best to get you back home soon."

"My whole life, I lived on my own. Independent," the old woman grumbles. "I feel so helpless now."

I can relate to the unique restlessness of being stuck in a hospital bed. I never want to experience it again. "We all need to accept a little help from time to time."

Her frown softens just a bit.

"I HEARD ABOUT your Code Brown earlier." Oisín runs a hand through his endearingly fluffy hair. The hospital's cafeteria thrums with the lunchtime rush. Physicians, family members, and patients who are well enough to sneak away from their rooms form a line that snakes through the bright space.

Code Brown actually means disaster. If Mrs. Serrano had better aim and had hit me with that bedpan, it certainly could've been.

Oisín stabs a grilled zucchini. "The nurses all said that patient was calmer after you spoke to her in Spanish."

"I read that speaking a memory patient's first language helps comfort them."

"Well, she's only asking for you now. Congrats on making a friend."

"Hey, I have friends. Don't you count?"

Oisín waves the fork between us. "I thought this was a 'keep your enemies closer' situation."

"Ass." I flick a purple Skittle at him, which bounces off the lapel of his white coat and lands in a pile of orzo. The purple ones taste different here. European food standards probably make these candies a better product than their American counterpart, but it doesn't matter. They're slightly off to me, even if Oisín insists they all taste like pure sugar. "Just because I've never passed out friendship bracelets in our lectures doesn't mean I'm enemies with anyone. I'm just . . . competitive."

As a woman of color in a male-dominated field, I have to continually prove my place and battle my own impostor syndrome. All with a non-confrontational smile on my face. Oisín and I have been neck and neck in our cohort for the past three years. While he enjoys the opportunity to be a dickhead from time to time, I'm the one who has been told to work on my bedside manner. *Curt* was the word on the A&E rotation feedback form—although the handwriting was messy and that *r* could've been an *n*.

My phone vibrates with an incoming text.

I raise a brow at Oisín. "See? People love me."

When I pick it up, there's a message from my mom:

You need to schedule your checkup.

A groan escapes my mouth. "Okay, maybe someone loves me a little too much."

"Clingy Tinder date?" Oisín asks.

"My mom, actually."

"Yikes." Things are rocky between him and his parents, too. He digs out his phone and scrolls through videos in between bites as I consider my reply.

Although my mom is a petite white woman, her contact photo in my phone is Godzilla. She has no idea. Before I can tell my mom that I called the cancer center this morning, she follows up with another text.

**I called the oncologist to schedule for you, but
they wouldn't let me**

Twenty-five, with a biology degree from UT Austin, in med school on the other side of the world, and she still treats me like a child. I shove a few Skittles into my mouth, concentrating on the sweetness instead of typing out a flurry of annoyance. My mom's never much respected American medical privacy laws like HIPAA, so it's no wonder she's trying to take over my care here in Ireland. But this is embarrassing.

Just got off the phone with them! Scheduled for next week, I re-
ply. My checkup has been carefully timed for me to give her the all clear in person when she comes next week for Lark's wedding.

It's not on the family calendar

Another Skittle crunches under my molars. I'd tagged it in my personal schedule and not the shared one. With a few strokes, I open the calendar app to correct the tag to our two-person family calendar that she insists on to keep tabs on me. It's populated mostly by my clinical rounds and study groups, with a few of her hair appointments and oil changes sprinkled in. There's also a standing Monday slot for when my mom and I give each other a full rundown of our week over video chat. If I skipped it, she'd probably hop on a plane immediately. The two-hour allotment for catching a show at the Hare's Breath tonight is tagged in my personal calendar, under a reminder to pick up Lark's dress from the bridal salon after clinicals today. Her bachelorette party is in there, too—a booze cruise I planned for the end of the week.

After a moment, another bubble pops up. I see it now.

Ten minutes remain on my break. The bag of candy crinkles as I stash it in my pocket. Mom stressing me out is nothing new. She keeps a close eye on my health. There's always a chance of recurrence with acute lymphoblastic leukemia, which my mother makes sure to remind me of frequently.

When I was diagnosed in middle school, she pulled me out of competitive swimming and public school to put me into a homeschool bubble. Then Dad became a traveling consultant for a tech company, leaving me home alone with a mom who became more and more protective. As I got sicker, our family broke apart. She clung on to any shred of control. It got worse during the divorce, especially for a teen ripped away from her social life and tethered to an IV half the time.

When I left for UT Austin a year after I went into remission, my mom insisted on having a spare key for my off-campus apartment in case of emergencies. She would let herself in when I was in class and raid my kitchen, tossing out the emotional-support junk food and replacing it with large containers of organic kale and vegetables, then stick articles to the fridge touting their antioxidant properties. I couldn't even gain the "freshman fifteen" in peace.

I could have enrolled in a med school out of state instead of across the Atlantic if I'd just wanted to cut down on my mom's unannounced visits. But then I vacationed with Lark in Galway and fell in love with the seaside city, too. I applied for the Atlantic Bridge Program and shocked my mom by announcing I'd study medicine in Ireland. Moving to another country felt like the closest thing I could get to rebellion, while still staying on track with my goals.

"Everything okay?" Oisín asks, glancing up from his phone, which is faintly playing "Come Here to Me." It was Ireland's unofficial song of the summer. I may have blocked Aidan O'Toole on Spotify, as well as the hashtag of his name on socials, but that hasn't kept me from hearing his music playing in boutiques and cafés, and as the background music to every other social media video, it seems.

Belatedly, he realizes who is playing and shoots me an apologetic look as the song cuts off mid-chorus.

"Yeah, it's fine. You don't have to do that."

"Listen, hearing my ex-boyfriend sing love songs would piss me off, too. I count myself lucky that at least mine is a talentless gobshite."

"Honestly? It still fills me with molten rage every time." It's only a slight exaggeration. How dare Aidan get famous for singing about how much he loves me, when I was so easily thrown away for the sake of that fame.

Oisín's laugh bubbles up over the din of the cafeteria. "I swear fealty to you—"

"Didn't you just call me your enemy?"

"—but it's criminally catchy!"

"Traitor."

"We all have problematic favorites." Oisín throws up both palms in a placating gesture. "Please don't pelt me with more sweets."

"I can't believe I'm gonna have to spend three days with my ex *and* my mom," I grumble, brushing my bob off my shoulder and watching a few dark strands stick to my white coat. "Look, I'm already stress-shedding and it's two weeks away."

"Are you sure you don't want me as your plus-one? I'm an amazing dancer. We can make Aidan so jealous."

"I'll be too busy with maid of honor duties and family stuff all night, anyway. I wouldn't want to leave you by yourself the whole time. Thanks, though." I stand, grab my tray. "Hey, want to go to the Hare's Breath tonight? Blow off some steam? I don't know who's playing, but they always have a band on Fridays."

He crinkles his nose. "Not my scene."

I END UP going to the Hare's Breath alone . . . if one can say that about a pub packed with hundreds of people and my own memories. Lark and Callum have been busy with work and wedding planning, so when I invited them to accompany me to the pub, Lark said they needed a quiet date night to reconnect before the festivities. But I still rushed to the bridal salon to grab her dress and veil before they closed today.

Cheerful lacquered yellow paint and green trim cover the pub's exterior, and mums fill the window boxes. A crowd spills out of the glass vestibule already stuffed with gourds and pumpkins, topped with garlands of autumn foliage. The only other time I've seen it this crowded was during World Cup finals.

The Hare's Breath has the best music in the city. I'll be damned if I let a six-month relationship with some dimpled, mandolin-playing fuckboy ruin it for me forever. I just make a point to avoid the cozy wooden snug where we had our first kiss.

I elbow my way to the bar, practically diving on a freshly vacated stool. A little Guinness toucan decorates the end of the bar, the finish on its beak worn away by hundreds of thousands of pats. I give it one more pat. Although I'm even more exhausted than usual lately, my soul needs some decent live music tonight. Call it self-care.

The guy beside me offers to buy my drink, but I decline. Flirting is the last thing I want tonight. One or two drinks to unwind and I'll go home, shower, pass out, and do the whole thing again tomorrow.

Hooray.

When the patrons erupt in shouts and whistles, I follow their attention to the small stage, tucked in the corner.

Oh. Fuck. Off.

CHAPTER 3

Aidan

THE HARE'S BREATH is, by far, the smallest venue I've played in two years. In fact, there's hardly a stage at all, just a platform elevated a couple steps up in a corner, but that's part of the appeal. During the right songs, it's like the crowd and I are one. Experiencing the elation and heartbreak of each lyric together. I've played across Europe, but there's nothing like a pub gig in Ireland.

Garlands of orange and yellow leaves drape around the vintage Guinness ads and Jameson signs lining the wooden walls, and the pub's carved logo of a Celtic rabbit hangs above the bar. Memories also reverberate throughout the cozy space.

Tonight, I'm wearing my own clothes. My stylist would probably turn up her nose at the well-worn Rory Gallagher tee, but Fionn reminded me that only a pretentious prick would show up in a hometown pub in designer gear. I'd almost forgotten how flashy my wardrobe is now.

Fionn waves to me from a corner snug and tilts his head toward the two women next to him. They're pretty, and he looks extremely proud of himself. That particular snug is the last place I want to sit. Still, I ought to say hello before he makes arses out of us both.

"Grab me one, please?" I ask Saoirse as I pass her on her way to the bar.

Her long black hair swings as she nods and disappears into the thick crowd. She played the fiddle on the "Come Here to Me" EP and on *Heaven-Bound*. Despite my shameless begging, she refuses to abandon her florist business to accompany me on tour.

Tonight is an impromptu show, but thanks to the wonder of a couple social media posts from fans who spotted me, the audience has already ballooned to three times its original size. I've never seen the Hare's Breath so busy, and Saoirse and I played it weekly for years.

Bodies are packed in, making it difficult to shuffle to the corner snug. Most nights, peat still burns in the fireplace, but it's not needed tonight. The earthy aroma lingers anyway and mingles with the faint scent of beer.

"I've listened to *Heaven-Bound* a hundred times," one of the women says when I arrive at the snug. "When's the next album out? Does it have a name yet?"

"We won't tell," her friend adds, voice silky with suggestion. "Promise."

Usually, I'd flirt right back. Maybe even spend the night with one, to help stave off the loneliness of touring off and on for the past year and a half. But being back in this city—in this particular wood-paneled snug in this ale-soaked pub—has me out of sorts. Too many memories linger here. The first time I kissed Cielo. Her cheering for me as I performed. Our heated discussions about what makes a film a "Christmas movie" (I say a single scene set during the holiday qualifies; Lo said more than 30 percent needs to be Christmas-centric), acceptable popcorn toppings (I'm a butter purist; she drowned the kernels in caramel and chocolate), or which Radiohead album is superior (obviously it's *OK Computer,* but Lo made a compelling argument for *In Rainbows*).

"I'm afraid I can't share anything yet," I reply. There isn't much to say about my upcoming album. Everything I've written in the last year has felt too shallow. The label wanted me to pivot to a more poppy sound if the best I can give them is mediocre material.

"Thanks for coming out," I tell the women. "Enjoy the show."

They share a disappointed glance as Fionn jumps in.

"We're brothers. Full brothers. Not step or half."

"That's nice." They already look bored. I push through the crowd toward the tiny stage where Saoirse is waiting and Fionn follows.

"Jaysus, the way they were looking at you, I thought they'd both go back to your hotel," Fionn says, sounding torn between resentment and awe.

"You have a vivid imagination. Most of my fans only ask for a hug," I say, stepping onto the raised platform. "Besides, I'm not at a hotel. I'm staying with Mam and Da. You know that."

Fionn scoffs. "I know Mam has been running around the place like mad and had me up on a ladder to clean the gutters for your visit. The gutters, Aidan. As if you would notice. I told her rockstars prefer to trash hotel rooms anyway."

"Oh yeah, this one's Jimi Hendrix reincarnated." Saoirse snorts.

I smile. Some rockstar I am. Turning down a night with a beautiful woman to stay at home with my mam.

"How long are you in town?" Saoirse asks.

"Till mid-October. Going to Callum and Lark's wedding in two weeks, of course," I answer. That'll give me about a month to spend with my family and write some new material. "Come on, let's get at it. Fionn, will you join us this time?"

He scans the crowd for the fans from earlier. He's a lot like I was at twenty.

"Don't worry about them." I wrap an arm around his shoulders. "I want to enjoy a ceílí with my brother."

Fionn's brow bounces as he picks up his bodhrán drum. "Women love a musician, don't they?"

Not the one I wanted to love me back. I force my mouth to mimic his smile. "Sure do."

Saoirse starts us off, drawing the bow across her fiddle in a tune from my latest EP. Fionn thumps the painted skin of his bodhrán in time. Under my fingers, the mandolin is soft and pliable, filling the pub with sweet notes.

It's simple. It's brilliant. It's home.

Caught in the electric buzz of performance, I grin at Fionn.

"Ah, look." He gestures toward the bar with his chin and mouths, "There's yer wan."

Can't he focus on the music for a bit, instead of women? My gaze drifts across the bodies packed in front of the stage to see what he's on about now. My jaw drops when I notice who is seated at the bar.

"Lo," I murmur, my hands on autopilot through the familiar song. But I can barely hear it now.

Even sipping a drink at the local, Cielo Valdez carries herself with a sense of sophistication and confidence. Lush, shoulder-grazing brunette hair frames her full cheeks, and an elegant top hints at her dangerous curves. She's a gorgeous mirage. If I dare blink, she'll disappear. Countless times before, I've spotted her in an audience, but it was only a trick of the stage lights and wishful thinking. This time, she's real.

Our eyes meet and I nearly lose my place. Arched brows raise in surprise, then form a scowl. If looks could kill, Cielo would cremate me on the spot. Unflinching, she stares me down, lifting her glass to the juicy lips that had kissed me softly and cut me deep.

Emotions knot in my chest. Nostalgia, the ache of longing, the pain of rejection . . . regret.

Two years have passed since we've spoken. I knew I'd see her soon what with the wedding, but I wasn't prepared for it to be tonight. Her life has been a mystery to me since we broke up. Callum never mentions her, good man, and I've never worked up the courage to ask. It's over; Cielo cuts ties to anyone who hurts her.

The way I really feel about her remains unspoken, but maybe I can put it into music for the sake of my own sanity. Not one of my original songs, that's hitting too close to home. Something else. After we finish the song, I lean close, whisper the next title to Saoirse.

Her attention darts to Cielo at the bar. "It's a bit on the nose, don't you think?"

"Maybe it is. So?"

Lo will know it's for her. She won't forgive me, but maybe she'll remember what it used to feel like, coming here together.

CHAPTER 4

Lo

BEING THE INSPIRATION for a hit love song is my villain origin story. It's been said that if a man writes you a sonnet or two, he loves you. If a man writes you a dozen sonnets, he just loves writing sonnets. Aidan is a man who just loves writing love songs. With lyrics so beautiful, it's easy to assume he feels more for his muse than he actually does.

Our eyes lock mid-song and I hold my breath. That voice, resonant and earnest. I used to believe the romance he's singing about was true. It sounds so genuine. Those blue-green eyes somehow always feel so warm when his attention is on you, but what is that worth when you're left shivering and alone in the end?

Aidan is devastating, if slightly different than I remember. Longer auburn waves hang over his forehead. A dense new beard covers his square jaw. A snug band tee stretches across his chest and broad shoulders, cotton softened by countless washes. His usually light, freckled skin is tanned, which is weird, but Celtic ink still twists up the corded arms that used to hold me tight.

Those days are long over.

Without breaking eye contact, I take another long sip of my beer. Bitter foam brushes my lip, but it's nothing compared to the bitterness I feel inside. I shoot daggers his way. If he's gonna show his face around the Hare's Breath, I'm making sure he knows he's unwelcome.

At least, to me. The rest of the patrons are going wild at this impromptu show and I can't blame them: His stage presence and talent are hypnotizing.

Aidan leans close to the microphone. "This is a song that means a great deal to me—"

"Just sing it already, ya spanner!" his brother, Fionn, calls out, bodhrán in hand.

"Don't rush me."

Aidan strums at his mandolin and warm sounds envelop the pub. It's "Boys Don't Cry."

Just like that, I'm transported back in time.

This same pub, three years ago. Our first date. The first time I heard Aidan sing.

To celebrate earning my bachelor's in biology, Lark had bought me a ticket to visit her in Galway. It was my first time traveling alone. My first time on a plane. Lark and Callum were in a rough patch, and Aidan had been the solicitor to simultaneously save Callum's business and his relationship with Lark. From the moment our eyes first caught in the law office where he worked, I haven't been the same. Aidan's dimple popped as he greeted me with a slightly gap-toothed smile and that was it. Game over.

Aidan took me to a tiny pub called the Hare's Breath. What I didn't expect was for him to borrow someone's guitar and step onto the corner stage. His rich tenor voice cut through the murmurs and clinking glasses, sweet and strong, and he watched me as if I were the only person in the room. Nimble fingers picked at the strings so effortlessly, I wanted them on my body. I'd never heard the song before, but he told me later it was "Boys Don't Cry" by the Cure.

Our first kiss was in the high-walled corner snug. I can still feel the warmth of his palm wrapped around my thigh under the table. His wavy hair mussed between my fingers. I'd wanted a vacation fling, and Aidan, with his lilting voice and inked arms, was more than I could have hoped for. One night that changed my life.

Now, from the stage, Aidan's eyes remain glued to mine. Something unnameable is there. Regret and longing and . . . He's always been an incredible performer, but even I didn't realize he could be this emotive.

Aidan reaches the chorus of "Boys Don't Cry," about knowing there is no second chance. No. I don't want to hear him sing those words; it hurts too much. I hop off the barstool, pushing my way to the door before Aidan can get the words out. When the vestibule door shuts, I lean against the wall, suddenly unable to take another step. I can just hear his voice, slightly muffled. I watch bustling tourists and locals on the cobblestone streets through the glass door and let the sound wash over me. And then, the song is over. The crowd inside, oblivious to the drama unfolding in my heart, breaks into a hearty round of applause.

Screw this. I open the door and a gust of September chill ruffles the bunting and flags over the busy street. I wrap my sweater tighter around my waist. Going out had seemed like such a good idea a half hour ago. I consider texting that Dev

Patel look-alike, before deciding what I really want is a kebab from one of the carts on Quay Street and a night of uninterrupted sleep.

Ten minutes later, I'm on a bench not far from the Hare's Breath and tearing into glorious, hot meat on a stick when a smooth, familiar voice speaks from behind me.

"You were watching me."

CHAPTER 5

Aidan

CIELO GLARES UP at me with the intensity of a laser beam, slowly chewing and swallowing her kebab. "I wasn't watching you. I only came out for a drink."

Every little freckle on her nose is still right where I left it.

"Lots of places in this town for a drink," I say. "And the Hare's Breath was mine first."

Lo points at me with the skewered meat. "Why don't you go hang out with Bono or something?"

"I don't know Bono." How famous does she think I am? "I just . . . saw you in the crowd and I didn't know if—"

"If it meant anything?" she interrupts. "It doesn't. I was just at the wrong place at the wrong time."

Ouch. There was a time when her smiling face in the front row meant everything to me. Hell, she was the one who convinced me to perform my own originals rather than just covers and traditional folk songs. She's the reason I was discovered. Lo supported me with her whole heart here in Galway, but long distance was a line she wouldn't cross. And if my music career was going to go further, I had to move to London. So I did.

"We need to find a way to coexist," I say. "For Lark and Callum. For the sake of their wedding."

She flicks her head to get her hair out of her face. "Look, it's easier for me to pretend we're strangers."

Does Cielo truly think that's possible? I'd never felt as close to another person as I felt to her. When my dreams were finally coming true and I was offered a record deal and a European tour, I'd expected her to be happy for me, but she broke it off instead. She wouldn't even *try* long distance. Bewildered by all the sudden changes in my life—including her lack of support—I didn't have the will to argue.

"We're far from strangers, Lo. Come on. This is me waving a white flag."

"Is that why you chose that song?" she asks.

In "Boys Don't Cry" Robert Smith admits that he'd apologize if only she would accept it. But Smith doesn't say he's sorry. Just like I never have. Lo would never apologize for prioritizing her career. I won't, either. Especially not when my family so desperately needed the money.

"You know things were complicated." It's not really an answer as to why I played that song.

Rerouting from the messy topic, she gently asks, "How's your family?"

"Well, Fionn's an eejit, as usual."

"He sounded good on the drum."

"Mam and Da are enjoying the garden at the new house."

"And Marie?"

I scratch my arm. Lo and I dated during Marie's cancer treatment. They'd bonded so quickly over that. "She's grand. She's in her last year of secondary school now. Still in remission."

"I think about her all the time, you know."

It slips out easily, not like the rest of her carefully chosen words, as if her tongue has betrayed her. Loud and clear, I hear the subtext along with them: that she thinks of me, too. Against her better judgment.

"Marie asks about you sometimes."

Cielo blocked my entire family on social media when we broke up and abandoned her old account for good measure. I stopped checking it long ago.

"I'm glad to hear she's doing well," she responds, all too diplomatically. She won't allow any more slipups.

"I—" My mouth shuts in an uncharacteristic bout of uncertainty, and I knead my palms. "I thought we could talk about the hen and stag do."

Lo looks me up and down icily. "I'm listening."

"I got Callum a hooker."

I mean one of the local, rust-red sailboats. Callum would probably rather get a public colonoscopy than a lap dance. I dig out my wallet and hand her a business card that reads THE HAPPY HOOKER: SAILBOAT TOURS FOR STAG PARTIES.

She doesn't even twitch a smile before handing it back. "I already have something planned for Lark." Cielo would be an absolute terror at a poker table.

"Callum told me they want to do a joint party. Come on," I reason. "Callum loves those yokes, but I don't think he's ever been out on one."

"So, you're thinking a group sailing tour instead of a typical bachelor party?"

"Yeah, one of those things where they take you around the bay and teach you how to tie a couple knots and let you sail the boat a little."

"Well, it's not a terrible idea. Have fun."

My brows furrow. "Why do you say it like that?"

"I think it's a fine idea. Knock yourself out."

"You're not coming?"

"I'll be busy with the real bachelorette party. Hen party, whatever it's called. We're doing a booze cruise."

"They wanted a group thing, not two separate ones."

"Lark didn't mention that to me. And we already have to spend enough time together. A whole weekend. At the rehearsal dinner. And the ceremony. And the reception." One by one, she ticks off the events with her fingers, then lifts them up and shakes her whole hand. "I'm jazzed."

"There's no way you'd miss your cousin's hen do."

"You don't know me anymore. And Lark didn't say anything about wanting her hen do to be with Callum," Lo snaps, before ripping another bite off her kebab.

I stare flatly as she chews. Then I snatch the skewer from her hand and steal a hunk of chicken from the top.

Cielo's scowl could cut steel. "Do you wanna get stabbed in the carotid?"

It's unwise to get between a med student and a decent meal at the best of times, but I can't help wanting to get to her.

I lick my lips and Lo's eyes are on my mouth as she swallows hard. We both know what I can do to her with this mouth.

When I hand the kebab back, she clutches the wooden skewer with a death grip.

"Buy some sunscreen, Lo, because the hooker is happening." I smirk as an angry flush reaches her cheeks. "Lark and Callum want to do this together. I'll text you the specifics later this week, so unblock my number."

CHAPTER 6

Lo

THAT POMPOUS ASS. I stomp home, dodging buskers and revelers stumbling out of cafés and pubs. I only agreed to the joint hen/stag party for Lark.

We've spent ten minutes together and Aidan's already pressing all my buttons like Buddy the Elf in the Empire State Building elevator. I'm lit up, and not from holiday joy.

Behind the swishing, gold-tinted foliage of willow trees next door, a figure watches as I approach my apartment building.

"Are you trying to give me a heart attack, lurking in the dark?" I exclaim, clutching my chest when I spot Lark sitting on the iron garden bench.

"You look like you're on the warpath." Dim string lights illuminate the sketch pad in her lap. We often spend time here among the willows and roses, me studying and her reviewing animation files on her laptop. For the past three years, I've sublet the apartment next door to the funeral home where she and Callum live and he's the undertaker. It's close to the university and the cul-de-sac is quiet thanks to the adjacent cemetery.

I wave her over as I unlock the front door. "Aidan was playing a pop-up show at the Hare's Breath."

She cringes and follows me inside and up the stairs to my apartment. I hang my bag and keys in their designated spots. Lark dumps her pink cowboy boots haphazardly on top of each other in the walkway. When we lived together in Austin that nonsense drove me crazy, but I swallowed it down because she was in such a dark place. However, once she healed, I realized that she's always been a bit of a slob. I resist the urge to move her boots into the correct spot for guests on the top shelf of the shoe storage unit for about four seconds before I cave.

When I began to sublet the semi-furnished unit from Lark, there wasn't much here. Now everything has a place. A decent hi-fi and record player on a salvaged side table. A bookcase populated by a mix of vintage rock, indie folk, and Latin alternative LPs, and riveting page-turners like *Principles for Clinical Medicine* and *Lippincott Illustrated Reviews: Biochemistry*. Between the demanding schedule of third-year clinical rotations, study groups, and lectures, I'm not home often, but I want a calm environment and decent music when I am. I drop the needle on a Vanessa Zamora special edition I found crate-digging at a record shop in the Westend. Soothing, groove-driven music plays as Lark heads to the kitchen.

"Are you sure you're okay with Aidan being part of the wedding?" Lark opens a cabinet in search of a glass. It's overflowing with bottles of vitamins and supplements sent over by my mom. I'd prefer if she sent Tex-Mex specialties that are hard to find in Ireland, like yellow habanero sauce, but if it's not for my health my mom's not interested.

"He just caught me off guard tonight." I explain how Aidan

got under my skin with that old song from the Cure, then proceeded to steal a bite out of my kebab and dictate my attendance at the joint bachelor/bachelorette party on the water.

Lark hums and plops down on the tiny loveseat. "I think it sounds fun to do it together, but you don't have to go on the boat if you don't want—"

"Oh, I'm going. Aidan is not going to stop me celebrating you. And I already decided to wear something ridiculously hot for the boat ride."

Suspicion fills her eyes. "You don't . . . want him back, do you?"

"Not to lure him back—to rub what he lost in his face. If he insists on being in close quarters with me, the least I can do is make him suffer for it."

When he saw me earlier, I'd just gotten off a twelve-hour shift and looked a little ragged. Meanwhile, Aidan could've stepped off a *Rolling Stone* photoshoot.

"He uses bottled tanner now," I speculate. "Or one of those booths that sprays you like a car wash."

"Or he's just gotten some sun on tour."

"And he got Invisalign. Or veneers. His teeth are different."

Every small change is unnerving. I didn't like the beard covering his dimples or that the gap between his teeth was now closed. His imperfect, gapped smile was so charming. The sweet, genuine guy I'd fallen in love with has been replaced by an airbrushed impostor.

"So? You had braces growing up," Lark reminds me. Not only braces, but headgear for eleven months.

"We agreed that you'd never mention my snaggletooth again."

"This isn't right. I've never heard you judge anyone for that kind of thing before. Why *are* you judging Aidan for it, anyway?"

She's right. What Aidan does with his own body shouldn't bother me. But two years after our breakup, my resentment still burns hot. Unfortunately, so does my attraction. I need to focus on whatever makes him less appealing. Right now, all I have is the lack of authenticity. Lark can pry it out of my cold fingers. "He's not the guy I fell for anymore."

Lark stares at me, her lips pursed.

"What? Stop looking at me like that."

"You never got over him. I knew it . . ."

"It was just a six-month fling," I lie to both of us.

As delicious as our vacation three-night-stand had been, I didn't expect more with Aidan. I'd worked too hard and come too far to risk getting distracted and washing out of med school. But once I relocated here for the Atlantic Bridge study abroad program, we kept running into each other. Every interaction with Aidan crackled with the knowledge of just how well we'd harmonized in bed. How easily our conversations had flowed, how satisfying it felt to make him laugh. How talented he is. The way this confident man had become tongue-tied after our first kiss.

I couldn't get him out of my head.

After a few group outings with Lark and Callum at the Hare's Breath, he asked me for coffee. We talked about our ambitions and passions for hours. Some guys are intimidated by intelligent women, but Aidan never made me feel like I needed to dull my shine for his sake. He learned about my family's culture instead of fetishizing my heritage. One latte soon became a standing date at the café down the street from the solicitor's office where he worked at the time, his dimpled smile the brightest spot of my day amid brain-melting lectures and exams.

Before long, I was counting down the hours until our penciled-in dinners and Aidan's performances, spending the night at his place more often than not because for once I wanted someone's company more than I wanted quiet.

Suppers with his family came next. Although they didn't have much, they welcomed me with open arms and offered me a seat at their table; made me feel like I belonged. I'd thought maybe Aidan and I could be forever. We were together just long enough for it to feel right. Long enough for my world to be rocked when he told me he was leaving to pursue his musical dreams without me.

Lark scoffs. "I know things ended badly, but it was more than a fling."

I don't need him, but I have missed him. Or at least I've missed the guy I thought he was. Mercifully, she ignores the fact that I haven't directly answered her accusation.

"Hey," Lark says. "Since we're on the subject of men you don't want at my wedding: Your dad finally RSVP'd 'no' today."

Equal parts relief and disappointment twinge in my chest even if we hadn't expected him to make the trip out to Ireland. Traveling cross-country as a tech consultant keeps him busy. Growing up, he was often absent from milestones. He made it to my high school graduation but missed my last day of chemotherapy. When I tearfully rang the "last treatment" bell as my mom and doctors looked on with bittersweet pride, he was on the other side of the country. It was hard to forgive him for that one, even though I now understand it was his tireless work keeping us afloat.

"It's not that I don't want my dad there. It will just be less complicated with only one parent to deal with. Our moms will already be kind of a handful."

"Amen to that," Lark agrees.

Eager to see me and my dad smooth things over, Lark had made sure it was all right with me before inviting him. He is her uncle, after all. Before he'd become all but absentee, he'd been a part of her life, too. Fireworks and cookouts for the Fourth of July (any excuse to set something ablaze and grill carne asada and fajitas, really), Nochebuena celebrations that ran late into the night every December. He hadn't always had to sacrifice time with the family to cover my medical expenses. Everything changed when I got sick, and it's never been the same between us since.

"Probably for the best, right?" I say. "At least my mom will be relieved he's not there."

"I don't know. Forgiveness is powerful."

Her words pluck a string in my heart that I'd rather ignore.

CHAPTER 7

Aidan

CRISP NOTES OF my mandolin reverberate through the funeral home where Lark and Callum live. Floral arrangements crafted by Saoirse provide a pleasant scent and add a bit of color to the traditional décor. We play in the parlor after hours because it's more practical than moving Callum's piano to Saoirse's flat.

Really, the only downside of playing here is that Lo lives directly next door. I know she's rarely home but being so close to her flat feels familiar in a way that makes me ache.

"It was a . . . bold move," Saoirse replies, rosining her bow as I recount what happened after I followed Cielo out of our impromptu show at the Hare's Breath.

Stealing Lo's kebab right out of her hand might not have been my finest moment, but I have no regrets. Getting a rise out of her is preferable to being treated like a stranger. And besides, slagging people off is practically a love language. I quite like her abuse.

I wouldn't know what to do with myself if she was suddenly

fawning over me. With Lo, you know where you stand, which is refreshing considering these days most people want my attention to raise their own profile. Except for Callum and Saoirse, who couldn't care less. Callum hates attention and refuses to perform for an audience at the pub, only for mourners and at these private jams.

Lark strolls in with a tray of biscuits that smell delicious. She stops by the piano and pops one into Callum's mouth, then offers some to Saoirse. I extend my hand with a thanks, and she pulls the tray away.

"Are you messin' with my cousin?" she asks. Cielo has definitely told her about our encounter.

"I mean, I enjoyed taking the piss when I saw her."

Lark frowns and sits on the piano bench next to Callum. "I'm serious. Don't play with her emotions, okay?"

"You're giving me more credit than you should, pretty sure I don't have any sway over Lo's emotions. But I wouldn't do that to Lo anyway." My stomach growls as I get a whiff of peanut butter.

"What was with the song choice, then?"

Saoirse bites down on a biscuit.

"It's just a good song," I lie. Even more than the straightforward lyrics; I wanted Lo to remember the good times. She's created an image of me as some prick who threw her away the instant fame called. And I suppose it does look like that, but that's not how I experienced it. Cielo let go of my hand first and balled hers into a fist. How could I hold on to her when she'd hardened herself against me?

"I'm surprised you two are speaking, honestly," Saoirse says.

"She tried to impale me with a kebab stick."

Lark shrugs. "Well, that's a start . . ."

"If you two, erm, *reconciled*"—Saoirse lifts a sardonic brow—"Lo would eat your head afterward like a praying mantis."

That mental image isn't as strong a deterrent as you'd imagine.

"Occasionally, the females will even d-d-decapitate the male before mating," Callum interjects mildly. "They're still able to finish the job."

His tone is so casual, it takes a moment for that horrifying fact to sink in. The man's full of morbid trivia.

"Once you cross Lo, she'll hold a grudge for eternity," I remind Lark before she gets any ideas. "So don't hold your breath for a reconciliation."

Lark knows firsthand how stubborn Cielo can be. Begrudgingly, she offers me the tray of baked goods. I bite into a chewy peanut butter biscuit. I'm not going to win back a woman who wants nothing to do with me. We just need to form a truce for long enough to survive this wedding.

"We're trying to get a new producer to work on the upcoming album," I say, grappling to change the subject. "You'll make it again for studio recording, Saoirse?"

She wipes rosin dust from her fiddle with feigned disinterest. "Maybe."

We both know she'll happily toss a bouquet of tulips aside and come running when the time comes. Like me, she can't resist the rush of performance.

"My manager, Martin, is working on getting us a meeting with Nigel Culpepper."

Callum's eyes snap to mine. "Stop the lights!"

"Honest. I hope we can get him. The lad's a genius."

Notoriously eccentric, he's known to go off-grid for years at a time, before reemerging with a fresh new act. With his slew of Grammys, Nigel Culpepper is well past the stage where he's expected to be polite to anyone in the music industry. Meaning . . . he hasn't returned my agent's calls yet.

Martin is keeping at it, convinced a collaboration with Nigel would be my ticket to stratospheric fame overseas. All I want is the opportunity to create something special with a legend. I'm not so sure global stardom is my goal anymore. Touring makes me feel untethered.

"I've a good feeling about it," I tell them. Maybe if I say it enough, I'll start to believe it.

These new songs are a far cry from *Heaven-Bound,* written during and immediately after my relationship with Cielo. Now all the songs with lyrical substance are melancholic. I envision textured analog production, but the label asked me to write something in an energetic pop-rock vein instead. They were awful. My contract demands a new album in production by the end of October, whether I like it or not.

Public relations for the label also asked me if I'd entertain strategic sightings with a popular English television actress. Martin argued that being spotted together would give me a healthy boost in the cultural consciousness, but it sounds so contrived. I don't need to be a celebrity; I just want to make music that matters.

"We'll be rooting for you," Lark says. Callum nods. "Nigel would be lucky to work with you. Remember that."

"Well, have you got any new material you want to practice?" Saoirse asks, tucking the fiddle under her chin. "That man won't be easy to impress."

She's absolutely right, this is no time to mess about. If I manage to secure a meeting with the legendary producer, I've only got one shot. Like Cielo, Nigel doesn't offer second chances.

I pull out my mobile and open the notes app, where snippets of inspiration coalesce into lyrics that eventually become songs. Soon, I find the one I began right after leaving Lo sputtering with indignation on the bench on Quay Street. The first halfway decent tune I've written in months, with a playfully irregular 5/4 time signature to reflect the excitement I felt at seeing her again.

"I started this one last night," I say. "It's called 'Stake Through the Heart.'"

CHAPTER 8

Lo

"ROOM 293'S FEVER finally broke," I tell Oisín as I pass the nurses' station. It's just after midday, but I'm exhausted. My shift officially started at six this morning, but I was here at four-thirty to pre-round, pulling charts and updated lab work. The competitive edge is worth it. Breaks are practically nonexistent for us students, but the attending encourages me to take a few minutes of downtime. Desperate for caffeine, I drag myself to the cafeteria.

My clogs squeak along the freshly polished floor as I come to an abrupt halt at the sound of a familiar woman's voice.

"The children will be so excited to hear 'Come Here to Me.'"

It's Aidan's mom, Ruth. Engrossed in their conversation, he and his family haven't noticed me yet. I consider hiding, but there's a tragic lack of potted plants or abandoned wheelchairs in this hallway. He's here along with his parents and sister.

Aidan used to visit the pediatric ward every week on top of working full-time as a solicitor, even when Marie wasn't here. He'd perform in the recreation area, then go from room to room, playing special requests for the kids who were too ill to get out of bed. That act of kindness had endeared him to me so much. Against my will, my heart stirs at the thought of him bringing much-needed smiles to our most vulnerable little patients again.

Aidan readjusts the strap of the guitar case more securely on his shoulder. An atrocious sweater covered in knit instruments and musical notes dials down his trademark sex appeal. Well, money can't buy taste.

"Ehm, 'Come Here to Me' isn't on the set list today."

"But everyone loves it!" Ruth insists. "And that's what we need more of these days. Good, clean, wholesome music."

Marie snorts. "Mam, it's far from wholesome."

Their mother looks offended on Aidan's behalf. "Why would you say something like that?"

"'Let's make up and bury the hatchet deep'?" she quotes from the chorus.

Ruth slaps a hand over her sternum. "Marie!"

"Don't look at me, your son wrote it."

"Aidan Francis O'Toole. My friends at church have heard this song. I've bragged to the whole parish about it. I sent a link to Deacon Kelly himself."

Marie does nothing to hide her delight.

Aidan ducks his head. "To be fair, I wasn't thinking about little old church ladies when I wrote it."

"Obviously not!" His mother sniffs before scrutinizing her husband, James—a silent witness to the conversation thus far. "And you never said a word, even when I included it in the parish newsletter!"

"I thought you knew," James replies.

"Our son is singing about—about *that*. I'm mortified!"

"Mam." Pink rises on Aidan's cheeks. "Can we talk about it later?"

Finally noticing my presence, he takes me in with an embarrassed smile. I'm probably the last person he wants interrupting this conversation.

"Lo!" Marie shouts. Exuberance radiates from her as she throws her arms around my neck. Plastic ID badges clatter on the lapel of my white coat.

"Hey, Marie." I pat her on the back as casually as possible. "You look amazing!"

I all but ghosted her for two years. Yes, I'm an ass for that, but are you really supposed to keep in touch with your ex's family after you break up? Marie was fifteen at the time; I'm sure she understood that our friendship was collateral damage. Even if it hurt both of us.

"I'm so happy to run into you," I tell Marie. "Hi, Mrs. O'Toole, Mr. O'Toole."

"Call me Ruth." With her maternal pat on my arm, the knot of tension in my stomach loosens. "It's good to see you, Cielo. Are you coming to the performance?"

Aidan steps forward. "It's just a little thing for the kids."

"I only have a minute, then I have to get back. Maybe one song?"

Construction-paper acorns and pumpkins line the walls of the rec room. Oncologists in cartoon-print scrubs look me up and down with curiosity while children in knit caps and pajamas gather in a semicircle. Every one of these kids ignites my protective instinct. They deserve to grow up, follow their dreams as I have. It's my purpose to help that happen; nothing in this world feels more important.

Aidan sits in a chair at the front of the room, plucking at his guitar strings to warm up. The kids are interested, but meeting Aidan O'Toole is no one's Make-A-Wish dream. "Any requests?"

"Can I get orange jelly today instead of the green?" one girl asks. "I don't like the green—"

James stifles a laugh and Ruth pinches her husband's arm. Aidan's mirthful eyes bounce to me before he answers her. "Erm, I don't handle the food. Sorry, love. If anyone has any requests . . ."

"Jaffa Cakes!" a bald boy shouts.

Aidan clarifies, "Song requests," but it's too late.

"Chocolate Hobnobs are better!" a girl missing a front tooth asserts.

Overlapping high-pitched voices start to yell the names of snacks, not even asking Aidan anymore. If anything, they are just naming every processed treat they know. I adore them.

Aidan blinks, and I have to laugh. "Well, there's my ego-check for the day."

The adults chuckle at his humility as he looks past them and straight to me, knowing that I'm delighted he's being upstaged by junk food. My heart trips against my will.

"How about some music? Maybe you'll know this song." He strums the guitar and half the kids immediately jump up when they recognize it as the theme of *The Magical Adventures of Havarti & Plague Rat*. Marie sits next to a friend, watching her brother win over these young hearts in only a few notes.

Some children join in, singing adorably off-key. Every nurse on the floor huddles around the doorway. There are a dozen things to do at any given time, and yet they're mesmerized by Aidan. It doesn't really matter who his audience is: rowdy college students at a pub, old-timers, or little kids. Sharing a song is just how he connects with people. It's beautiful. His rich tenor voice is beautiful. *He's* beautiful, doing a goofy dance in that horrible sweater.

It's been a long time since I've allowed myself to enjoy his voice.

Aidan's smile is infectious. Then again, so is tuberculosis. Being good at lifting the spirits of these kids doesn't mean he's good for me.

I stand next to his parents as Aidan transitions into a Disney sing-along classic. We clap to the beat, and soon everyone joins in. One girl's IV cannula jangles as she dances in a momentary reprieve from the gravity of her illness.

Music was a lifeline when I was a teenager isolated in a hospital without my usual outlet of swimming. Even on the hardest days, I could always find a song or genre that brought me solace.

In my med school application essay, I'd written about the firsthand patient experience that galvanized my desire to practice medicine. Only 2 percent of physicians in the States are Latina, yet our community has disproportional rates of blood cancers. One empathetic member on a medical team can make all the difference to a scared little kid—especially one who looks like them. A lot of cancer survivors do their best to avoid hospitals, but I needed to pay it forward. No one gets into such an emotionally demanding specialty for the money. This was personal.

Aidan pours himself into this performance, the same as he would at any venue. Pride shines in James's eyes as Ruth rests her head on his shoulder. They've been through the same nightmare as my parents, yet somehow, they managed to come out stronger on the other side of Marie's diagnosis. Unlike mine.

Tension returns to my shoulders when I glance at the clock and realize it's time I got back to the A&E. I give Aidan's family a polite but rushed goodbye as he wraps on the sing-along. I gesture to my wrist to let him know it's time to get back to work and head to the door.

I slip down the hallway, and hear Aidan call my name. He jogs over with his instrument still strapped to his shoulder.

"Thanks for coming here for the kids. When I was in a unit, the most entertainment we ever got were some dingy sock puppets."

Aidan rubs at his bearded jaw. "The white coat looks good on you." He knows how hard I've worked to get here. Countless nights he'd clock out of his solicitor job and come rub my shoulders after I'd been hunched studying for hours. I did the same for him when stress over his sister's health and parents' finances kept him up at night. Sweet memories that carry a bitter aftertaste.

"Thanks." I gesture to his obnoxious sweater. "Nice outfit. Are you trying to trigger an ocular migraine?"

"My mam knit it for me, actually."

Oof. Ruth is a sweetheart. I'd never want to hurt her feelings. "It . . . really suits you."

"It's an eyesore. Ready for the party this weekend?"

"Aye-aye, cap'n."

"Oh, and it's a very small boat, so just bring yourself. No date."

I realize for the first time that Aidan might bring a plus-one to the wedding. Watching him dance and flirt with someone else sounds like a special kind of torture.

He must have noticed my face drop because his expression grows serious. "Did you invite someone already?"

"No, there's—" *There's been no one since you.* My tongue transforms into cotton at the thought of saying that out loud. I clear my throat. "I'm focusing on school. No time for that."

"Right, right." Aidan nods vigorously, the way he does on those rare occasions he's nervous.

"Are you bringing a plus-one?"

We've never had a post-relationship debrief, no sense of closure. One day, he got the call every struggling musician dreams of, but it came at a cost: us. We both knew things couldn't be the same between us if he was on the road. For the sake of my sanity, I decided I'd rather not know what his shiny new life looks like. For all I know, he has a famous girlfriend.

"I'm taking some time with my family. Working on new material," he says. "Keeping out of trouble."

Relief rushes in and my mask of casual indifference slips into an unconscious smile. *Fuck fuck fuck.* The corners of my mouth drop. I jerk my thumb back toward the A&E unit like a hitchhiker. "I need to get back to work now."

CHAPTER 9

Aidan

THE GHOULISH GRINNING face of a ventriloquist dummy peeks out from the darkness when I open the wardrobe in the guest room.

"Holy shite!"

I stumble back, slamming it shut. "Fionn! Marie!"

Laughter rings out from the hallway. Their Christmas bathroom prank had been so successful, our da thought it was Marie shrieking and not me. Blame the R. L. Stine books I devoured as a kid, but nothing is creepier than a ventriloquist dummy. Fionn tumbles into the room with a shite-eating grin.

I rip the wardrobe open again and grab the dummy, tossing it at his chest. The wooden body hits his sternum with a thud. "You will cry when I exact my revenge."

Marie walks in and he thrusts it at her as if we're playing a game of Hot Potato. She launches it onto the bed. Fionn plops down beside it, unfazed. I resist the urge to snatch up the demonic thing and throw it in the bin, only because it belongs to Marie.

"Where are you headed?"

"Callum and Lark's stag/hen party," I remind him. "Lo will be there."

Fionn picks up the dummy and shoves his hand inside. Speaking from one corner of his mouth, he goes, "Oooh! Can I come, too?"

"Stop that right now. It's . . . unsettling."

"The dummy isn't what's unsettled you," Marie says. "I saw you and Lo talking at the hospital."

The relieved uptick of Cielo's mouth has haunted me since. When I told her I'd be attending the wedding without a plus-one, a brief smile had flashed across her face. That had to mean something, right?

"Don't get excited." I ought to listen to my own advice.

Marie looked up to Lo so much during our relationship; she'd always wanted a sister. Growing up an only child, Lo had wanted that, too. For a time, they filled that role for each other. Lo helped her with homework and taught Marie to apply feathered eyelashes after she'd lost hers to chemo. It really felt like she was a part of my family in that moment. I imagined her being a part of my family, my life, forever; something I'd never thought before.

"We were just trying to get over the awkwardness between us before we spend all afternoon trapped on this tiny boat together."

Marie raises a brow. "Didn't *you* arrange this party?"

"Yes."

"So you planned a party where you'd be trapped together in close quarters . . ." Fionn says, tenderly tucking the dummy under the duvet. Sick in the head, that one. When we were kids, he trapped me in the pantry and stuck a mop in the handle to lock me inside. The little bastard took full advantage of his younger age with the knowledge that I couldn't retaliate. Him and Marie both.

"Callum has social anxiety. We needed to keep it small for his sake."

"Right," Marie mutters skeptically.

It is true. And I wanted to do something special to make up for missing their engagement party last year since I'd been touring. I knew Callum would enjoy a chance to experience the bay from one of the sailboats he loves to watch. It was only a convenient coincidence that I chose a tour in the smallest ship: a twenty-footer with a fixed boom and stays. One that would practically keep Lo in my lap the entire afternoon.

"Hey, remember that shirt Cielo liked? You used to wear it all the time?" Fionn asks. "You should pick that one today. I found it in the wardrobe when Mam made me clean up. Surprised you left it behind last visit."

I shrug. "I didn't leave anything here over Christmas. What are you on about?"

He sighs in exasperation. "You did. And I remember her making a big deal about how great you looked in it during one family dinner."

"Put me off my food," Marie adds. "No one wants to hear what a ride their brother is. And I hear it all the time in school now, too. Ugh."

"If you cared about us, you'd wear a paper bag over your head," Fionn says.

I have no recollection of that meal or that shirt, but if it made such an impression on Lo . . . "Where is it now?"

"It's all the way in the back, I think. Behind the winter coats."

Wooden hangers slide out of the way and I'm suddenly nose to nose with another grinning ventriloquist face.

"Gah!" I stumble back as Marie cackles. I'd forgotten we had two of these awful things in the house. I poke a finger at my siblings. "You're twisted."

"'Reach further back . . . '" Fionn says with mirthful eyes. "I can't believe he fell for it!"

"The biggest dummy here is the one who *doesn't* have a hand up his ass," Marie hoots.

———

AN IMPRESSIVE HOOKER is anchored before me. Crimson sails gently flutter in the salty breeze and traditional, shiny black tar coats the hull.

"It's pretty." Lo's lightly accented voice comes from behind me as I watch the waters of Galway Bay shimmer from the pier.

I point to a vessel in the distance. "Actually, our boat's the last one there on the end."

Passionate locals keep the sailing tradition alive, lovingly restoring and racing the iconic red-and-black boats. However, the one we chartered for the day looks like a "before" picture. Barnacles encrust the hull, tattered sails hang in a faded mauve instead of the signature blood red. Maybe I can get a refund. It's not even decorated for a stag do, other than *Happy Hooker* in worn paint on the stern.

"I canceled what I had planned for Lark for this shipwreck waiting to happen?"

My cheeky response to Lo's skepticism evaporates when I

turn and get a look at her. A sleeveless cotton sundress offers a peek at her cleavage before flaring out over her thick thighs. Understated and effortlessly gorgeous. She watches me stare, but I can't help myself. Self-conscious, I tug at the too-short, too-tight GAA shorts Fionn loaned me when I realized that I'd only packed trousers. Lo's eyes drop to my thighs and bounce away a split second later.

Saoirse strolls up and peers over her sunglasses at me. "Who invited Paul Mescal?"

Thanks, Fionn.

"Ha," I reply dryly as she and Cielo exchange an amused glance.

Lark's mates from the KinetiColor studio appear on the boardwalk next. Anvi's glossy black braid is thrown over her shoulder, and the platinum-haired, androgynous Rory is decked out in lime-green board shorts.

"I brought sandwiches and TK lemonade!" The brim of Deirdre's sun hat flops as she ambles down the wooden path, holding a cooler aloft. She's old enough to be Callum's mother—and she acts like it—but the wedding party wouldn't be complete without the funeral home receptionist.

"This is ridiculous." Lo whips out her phone. "Let me find something else. Anything else."

But just then, Callum and Lark stride down the pier. He's pale as a glue stick all in black and she's sporting pink polka dots. Hand in hand with Lark, he takes in the handsome vessel with an almost boyish wonder.

"Hate to break it to you, but ours is the homely one on the end," I tell them. "Captain McGrath told me his family has been Claddagh sailors for generations. I didn't know."

Anvi's jaw drops.

Deirdre makes the sign of the cross. "The state of it!"

Callum squints at the boat a moment then breaks into a grin. "B-b-brilliant."

Lo's eyes dart to mine in disbelief. Perhaps this isn't so bad after all.

Lark uncaps a tube of zinc cream. Taking care not to get it on Callum's glasses, she thumbs a thick white smear across his nose. It makes him look like the unfortunate victim of seagull target practice, but there's something about the gesture that makes me stop and watch as he kisses her on the cheek in thanks. When was the last time someone touched me in such a tender way?

Naturally, when I turn my head, the first thing I see is Lo.

"Let's see if we make it back to the pier dry before you start congratulating yourself," she quips.

Captain McGrath is a man weathered by the sea, with a wiry silver beard and a no-nonsense demeanor. Not the kind of man I'd expect running a stag party operation. Waving us down the boardwalk for a crash course in boating before we board, he announces that we must learn a couple basic knots. Bundles of rope are laid out on a folding table for us close to a railing. Callum takes one and claims his place on the end, leaving me sandwiched between Lark and Lo, while Saoirse, Deirdre, Rory, and Anvi spread out at the end of the rail.

Captain McGrath begins with a bowline knot, explaining that it doesn't tighten much under tension, making it both secure and easy to untie. He demonstrates the entire process first, then walks us through it.

Sunlight pours across Cielo's bronze shoulders and up her

graceful, exposed neck as she loops a length of rope around the railing. Kissing that junction of sensitive skin used to make her squirm. I still remember the taste. Her full lips purse in concentration as she follows each the step.

God, those delicate, nimble hands.

Annoyed at myself for the lapse in focus, I double back and yank at the end of the rope to tighten it, then loosen the knot and try to repeat it on my own.

Beside me, Lo moves with confidence. Smooth braided nylon glides against her soft palms. Slow, deliberate movements manipulate the rope. Always in control. Her hazel eyes slide to me, seductive and smug. With a swift tug—bordering on aggressive—she undoes the whole thing. I suck in a tiny breath. She knows this will plant ideas in my mind: rope tied across my chest, snugly binding my wrists as she takes charge.

I swallow thickly.

We'd flirted with light restraint before but had never gone for all-out rope play. I didn't know I'd find it so exciting until I saw the rope in Cielo's elegant hands.

Focusing on the captain leading us through a clove hitch is impossible when Cielo bends closer to the rail, giving me an eyeful of her chest while tilting her ass up. The sea breeze stirs the hem of her dress around her powerful thighs. Following along is futile when all I can think of is being tied up and smothered between them. My own rope has become one messy tangle. I find myself holding my breath when she crosses the rope back over itself, sliding it through her fingers. I nearly collapse when the tip of her tongue darts out to glide over her plush lips. Diabolical woman.

"Hey!" Anvi hip-checks Rory. "Let me help you."

That snaps me out of it. I blow a shaky breath through pursed lips and try to ignore the flare of heat between us.

Captain McGrath hands each of us a life vest, laying down some basic safety instructions. The boards creak underfoot as Lark and Callum zoom toward the ugly hooker at the end of the pier. Lo walks ahead of me, head high and hips swishing with each step. It's awkward to board the boat, so I reach out to steady her. The touch of our hands, however brief and practical, hits me like a lightning strike, shooting up my arm and spreading through my chest before I can pull away.

The pungent aroma of fish assaults my senses when I step on the boat last, and I welcome its cooling effect on my libido. Lark and Cielo exchange pinched expressions. Is it the far end of the pier that smells so rancid, or the sailboat itself?

"Listen, Lark," I begin. "If you want to do something else—"

"This is class!" Callum pulls me into a hug for the first time ever.

Surprised, I look over his shoulder at the rest of the wedding party. Deirdre grins and gives me a thumbs-up.

This really means a lot to him—and he doesn't seem to notice the smell of rotting fish—so of course we're doing this.

The boat is small, with no space wasted. There's no techie equipment, not even a steering wheel, or winching handles or cleats to fasten down the ropes. Most modern hookers are used to race—a biannual event that brings locals much pride—not for sightseeing excursions. Callum goes right to the bow, craning up to examine the frayed sails. Dierdre wastes no time opening the cooler and distributing cans of red lemonade.

"We could be having brunch right now like normal people," Lo mutters as we untie the moor lines and cast off.

"You can get a mimosa and some eggs Benedict anytime," I say.

Deirdre thrusts a sandwich at Lo. "Here, have an onion and egg!"

Looking queasy, Lo politely declines and shoots a pointed expression at me. "I've lost my appetite."

"Play nice and don't throw Aidan overboard," Saoirse replies through the hand covering her mouth and nose.

"I'm right here."

"I said '*don't*.'"

"Lark," I ask, "does Callum have a sense of smell?"

"Pretty sure he does, but nothing seems to faze him."

Deirdre shrugs and starts eating. Maybe formaldehyde exposure has affected them both.

Salty wind blows through my hair as we pick up speed. The smell abates as we head into more open water. Thankfully, it must've been the docks. Or else I've already gone nose-blind to it. Captain McGrath settles into a mystery paperback once we're out in the bay, letting us take our places as the crew. Callum and Lark go first, delighted to steer the vessel.

"Okay, loveen, turn the tiller to bring it left here," the captain directs Lo next, half paying attention. Something about the rudder or a sail, but it goes fuzzy when I recognize the bright yellow diving tower to our right. Salthill Promenade.

She and I have history at this spot. A memory I occasionally return to during long showers. The faint taste of ocean water beaded on Lo's skin, the way she whimpered into my palm as we lay on the wet sand together after the sun went down and the Ferris wheel at the fun park lit up in the distance.

When Cielo turns back in my direction, it's clear that she

recognizes it, too. Well, that's a nice change of pace from earlier, when she had me practically panting. Two can play that game.

Without breaking eye contact, I wrap my hand around a rope attaching the sail to the mast. Her attention drifts from my eyes, down my chest, across my arm, to my hand. My grasp confident around the rope, I caress the braided surface with my index finger. She tracks the movement, then slides her gaze up my hand to the strong tendons of my forearm and her mouth drops open.

CHAPTER 10

Lo

MY EYES GET lost in the whorls, tracing Aidan's toned arms. Celtic knotwork envelops the sinewy muscle, a bold black-and-white take on a traditional motif. Something without beginning or end. It's especially jarring to see what he's added to his tattoo sleeve, tucked into his inner biceps: a pair of gleaming scissors hovers above the intact string. So realistic that I'm almost convinced it would cut me if I reached out to touch it. A threat to sever something meant to be eternal. The art is beautiful, but so jaded. I wear cynicism like couture, but it doesn't suit Aidan. He was an idealist when we met.

What am I supposed to make of that? Is it about us? No. Of course it isn't. I'd be even more of a fool to think I'd made that kind of impression on him.

I'd been overwhelmed by a tsunami of memories when I noticed the diving tower. Aidan's hand in mine as we climbed the slippery steps and thundered down the diving platform. Momentary weightlessness before plummeting into the frigid water.

His laugh as I shrieked. How he'd rubbed my arms to warm me up after we were back ashore. Then he'd slipped his fingers into my bikini bottoms. Aidan's touch was always irresistible, no matter where we were. His wide palm had clamped over my mouth to quiet my cries as I came undone there on the beach. I can practically feel those talented hands on me now . . . see a glimpse of the man I used to know.

The soft nostalgia in Aidan's expression becomes something hotter. It's like he can sniff out my every hormonal thought. But then his face morphs from seduction to surprise as the captain pushes him out of the way and tugs on the sail.

"I said turn it!" the captain shouts.

I snap back into the moment.

"What do I do?" I say, embarrassed that I'd zoned out thanks to a little mental trip to my spank bank. Lark and Callum look alarmed; he's holding on to her like he's bracing for impact.

"Son of a b—" the captain mutters while Anvi yells, "Hold on!"

The sailboat lurches to a stop, flinging me forward until Aidan's arm hooks around me. I make an inelegant *oof* sound and our life jackets chafe together. He steadies us by gripping the rope.

Lark spits out a mouthful of blonde hair. "Y'all okay?"

Callum has her in his arms.

Aidan's arm remains protectively around me and I feel my pulse race. Our bare legs touch. Did he really need to wear those shorts?

"What happened?" he asks.

Admit that we crashed into a sandbar because I thought he

might've gotten a tattoo inspired by me? I'd rather dive into chummed waters.

"Is anyone hurt?" Rory asks, adjusting their grip on a rope.

We glance at one another, confirming the group is rattled but unscathed.

"We've run aground!" The captain wags his finger at me.

I crashed the boat thanks to Aidan distracting me with his indecent exposure. Huffing in embarrassment, I extract myself from his very warm, very toned arms.

"Did you not hear me holler to move the tiller!" the captain shouts at me.

Oh, I cannot wait to eviscerate this business on Yelp.

Aidan steps forward. "Hey. It was an accident."

The captain scowls, but the rest of the group stares him down.

"If this area's that treacherous," Aidan continues, "you shouldn't have let her sail. Considering you neglected to give her any direction until a sudden turn was the difference between crashing or not."

Him coming to my defense is perhaps sexier than his arms. Jesus, I've just ruined my cousin's bachelorette party and I *still* can't stop thinking about Aidan's biceps.

"Lark, I don't know what came over me. I'm so sorry."

Lark looks out over the side of the marooned sailboat. "Don't worry about it. We're all safe."

I stride toward the red-faced captain, putting on my sweet bedside-manner voice. "Is there anything I can do to help?"

Captain McGrath crosses his arms. "You can get comfortable. We'll have to wait for the tide to come back in."

"I— When is that?"

"About five."

"Oh god."

My days are scheduled down to the hour, even on the weekends. Laundry in the morning, meal prep for the week at eleven, this bachelor/bachelorette excursion at one, study group at five. Dinner at seven-thirty. Early to bed so I'm ready for my six o'clock shift tomorrow. I'd come to terms with sharing the small vessel with my ex for a couple hours. I hadn't anticipated being stranded together on a sandbar.

I pace the short length of the boat, anxiety rising. "There's a tugboat, right? They'll pull us out."

"No."

"Harbor rescue?"

Captain McGrath stares at me blankly.

I snap my fingers as the solution dawns on me. "Can we call the coast guard?"

"We wait for mid-tide."

For real?

"Fine. I'll do it myself." I pull out my phone, only to find that you can't get cell service out on the water, though we're only a few miles offshore. "Don't you have a satellite phone?"

Silently, he rummages through a storage tub. Relief fills me that he's come to his senses—until he pulls out a fishing rod and tackle box. Saoirse and I exchange an incredulous look. Rory plops down and asks Deirdre if she's got anything stronger than lemonade. She doesn't.

Drawing in a deep breath, I dump a packet of Splenda into my voice. "If you're worried about how it might look for your . . ." The captain impales a writhing worm with a fishhook. I wince. ". . . reputation as a sailor, just let them know it was me."

Captain McGrath props the rod over the edge of the boat and returns to his novel. I force myself to sit before I lose it. Gazing out at the slate-colored waves licking the hull of our stranded boat, I fantasize about garroting him with that fishing line. Unfortunately, we'll need him to sail us back to shore.

The lack of movement and progress—any semblance of control—makes my skin feel too small. I'm a fixer; I can't calmly wait in the middle of the bay for the tide to come.

Unbothered, Deirdre sips on her lemonade while Rory and Anvi joke about throwing a life preserver overboard and making a break for the shore.

Aidan takes a seat on the bench next to me while Saoirse, Lark, and Callum point out the Ferris wheel on the shore. Aidan's body heat still lingers on my skin, a map of where he steadied me earlier, so I scratch at the spot, as if that will cancel it out.

"Things could be worse," he starts.

I hold up a hand before he can jinx us with a sudden downpour. "Do *not* speak a word about the weather."

"I was gonna say at least you're not the one footing the bill for this maritime disaster. I'm paying by the hour."

"That does make me feel better, actually." My smile flickers then flattens. "But I ruined Lark and Callum's party."

Aidan watches them, heads bent toward each other as they smile and point out landmarks along the promenade. "They don't look too broken up about it."

"Lark's just too sweet to say anything. No one wants to spend an afternoon marooned." I drop my shoulders in defeat. "I really wanted this to be perfect for her. For both of them."

"Sometimes perfect is more about who you're with than the circumstances you find yourself in."

My gaze returns to Callum and Lark, whispering into each other's ears. Our sailing adventure was upended thanks to my inappropriate thoughts, but they seem content, even when forced to a standstill. They are so sure about their commitment to each other that they're ready to promise forever.

The last time I truly felt content . . . My eyes drift back to Aidan.

"Your response time was a bit slow earlier," he says. "Are you okay?"

"I'm mortified."

"It was an accident. So you're no Grace O'Malley," Aidan says. Of course not. I'm a sheltered girl from Austin, not an Irish pirate queen. But I do envy her access to cannons and swords. "And that's okay. I'm no Blackbeard."

"Although you made a real effort with that facial hair."

Afternoon light illuminates the ginger threads in his beard as Aidan swipes a hand across his jaw. "My manager says it makes me look virile."

"Blech. Something about that word just rubs me the wrong way."

Aidan grins. The perfect teeth peeking out from his new beard still throw me off, but it's a great smile. "I remember."

A splash rouses my attention. A thin slice of silver cuts through the waves gently sloshing against the hull and a porpoise breeches the surface.

"Lark! Look."

She squeals and clamps on to Callum's arm as the porpoise circles our stranded hooker. A second fin and sleek back cuts through the surface. Briefly, a rainbow forms in the misty exhalation through its blowhole. The rest of the group shuffles across the deck to watch.

"There's another one," Aidan says. Soft laugh lines frame his eyes when they meet mine.

I grab the rail to lean closer for a better look. My fingertips brush the familiar warmth of Aidan's knuckles curled around the same piece of wood. Electricity shoots up my arm.

And . . . I don't pull away. I let my pinkie and ring finger rest atop his hand. There's a certain magic in sharing an experience with him. He knows how to be in the moment more than anyone else I've ever met. We used to lie on his couch and play old records in the dark, basking in the sonic landscape. He'd trace his fingers along my scalp as we listened. Holding each other, letting the music wash over us, every sensation heightened and my heart rate slowed because there was nowhere else I needed or wanted to be. These few seconds while we watch the porpoises surface, feel the gentle breeze, and hear the lapping waves are the closest I've gotten to that feeling in two years. For so long, I've been working relentlessly toward the future, playing the role of the perfect daughter. Aidan always gave me permission to live in a moment that was perfectly imperfect. When we're together, he's so present that I almost forget the past.

I've missed that.

"Can you believe this?" Saoirse says.

At the sound of her voice, my hand slips away and tightens around the rail.

Callum exchanges a glance with Aidan before he guides Lark by the elbow. "Let's see if there are more porpoises on the starboard side," he says.

"But these ones are so close—" Her voice shifts higher, and she scuttles across the deck. "Oh! Yeah, let's see."

Rory, Deirdre, and Anvi follow suit and move to the other side of the boat. Subtle. Real subtle.

Lark loves to fix people up. She'd even tried to matchmake for her own fiancé before they got together and keeps an eye open for eligible men and women for Saoirse. She'd better not try to pull anything with me and Aidan. Moving backward isn't an option and there is no future with him.

The moment is ruined, anyway. The captain's fishing rod twitches and Aidan goes over to look.

Lark notices I'm alone and scoots onto the bench beside me. "Hey. I don't want this maid of honor thing to be one more stressor. If there's too much on your plate with rotations—"

"No, no, no! I'm good."

"Are you sure? You looked kinda out of it earlier."

I nod rapidly. "Yeah, I just zoned out for a second, but you can count on me. I won't ruin your wedding, too."

Lark gestures to the bay around us. "How is this ruined? It's beautiful—the sun is shining and I'm enjoying this view with the man I love and my favorite people. Seriously. Chill, Lo."

She waves the rest of the wedding party back over.

"Lark and I were talking earlier," Callum begins. "And we're gonna need some help on Wednesday."

I already had to request Wednesday afternoon off for my follow-up care appointment at the oncologist's office, so it's good timing.

"We'd planned to put favors together for the guests, and welcome baskets for the out-of-towners," Lark explains, "but one of my animators is out with the flu and I need to put in some extra hours so production doesn't fall behind."

"I'll do it—" Aidan answers at the same time I say, "I can handle that."

We glance at each other. Amusement is splashed across his face.

"Great!" Lark says. "I was going to ask you two to do it together. Thanks so much, you're both lifesavers."

———

NO MATTER HOW many times you wear a hospital gown, you never quite get used to the feeling of your ass hanging out the back. Every year since I got the all clear, I've had a full annual workup to monitor my health. Poked, prodded, the whole nine yards.

The phlebotomist gives me an apologetic smile as she labels the last blood sample vial with my name, birth date, and patient ID number. I smooth down the bandage she'd placed in the crook of my elbow.

Acute lymphoblastic leukemia has a good remission rate, but my case had required three treatment cycles of chemo. I always figured if I could get through that, I could get through anything.

But I didn't do it alone.

My mom gave me a bone marrow donation for a stem cell transplant. It allowed me to take a higher dose of chemo, which ultimately saved my life. Finding a family match was a stroke of luck; it's not always so easy.

When my dad learned that leukemia rates are higher among Latine people and ethnicity can be important in tissue matching, he organized a local drive to get hundreds of his coworkers' cheeks swabbed. My dad cared—but whether it was due to stoic machismo or depression, or a mixture of the two, he struggled to connect with me when I was actually in treatment. If there's any way we're alike, it's that we both hate feeling powerless. We just handle it differently. I made treating cancer my own life's mission. He could never quite handle the loss of control and stayed away.

"Any concerns?" the doctor asks, breaking my reverie.

"Not really. I'm a medical student. Stress and insomnia are part of the deal."

She nods. "Yes, I remember."

I don't mention that my stifling mother is adding to the stress load. She's already texted me twice: once to remind me of the appointment—as if I've ever overlooked my calendar—and just a few minutes ago to follow up. When it comes to these annual visits, she practically foams at the mouth until we get the all clear. Honestly, I can take feeling like a pincushion; it's the wait between the exam and another *No evidence of disease* on my chart a few days later that is the worst part.

When the appointment is over and I'm back in clothes that don't expose my backside, I confirm with my mom that (a) I am alive and (b) I made it to the cancer center. She always assumes I'm kidnapped or in a roadside ditch when I don't answer and sends me increasingly unhinged messages until I do. Having an ocean between us makes her even jumpier than normal about these visits. Which, in turn, kind of makes me anxious about them.

My greatest fear is a relapse that would derail my medical training. Of course, I don't want to go through chemo again either, and there are always those big mortal fears that revolve around the diagnosis—especially considering how difficult it was to treat—but I'm worried it will interfere with my purpose. Everything I've worked for can't be rendered moot. It just . . . can't.

Shaking off the itch of anxiety, I exit out of my mom's text and click on Aidan's contact.

Hey, are you around to take care of those wedding favors?

CHAPTER 11

Aidan

FRESH LYRICS AND melodies have spilled out of me in the days since the boat outing when Cielo and I shared a moment. And the songs are *good*. Emotionally loaded and as lively as the waves that shimmered around us. Yes, her resentment for me burns hot, but now I know the glowing ember of our connection is still very much alive. If I tend to that cinder, it just might warm us both once more.

I have to try. I want her back.

Beams of concentrated malice aren't shooting from Cielo's eyes when I arrive at her flat, so that's a start. She answers the door in a simple top and jeans. Shiny lipstick accentuates her modest smile in the most distracting way. In the past, I would have greeted her by tugging her close and testing just how color-fast her lipstick was.

I clear my throat and stow my shoes by the entrance. "Hey."

"Um, hi."

Her meticulously tidy flat hasn't changed. Big Thief spins on the turntable under a framed Austin City Limits poster. Notebooks are stacked on the couch, as if she'd been studying. An example favor sits in the center of the kitchen table: a jar of homemade bubble liquid wrapped in fabric, tied with a double bow, and finished with a stamped name tag.

Lo holds up another bundle. An absolute mess. Lark's and Callum's stamped names and wedding date are crooked on the label, the guest's name crammed onto a tag that hangs from a limp ribbon. This one's definitely hers and I know the perfectionist in her *hates* it.

"You've made hames of it, haven't you?" I tease.

"I'd like to see you do any better. The fabric barely fit and if you even look at one of these favors wrong, it pops out of the wrapper." She scowls at the bubble jar favor. "So, how do you want to do this? Assembly line?"

"Works for me."

She's all business, and while it's . . . civil, it just won't do. Lo was embarrassed when the boat ran aground, but we'd shared a moment there . . . before and after the mishap. The chemistry between us is still electric, even if she's doing her best to ignore it. But I won't let her ignore me.

Silence feels loud when there's so much to say. It's overwhelming. Adrianne Lenker's raw, timeless voice laments how all the money in the world can't buy forgiveness. It's the reminder I need.

We collect the supplies Lark left us and line them up on the table.

"Okay." I sit down beside Lo. "Show me how to make one."

She starts with the label that wraps around the tiny plastic jar. There are individual stamps for each letter of their names and each number in their wedding date. She lays out only the letters and numbers we'll need, putting the rest of the set aside. Two stamp pads: black for the text and gold for the claddagh. It's slow going, and by the time I'm finished with one, I'm sure this is going to take all day.

Perhaps that's the point. Surely, Lark knows they make custom stamps and printed labels for these sorts of things. It feels like a deliberate choice, just like pairing us together for the task. I have to admit . . . I'm not upset about it.

"How about we focus on the stamping first? All the labels and tags." Lo pulls up a guest list on her phone.

"Fine by me."

She grabs the tags; I take the labels.

We go about stamping in silence. The faint rosemary scent of Lo's shampoo catches my attention and I inhale greedily. Memories of tea in bed on Sunday mornings swirl in my mind as Lo moves brusquely in my peripheral vision. I watch for a sign that our proximity affects her, too, but she's unreadable.

We reach for the same stamp and our hands bump.

"Sorry—"

She yanks her hand back. "No, you go ahead—"

"I insist—"

I reroute, reaching for the gold pad instead at the same time she does. We freeze mid-motion and I huff at the synchronicity.

"You can talk to me," I say. "This doesn't have to be awkward."

Lo sighs. "I . . . don't really know what to say."

"Well"—I dab the stamp onto the ink pad—"we can start with the basics. You had clinicals today?"

"Yeah, most days on top of coursework. But I took the afternoon off for an appointment," she says, keeping her hands moving.

"My da and I went fishing at Salmon Weir Bridge this morning. The season's nearly over and it was the first time I've had a chance to go with him." From the old stone bridge, we watched a pastel sunrise against the cathedral's impressive green dome. Da's a decent angler, and the River Corrib had been generous. "So, Marie picked up ventriloquism last year—"

Lo pauses. "Like, a talking dummy?"

"Unfortunately."

"That's . . . pathological."

"The whole family has been pranking me with them ever since! This morning, my da asked me to get his tackle box from the shed and the awful thing was sitting on top of it."

A light laugh escapes her. "Fantastic."

"You would think that."

We find our rhythm. I sync the inking of the stamps to the bassline of the song, looking up to see a glint of amusement in Cielo's face. We match each other's pace, stealing glances at each other. She speeds up; I follow suit.

Next thing I know, we're racing. Lo is a blur of motion, frantically spelling out the names of the bride and groom. She slaps her tag down in the center of the table with a triumphant grin. I want to kiss it off her face. God, I've missed her.

"Best out of three?" I ask. Anything for this easy energy to continue between us.

Cielo purses her lips as she considers. "Only if we raise the stakes. Loser stamps 'loser' across their forehead."

"You'd do that?"

"I won't be the one who loses." She's always shit-talked with extreme confidence.

Now it's war. I open a one-minute timer on my mobile.

"Bring it on, babe," I say nonchalantly as the countdown begins.

Fire flares in her eyes. "I'm not your babe."

Ignoring her outrage, I start the timer and we're off. I'm stamping three letters at a time when she pulls the ink pad out from under them.

"Cheat!" I reach for it, but she passes it to her other hand and playfully holds it out of my reach. Of course, I could just stand up and take it, but where's the fun in that? "Give that back right now."

"Not a chance." She starts furiously stamping.

I grab her by the wrist and her eyes dance with mischief.

"You wouldn't dare," she says.

I lunge for the supplies.

"Get"—she stamps my arm with a letter *L*—"off."

Now it's on. I snatch the ink pad and press a big gold blob to her arm as she bats me away with shrieking laughter. She presses the stamp into my forehead just as the timer interrupts the playful tension. Sixty seconds went by far too quickly.

Lo's eyes widen, as if she's just realized how easy it was to sink into that familiar comfort. As if she'd momentarily forgotten the past. She pulls away and turns off the phone's beeping timer.

I'd finished one favor and got three-quarters of the way through another. Lo got two and a half done.

"Okay, you got me." My chair makes a honking noise as I scoot closer. "Get your kicks."

"Really?"

"Really."

I assumed she'd relish the opportunity to brand me a loser, but Cielo hesitantly taps the wooden stamp.

"Get on with it, then," I dare her, voice soft.

"You asked for it, pretty boy." Amusement fades into an intense expression. Scrunching her nose, Lo presses each letter into the ink, then onto my skin. *L-O-S-E-R.*

"You're taking this more seriously than the favors," I mutter to break the tension.

She snaps the ink pad closed but doesn't lean back to appreciate her work. She stays in my personal space, breathing in the same air as she stares at my marked forehead, then lingers on my mouth. After a moment, her gaze drops back to the ink pad.

"Um, Aidan? This doesn't say 'washable.' It says 'highly pigmented, artist-grade permanent ink.'"

"Very funny."

She holds the ink pad up, her face equal parts chagrin and glee. "I swear, I didn't know."

The last thing I hear is her cackle as I race to the bathroom. To hear that mirth in her voice, even directed at me—it was worth it.

CHAPTER 12

Lo

"IT'S A NICE area." I point my mom's attention to the window and the willow trees lining the cemetery. "Very quiet neighbors, except for Lark."

The joke doesn't land. My mom purses her lips and surveys every inch of my living room. She's visited me twice since I moved here, but insisted that she wanted to see it again before I drop her off at the castle. She examines the contents of my fridge, then surveys my coffee table, opens a decorative box and holds up a matchbook inside, printed with HARE'S BREATH: COLD PINTS, GOOD CRAIC.

"Cielo Valdez, are you smoking?"

I point to the jar next to it. "Mom, they're for candles."

She takes a sniff and pulls a disapproving face at the "Autumn Leaves" scent. "Burning paraffin releases carcinogens." She marches to the kitchen and unceremoniously dumps the candle into the trash. "Aunt Sharon has been selling soy candles that smell marvelous. I'll send you one."

Indignation flashes through me. Keeping the peace is important for the wedding weekend to go well, but she's literally throwing my belongings in the garbage.

"Mom." Clenching my teeth, I cross the room and pull the candle out of the trash. I rinse it under the tap. Having a task to do somehow makes this interaction easier. "You don't get to choose how I decorate my house."

"I said I'll send you a new one."

"This isn't about a candle. I can take care of myself. I exercise and take my supplements religiously. I eat well most of the time—"

"There's a candy wrapper in your trash."

I draw in a deep breath, willing my anger away. For years, I've been following a guide set by an oncology dietician. It's true that Skittles and popcorn are my favorite cheats. I indulge more when I'm stressed, but overall, I'm pretty disciplined. Not that I need to explain the contents of my garbage.

"You're my only child." Exasperation colors her voice.

"But I'm *not* an actual child. Just trust me, okay? I have a vested interest in keeping myself alive."

She huffs as if she's the one aggrieved.

I snatch my short white coat from the hook along with the engraved stethoscope my dad sent when I was accepted to the University of Galway. "Ready to see the castle now? I have to get to the hospital by six."

She plants a hand on her hip. "You're working? Tonight? You're not even going to visit with me?"

Guilt mixes with my still-simmering anger. She did come 4,500 miles.

"Every clinical hour is important. I'm already taking a three-day weekend." Not to mention, I'd lose all my hair again if I spent too many days with her. "We'll get to see each other, I promise."

My mom is moody the whole ride there, feigning indifference as I point out landmarks along the way. I silently wonder if I'm a crappy host, dumping her at the accommodations right after picking her up. If I'm a crappy daughter for deciding to go to school in another country.

Castle Teachan's medieval silhouette and ornamental trees come into view. I carry my mom's suitcase to the door, where we're met by a concierge. Before I picked up my mom at the airport, I'd delivered the guest baskets Aidan and I had assembled last night.

With a glance back at my idling car in the drop-off lane, I say, "I'm glad you're here, Mom. See you tomorrow."

———

THE NEXT AFTERNOON, the contents of my suitcase are laid out on the hotel bed like a postmortem exam. I've brought anything and everything that makes me feel more prepared for the emotional gauntlet that is this weekend.

Castle Teachan has just as much romantic ambiance on the inside. My room is anchored by a massive four-post bed and lined in tapestries, a decorative sword, and sconces that I'd swear were lit by real candles if I hadn't just turned them on with a switch. Touches of modern luxury balance out the traditional opulence.

My reflection peers back at me from an ornate mirror. I got less than three hours of sleep after returning home from my twelve-hour shift at six-thirty this morning. Between a double espresso, a caffeine-infused eye mask, a metric ton of concealer, and a chic linen jumpsuit . . . I actually look good. It's a miracle.

The way Aidan stared at me when we were assembling the gift bags still ricochets through my brain. His melodic voice, daring me to go on.

I want him to look at me like that again. I want to tempt him. I want . . .

There's a cheerful rap at my door; it's Lark and Callum.

"Hope you're hungry. The lunch buffet is starting," she chirps.

I step out, practically running straight into Aidan as he emerges from the room next door. The idea of him sleeping so close, just beyond a wall, makes my chest feel like it's filled with lead.

"Hey," he says casually.

Dressed in a simple white shirt and dark pants that somehow look absurdly expensive, Aidan's distractingly hot—but I still have a hard time shaking the fact that this isn't *my* Aidan.

"Hey. Nice place. My bed is huge," I say. His mouth pops open. He probably thinks I'm trying to make a pass at him. "I mean, it's large. Good for bouncing."

"Bouncing?" Aidan repeats.

Lark delightedly elbows Callum. There is no way the side-by-side placement of our rooms is a coincidence.

"Jumping! Jumping on the bed," I correct. What am I saying?

This meeting has already gone off the rails; I've got to regain control. I turn to Lark. "Can you give us a second?"

Lark smiles knowingly. "Meet you downstairs."

There's an openness to Aidan's expression, and I feel even worse now for what I'm about to say.

"Hey, before I forget: I just wanted to ask that you not mention . . . us . . . to my mom when you meet her. Please."

Hurt flashes across his face.

I'd wanted to tell her about him a dozen times, but every time I started to work up the nerve, she'd remind me of just how neurotic she could be. His parents are so easygoing, he just doesn't understand that there is no way to impress my mom. I'd simply wanted to keep him to myself for a little longer. Then it all ended anyway.

"You know how she is," I explain. "She only wants me with some cardiologist or a stock trader or a lawyer."

Aidan raises a brow and I pause to process the irony of that last one.

"Shall I tell her we met while I was practicing law? Might win her over," Aidan asks with an almost melancholy smile. Here, you can sit for the entrance exam without a law degree. Before we met, he'd studied on his own for months in between busking, trying to balance his musical dream with a practical job when his parents needed help. I'd always admired his tenacity, his intelligence, his devotion to family.

"For my sanity's sake, let's just let her think we're friends," I plead. "I don't want to get into my love life with my mom. There's enough on my plate this weekend."

"So, we're friends now?"

My lips part, but I honestly don't know how to reply. Could I learn to be friends with Aidan over the course of this weekend? Do I even want that?

"I won't say anything to her," he promises before I can answer. Layers of emotion shift across Aidan's face. Hope and hurt and something else that I can't quite identify.

My hand reaches out on its own accord, but before I touch his cheek, I pull my hand away and lift my index finger instead.

"One minute. I'll meet everyone downstairs. I forgot something."

I slip back into my room to compose myself. What about my comfort? My boundaries? I put them in place with good reason.

The mattress shifts under my weight as I plop down on the bed. Three days with my ex. I thought I was ready for it, but I'm far from over Aidan.

CHAPTER 13

Aidan

A TERRIFYINGLY INTENSE middle-aged woman stomps down the ornately woven runner in the hallway. From the arch of her brows to her determined gait, the family resemblance is clear. Cielo's mother, Tracy, I realize, just before she bangs on the door to Lo's room.

My heart sank when she asked me not to mention our relationship to her mom. What hurt more was the realization that she'd never told her about us before. But apparently even back then, Lo had suspected we wouldn't go the distance. No wonder she didn't try to hold on to me when my career started to take off.

I pause at the banister and watch her mother slip inside the room.

Lo's parents always exerted so much pressure on her, expecting her to be the perfect daughter and student. I may not be able to repair their relationship, but I'll make this weekend easier on her in any way I can, even if it means pretending that we're nothing more than friends.

Before I reach the banquet hall, my phone buzzes in my

pocket. My manager's contact photo lights up the screen. I step into the garden, where dahlias the size of dinner plates sway under rust-colored trees.

"Great news!" Martin says. "I have a last-minute gig for you."

He knows this weekend is blocked off my schedule for the wedding.

"Don't worry, it's in a couple weeks," he assures me before I can remind him. "The Harvest in the Park."

Indie legends and the hottest new acts flock to the annual festival in New York's Central Park. In fact, Nigel Culpepper will be performing for the first time in years. He still hasn't returned Martin's calls, so we're continuing to shop for a suitable producer, but simply hearing the man perform live would be a dream come true for me.

"Yeah! I'd love to play it." Dry leaves crunch against the stone under my feet. "Did you listen to the demo I sent? A few more weeks in Galway and you might actually get a decent album out of me," I joke, though it's not funny this close to the deadline and with the label ready to force me to make an album I'd rather quit than create. Thankfully between flashes of lyrical inspiration in Lo's company and getting back to basics practicing with Callum, Saoirse, and Fionn, I'm starting to think that I can do it.

"Don't bother, the label's heard enough," Martin says dismissively. "The stuff you sent earlier this year will sound good once it's properly produced."

"But that's all rubbish and this song is already better—"

"Look, maybe you impress Nigel Culpeper enough at this festival that we get him on board and then the label will reconsider. But for now, we've got to pivot genre a bit. Which leads me to my next bit of good news: Neon Joy agreed to produce. With any luck, we'll get that sad bastard music listenable by the end of October."

Did I hear him wrong? Neon Joy, as in the auto-tuned duo that just happens to be Martin's other management client? Martin does know what he's doing, but he's making moves without me. I wasn't even aware he'd asked Neon Joy to collaborate or that he'd been speaking to the label behind my back. The executives lost confidence in me as a singer-songwriter after the half-hearted crap I sent them this spring, but if they only gave the new demo a chance, they'd see that I was just in a temporary funk.

"Trust me, the new demo isn't sad bastard music," I tell Martin. "If I play something fresh for Nigel during the festival, maybe he'd take notice."

"It isn't the best time to debut new material. Better to wait until the first single is decided." Decided for me, not by me.

"So the label would let me record the songs I want if they have his stamp of approval?"

Martin sighs. "With that kind of endorsement, you'd earn their trust back."

"Sign me up for the festival, then."

"Already done," Martin admits. "Forwarding you the contract now. It's a great slot. Both nights. Second stage. Not too early."

While I appreciate his efficiency, it would've been nice to agree to the performance first. I push down a flare of frustration and reroute the conversation. "How did you get me a spot so late, anyway? This show has been booked for months."

"Bayou Diamond broke up and canceled all their tour dates. I called the moment their very public meltdown popped up on TMZ."

"The devil works hard, but you work harder." What kind of unholy pact had Martin made to be able to secure these deals?

We schedule another call to discuss the festival's logistics and prepare the band for travel. He still doesn't approve of performing unreleased new material at the festival, but I know this new song is special. And what is he gonna do, unplug my mic?

Stuffing my phone back into my pocket, I finally enter the banquet hall for lunch. Vibrant sunflower arrangements blanket the traditionally elegant space, suspended from the chandeliers and covering nearly every surface. Saoirse has outdone herself.

I scan the area, looking for anyone I know. Lark is across the room, intently listening to a story told by her colleagues. Her female relatives surround Callum in the buffet line. He looks petrified despite towering over them.

"That's adorable," Lark's mother drawls. "He can't say the 'th' sound."

"Say it again!" another pleads.

His eyes are wide when I approach and clap a hand onto his shoulder. If these Yanks want to hear an *Irishman*, I'll give them one.

"Top o' the mornin', ladies!" I say, exaggerating my accent with a shite-eating grin. I hate myself for it, but I'll do anything for Callum, who is obviously in distress.

Immediately, their faces turn toward me. These ladies aren't malicious. Just clueless. They might not realize they've cornered a man with a speech impediment.

Lark's mother, Sharon, claps in delight. The wide sleeves of her caftan flap with each movement. "Oh my lord, they really say that here!"

"We d-d-d-don't," Callum says.

I cast a look over my shoulder that says, *Relax, I'm on your side.* "We most certainly do in County Cork!" I gleefully lie.

Just like that, their attention is redirected. They crowd around, speaking over one another, asking me to pronounce a battery of words so they can hear my accent. I oblige as they fill their plates. After a couple minutes, they head toward the tables.

Callum ladles gravy over the mountain of mash on his plate. "One of them asked me what time it was, and when I said 'twelve-thirty,' she called another one over and had me repeat myself. Suddenly I was surrounded."

Cielo appears behind us at the buffet line wearing a jump-suit that perfectly accentuates her hips. I want to tell her about the festival. She said we were "friends," though my instinct to share good news with her stems from something more. Now isn't the right time, but I wonder if it will ever be the right time to share news that reminds her of my career and how far it takes me, if I truly want her to give me a second chance.

"I apologize for the unprecedented levels of paddywackery," Lo says to Callum, then directs her attention at me. "That was sweet, rescuing Callum from my family."

She examines the buffet's food options with all the gravity of studying to pass the medical licensure exam but doesn't reach for anything.

My brow furrows. "Are you okay?"

Lo's nod is unconvincing. She glances over her shoulder to

where her mother is sitting before seizing a plain chicken breast with a set of tongs. "I'll see you later, Aidan."

Something is up. Cielo once insisted we try an Indian take-away because she read a review that said, "I couldn't feel my face, but I couldn't stop eating."

Her spine stiffens when her mother waves her over to the table where she, her aunt, and Lark are already seated. It's subtle. Chin up, shoulders back, she's poised and battle-ready. Is her mother's judgment the reason why unseasoned poultry and steamed broccoli are the only things on her plate? My hand tightens into a fist at my side. She's perfect just as she is. Power-ful, soft, and incredibly sexy.

"I've no idea how to talk to Lark's family," Callum says. "I just stuff bread into my mouth, hoping they get caught up in their own conversation and forget I'm there. This morning when we had b-b-breakfast with her mam, I ate four pieces of toast. Consecutively."

"You've already made a good impression." I transfer an emergency piece of boxty from my plate to his. "Lo told me they loved you when you went to Texas for Christmas."

Some of Callum's wariness lifts. "Really?"

"It's obvious that you're good for each other. They're happy for Lark."

Cielo's parents are pickier about her relationships. What would her family think of me if they knew the true extent of our history?

"If it makes you feel any better, I have no idea how to talk to Lo anymore," I admit. "It feels like I'm in the second grade, tugging on her pigtails to get her attention."

"Can you believe there was ever a time where I saw you as some sort of ladies' man?" Callum asks.

"I resent that."

Before I know it, the bubble of this weekend will have popped, and Cielo and I will go our separate ways. I need to make the most of our time together before she disappears back into rotations and pretends that I don't exist for another two years.

Callum pulls a gray velvet ring box from his pocket and puts it in my hand. "This belonged to my grandmam. Would you mind holding on to it?"

I open the hinged lid to find a gold claddagh shining inside. He's trusting me with something irreplaceable. I swallow hard and tuck the ring box into my back pocket. "Of course. I'll guard it with my life."

"No need to be dramatic."

"Go on, talk to your mother-in-law and stuff yourself with gluten."

I scan the impressive arrangements of sunflowers, wildflowers, and baby's breath piled on the tables, and quickly locate Saoirse, Anvi, and Rory.

"It looks amazing in here," I tell Saoirse the moment my plate hits the table. At her own insistence, she's on double duty as both floral designer and bridesmaid.

"I've never had the opportunity to decorate a venue like this. It'll be huge for my portfolio."

"You want to do more weddings?" Rory tucks a lock of platinum hair behind their ear.

"I'd like to do event design. Sure, that includes weddings, but it's really the opportunity to do something daring and immersive." She gestures to the swirling yellow blossoms. "Whimsical, in this case. Most of my arrangements are for wakes, so it's a nice change."

From across the room, Lo laughs at something her mother said. The unmistakable, robust sound is burned into my memory. I want to turn it into a song. To make her laugh like that again.

Heaven-Bound was one big musical prostration, but admitting wrongdoing in person is another story. I lost her because I let her believe she wasn't worth fighting for. I want to tear down the fortress Cielo has since built around her heart, but I have to remind myself that Lo has always been the more patient of us, and she'll need a methodical approach. Brick by brick. Word by word. Action by action. Earning her trust back won't be easy.

The clink of silverware against crystal rouses the attention of the dining hall. Lark's mother, Sharon, stands up, her flowing caftan nearly knocking over the remaining glasses on the table as she swings her arm. "I hope y'all will join me for yoga in the aviary after lunch. The castle staff will provide special workout clothes to change into, so come as you are. It's important to feed the soul as well as the body . . ."

Beside her, Lark is clearly fighting the urge to cover her face. Yoga isn't something I'm usually keen on, but I know Lo will be there. If it means a chance of seeing more of Lo than she's let me yet, I'm game to try.

RICH TAPESTRIES AND portraits line the halls of Castle Teachan. A fully articulated suit of armor stands on either side of the stairs. I bump into one when I catch sight of Lo rounding the corner and heading to the yoga session and apologize to it out of habit. Pulled-back hair now exposes her graceful neck and soft jawline. The way that jumpsuit hugs her ass makes me feel the opposite of zen.

"Headed to yoga?" she asks.

"I'll give it a lash."

We exit the impressively carved double doors at the front of the castle and enter the manicured garden. Lush dahlias dot the path to the falconry buildings, but Lo isn't much for a relaxed stroll to appreciate them. Wherever her destination, she travels with intention. She's speed-walking, her jumpsuit swishing and hips swaying with each step.

I match her pace.

You're not getting rid of me that easily, my raised brow says when she casts a furtive glance my way.

We're nearly nose to nose when she barrels ahead. I catch up. The corner of Lo's mouth ticks up in a competitive little smirk and her breath quickens from the mild exertion. Mine, too. We're almost to the arched stone bridge over the creek to the aviary when a shadow passes overhead.

A raven squawks loudly as it circles us, then dives so close that I can feel the rush of wind.

We turn to each other, still locked in a ridiculous speed-walking race. Confusion on her face shifts to alarm when the bird comes back for more, dipping low and circling as we approach the edge of the bridge.

"Fuck me!" I duck before it nearly scalps me. We need to get indoors, now.

"It's like a feathered Liam Neeson!" Lo covers her head when the raven picks up speed and whooshes close. It passes her and sets its sights on me.

Talons drag across my scalp when it returns. Not forceful enough to draw blood—yet.

Lo goes to shoo it off, but she could be next. I shield her with my arms. She pushes me away, amused at my misguided chivalry. "Run! It's you she wants!"

For a moment, it's almost flirtatious. Or at least, it would be if there wasn't a murderous bird attacking us. "Go!" she says and laughs, shoving her palm into my chest. I'm thrown off-balance by that laugh, by the sparkle in her hazel eyes. Knocked completely off-kilter, I rock back on my heels, and my stomach bottoms out as I realize I'm falling.

It happens fast, before I can even shout. And then I'm submerged. It's shallow, perhaps five feet deep, so my arse hits the river stones. I break the surface and gasp in shock.

"Aidan!" Lo sprints from the bridge to the creek's edge, crunching reeds along the muddy bank. "Are you okay?"

I stand in chest-deep water. Rivulets stream from my soggy hair. "Did you see that? An unhinged harpy just tried to drown me."

"I took a Hippocratic oath. I was just trying to get you away from that raven. I didn't mean to actually push you off the bridge." Now she's in up to her ankles, sandals coated in mud. That woman neurotically cares about her shoes. Maybe she cares about me, too. "I mean . . . have I thought about it? Maybe."

"Were you worried about me?" I trudge back to the creek edge in waterlogged clothing, failing to suppress a delighted grin.

"Worried I'd have to haul you out of the water to administer CPR."

"Don't act like a little mouth-to-mouth would be such an imposition."

Cielo's teeth press into her juicy bottom lip, and the energy shifts between us when I realize it's because her gaze is fixed to the wet shirt plastered across my chest that's become all but transparent. I attempt a seductive swagger back to the grass, but the marshy surface pulls me down. As Lo reaches out to help me out of the mud, I consider pulling her into the water, just to hear her squeal in protest and have an excuse to hold her tight to my body—but we're not there yet. Maybe not ever again.

From a nearby tree branch, the raven caws another warning before flying off in search of its next victim. Cielo shakes her head.

"What did it want? We haven't got any food," I say.

"It thinks we're about to send a falcon out to hunt. The guide earlier said some of the other birds in the area get territorial."

Plodding awkwardly up the bank, I try to recover some semblance of the effortlessly cool musician I'm supposed to be. Mud squelches in my shoes. I smooth a hand over my heavy trousers to wick some of it away. When my palms skim over empty pockets, my stomach drops.

The ring box Callum had entrusted to me is gone.

"No, no, no, no . . ." I pat the pockets again in hopes that it will magically materialize.

"What?" Lo asks.

"The ring! Callum gave it to me for safekeeping."

"You lost it?"

"Only because you threw me off a fecking bridge!"

"I didn't do it on purpose!"

A wave of nausea washes over me. "It's an heirloom, it belonged to his grandmother. God. I'm the worst best man ever."

"Untrue," Lo assures me. "You're sure you had it before you fell?"

"He'd just given it to me. It was in my back pocket, in a ring box. I'm going to be sick."

Without hesitation, Cielo marches toward the creek again, craning her neck and moving aside reeds. "What color is it?"

"Dark gray, rounded edges. Gold hinge."

"Seriously . . . ?" She peers grimly at the thousands of smooth gray stones composing the creek bed. "It'll be like finding a needle in a haystack."

"Afraid so."

I follow our footprints through the mud back to the water. Nothing. Wading into the creek slowly, I nudge stones aside with my foot in search for the telltale seam of the gold-hinged lid. My unease rises with each stone overturned.

Lo follows me in, hissing as she is engulfed in cool water up to her chest.

It's impossible to make out any difference between the stones, so I bend down, angling to keep my nose above the surface as I navigate them by touch.

"I won't forgive myself if I lost it."

Lo's wet hand rests on my shoulder. "Hey. We're going to find it if we have to turn every stone in this creek."

Determination blazes in her hazel eyes, but something softer lies just under the surface. This small touch fans the flame of hope within my chest. I curl my fingers into a fist to stop myself from pulling her into an embrace. The instinct to wrap her in a hug is so strong, like muscle memory. When I was worried sick for Marie, Lo was always there. When I was burnt out, working to support my family while still playing music, Lo was there. And now . . . she's here. Mere centimeters away.

Cielo isn't quite tall enough to reach the bottom without putting her head underwater, so she takes a gulp of air before submerging her whole body in the creek. Her hair dances in the stream's flow, lending her an ethereal quality. She gasps as she breaks the surface, hair sleek against her forehead and peaked nipples visible through her clothes.

Our eyes meet and I'm transported back in time, to jumping off the diving board into the bay at Salthill Promenade. The freezing crash of the sea and contrasting warmth of her skin. Licking salt from her lips as we treaded water. My blood stirs as her droplet-covered lashes lower to rove over my wet body. In an instant, the cold creek feels like a hot tub ready to boil over.

Cielo breaks first, drawing in a deep breath before submerging herself again to search for the ring box. I open my eyes underwater to search, and see Lo groping blindly at each stone before casting it aside. She rises to the surface and I follow, empty-handed.

Heart growing heavy with the acceptance that I've lost Callum's ring, I shake my head. Ripples surround us as Lo wades closer.

"Thanks for trying," I say.

She frowns. "That's it?"

A gentle wave sloshes as I gesture at the countless stones. It feels like one's lodged in my chest. "It's a lost cause."

The disappointment in her eyes says it all. She needs to see me try, against all odds.

The thing is: If I could go back in time, I wouldn't do things all that differently. Yes, I'd tell Lo that we're stronger than the statistics against a long-distance relationship . . . But I would still go to London. She understood that if I didn't take that risk, I couldn't respect myself—as an artist, as a son, as a man—but she didn't believe we stood a chance if I left. How was I supposed to convince her we could make it work, no matter how many miles lay between us, when she wouldn't hear me out? Discouraged by her lack of faith, I hadn't bothered arguing.

I have to try now, even if there's little chance of success. I gave up too easily before, but now is my chance to prove to Lo that I'm willing to put in the work. If only I didn't have to return to London at all. My career is just too unsteady to risk leaving right now.

"Go ahead and get dry. I'll stay and look," I tell her.

"I'm not gonna let you search for it alone." Lo makes her way toward a half-submerged fig branch close to where I fell in.

I reach down to the creek bed again, fingers gliding across the smooth stones.

"Aidan!" she cries, clutching something in her fist. "I got it!"

"How?"

"Maybe the branch kept the ring box from bobbing along under the surface." Reluctant to trust me with something precious again, she holds it in a viselike grip.

"Come on, let's get you inside and warm." I gesture toward the castle.

We wade to the marshy embankment, pushing aside the reeds. I reach out, unsure if Lo will accept my meager assistance. She pauses for the briefest moment before her freezing fingers grip my palm. It's not an embrace, not even a hug. It's a utilitarian arrangement of our bodies for the sake of balance on a squishy patch of waterlogged earth, but the proximity has my heart beating faster. I tell myself it's the residual panic of losing the ring, but no. It's all Lo. She's always had that effect on me.

"Wait." There's so much to say, but I settle on, "Thank you for helping me. I'd never have found it on my own."

Lo's eyes dart between mine, searching. Water droplets still coat her eyelashes. She hasn't yet pulled away and I'm grateful for every moment our skin touches. Every inch of contact. "I think you would have . . . if you didn't give up so fast."

Was Lo now saying that she believed we'd have found a way to stay together, had I just fought harder?

Did she want me to fight for us now?

The sadness in her voice pulls the breath from my chest. I want to say something, but for a songwriter, I can be awful at coming up with the right words. When they're set to music and not uttered face-to-face, it's completely different.

"Aidan . . ." She says my name like a dare. An invitation. A plea. Two years of pent-up desire crackles between us.

Before I realize, I'm leaning in close. Cielo's hand slides up my arm and sends a jolt of adrenaline through me. Tentatively, I hover a breath away from her mouth, terrified to close the gap. Her eyes flutter closed. Cupping her chin, I bring our lips together. Momentary cold melts into warmth as Lo returns it eagerly. How I've missed this. Kissing her again after two years apart feels more vivid than I remembered, like a digital remaster of an old demo. My body recalls the sweet melody, and my heart races to its pulsing beat. When I skim my tongue along the seam of her lips, she opens to me beautifully. My hands drift across her chilled skin, from her chin down her neck. A delicious little moan is my reward.

Lo steps forward, close enough to brush the front of my pants. I nip at her bottom lip in retaliation instead of giving her the friction she wants. She kisses me hard and hot. Can Lo feel my hands tremble?

Her eyes snap open. "I don't think this is a good idea."

Too far. I took things way too far. What is wrong with me?

Although my arms ache to hold her, I drop them to my sides. "Sorry."

With a suction sound, Cielo extracts her foot from the mud and plops into the grass. The intimacy of the moment vanishes. Her sandals are toast, but she wipes them on the grass anyway while I try to process the abrupt change in mood.

"We'd better go tell Lark's mam we're not coming." Although they're providing dry athletic clothes, our hair and undergarments would still be soaked.

"Yeah," Lo agrees. "Her heart would be broken if she thought we just blew off her sun salutations or whatever."

My lips buzz from where they touched hers. My brain is replaying that kiss, again and again.

CHAPTER 14

Lo

I DO EVERYTHING I can to avoid Aidan's eyes as we enter the castle.

"I'm gonna get changed for the rehearsal dinner."

Falling into his arms had felt amazing; his soft lips and firm touch almost made me forget what went wrong between us. But I refuse to fall into old patterns for the sake of comfort.

I'd underestimated the power of his presence, but he's bound to leave me behind. Alone. It's his job to tour and travel. He thrives on it. Life is no less complicated for us now than it was two years ago, no matter how good it feels to be with him.

"Lo . . ." Aidan pauses in the foyer. "Can we talk later?"

"After the rehearsal."

Does he want closure or to try again? Because this feels like picking a scab, and I can't reopen that wound.

———

LUCKILY, I BROUGHT several nice outfits—I like to be prepared. After drying off, I change into a sleek maxi dress and re-do my hair and makeup. In an attempt to distract myself, I decide to check if Lark is back from yoga and if she needs any help before the wedding rehearsal. She and Callum are sleeping separately until they tie the knot.

I knock on the door and she pulls me inside. Workout clothes lie in piles on the floor, hairspray cans and contour palettes strewn across the bed.

"It looks like a Sephora exploded."

"Help me with this, would you please?" Lark points to the open back of her short, ballet-pink dress. The state of this room looks like evidence of a crisis to me, but she grins beatifically.

I oblige, tugging the zipper up her lower back.

She casts a glance over her shoulder. "So, I noticed that you and Aidan weren't at yoga . . . Interesting that you both disappeared."

"Yeah, I kind of threw him off a bridge into the creek."

"You didn't." Lark swivels to face me directly.

"Accidentally! There was this raven, and—"

"Forgive me for not believing that."

I don't want to tell her that I kissed Aidan, because nothing can come of it. And I definitely won't be telling her that he nearly lost the Flannelly family claddagh ring to the creek.

"I felt so bad that I jumped in to pull him out. So I had to go back to my room and change."

Something like vindication spreads across Lark's face as she blots her lipstick.

"Uh-uh. Don't do that." I wag a finger. "It doesn't mean anything."

"Whatever you say."

My phone chimes with the event reminder.

"You look beautiful. Time to go, Bridezilla," I say affection-ately.

We walk downstairs together. It's just the rehearsal, but Lark crackles with anticipation beside me.

Aidan stands by the French doors leading out to the garden where the ceremony will take place. He's delicious in a crisp white dress shirt, sleeves rolled up exposing his tattooed fore-arms. While he's still deep in conversation with Callum and the officiant, I take the opportunity to drink him in, but it doesn't take him long to sense my attention. His aquamarine eyes pin me from across the room. Their intensity hasn't wavered since our searing kiss.

If I knew what was good for me, I'd look away. But I haven't been great at self-preservation since Aidan came back to town.

He's pushed his damp hair off his forehead. As I walk closer, I can make out *LO* stamped against his skin.

"It didn't wash off?" I whisper-yell, gesturing to the faded ink. I try to resist cracking a smile as he arranges some hair to cover the letters, but it's stuck together in a wet clump that won't photograph well.

"I've been marked," Aidan says with amusement.

The scissors tattoo I'd glimpsed on the boat returns to my mind. Was I reading too much into the imagery of it about to cut through a knot?

"Come here." I rake my fingers through his hair to separate the strands. Mirth twinkles in his eyes. He's so damn pretty. "I have an exfoliating wash that might help scrub this off. I'll give it to you later."

"All right, everyone, here's the run of show." The wedding planner's voice cuts through the rush of adrenaline brought by

Aidan's silky strands between my fingers. She gives us an over-view of the ceremony layout in the garden. A white aisle runner cuts through rows of slip-covered chairs, leading to an arch of willow branches that Saoirse and her assistant will adorn before the ceremony tomorrow. The planner props the doors open and directs Callum to wait at the end of the aisle with the officiant. Up next is Aunt Sharon. Then, the wedding party—including Aidan and me—and finally the bride will meet her groom. Easy enough.

"Okay, Best Man and Maid of Honor! You're up," the plan-ner shouts from across the room. "Walk down the aisle together, please."

Aidan offers his arm and I take it. Golden evening sunlight spills across his face as we step into the garden. Unlike the flir-tatious race on the way to yoga, we easily match each other in an instinctual stride.

I lean gently into the sense of contentment when Aidan's fingers rest atop mine. But I need to stand on my own two feet. Leaning on Aidan hurt me once before and I can't—I won't al-low it to happen again.

My mom sits in one of the guest seats. Protectiveness surges in my chest as she coldly examines Aidan while we pass. This is why I don't want her to know our history. He doesn't seem to notice her silent judgment, but I've become attuned to it.

We take our places on the bride's and groom's sides of the aisle, but throughout the rehearsal, Aidan and I keep finding each other's gazes. Saoirse and Deirdre, then Anvi and Rory take their turns down the aisle, then Lark begins the measured walk toward her groom. Of course, all eyes will be on the bride to-morrow, but for now, Aidan's attention is on me alone. It feels like I've stepped back in time, to that first gig I watched him play, when he stared at me the entire set.

Clapping, the wedding planner brings the ceremony portion of the rehearsal to a close. We reverse the procession, and it's time for dinner in the formal garden.

Squared-off hedgerows and topiaries anchor the outdoor dining space composed of large round tables. Twinkly lights glow in strands overhead as the sun drifts below the horizon and the sky shifts to indigo twilight. A faint fragrance fills the air, courtesy of flowering vines snaking up the castle's exterior wall.

When I notice Aidan's name on the place card beside mine, my chest seems to constrict and expand simultaneously. Part of me wants to run from him, another part longs to sprint straight toward him. Well, I can't very well run away from Lark's rehearsal dinner when I have a speech to give.

Sharing a table with both Aidan and my mom is a study in tension. From the concerned glances Aidan keeps throwing me to the way my mom grills him on his career, it's a strange energy for a celebratory dinner. But my maid of honor speech goes better than planned, earning a few laughs as I lead a toast to the couple.

Halfway through the salad course, my mom rubs her temples.

"Everything all right, Mom?"

"All that patchouli oil Aunt Sharon wears gives me a headache."

I offer a small smile and make a mental note to ask my aunt to tone it down before the ceremony. "I have some medicine in my room. Let me grab it."

As I ascend the stairs, the soft concern etched on Aidan's brow flashes in my mind. I don't love leaving him alone with her.

It doesn't take long to retrieve the headache remedy and tuck it into my clutch. Soon I'm back in the formal garden, striding toward our table. Aidan catches my gaze and then flits his eyes to the man beside him. My ankle rolls as I come down wrong on my heel when I see who it is. My stumble catches the eye of the whole table, and now everyone is staring.

"Dad?"

My eyes snap to my mom, who is staring at her empty place setting, and my blood goes hot.

I shoot a questioning scowl at Lark. She told me he'd RSVP'd *no* and hadn't said a word about him since.

My dad rises from his chair and spreads his arms. "Surprise!"

"Yeah," I sputter. "Very. Hi, Dad."

People say to forgive and forget like it's easy, but neither response feels natural to me. He provided for us, but he also left my mom and me alone when we needed him. My bitter heart clings to those transgressions.

My dad comes around the table to hug me, and we do an awkward tango before he wraps his arms around my shoulders. It feels so stilted. Growing up, I'd convinced myself that if I was the perfect, low-maintenance daughter, he'd stick around. Maturity was realizing that no matter what I did, he wouldn't stay. I needed to succeed for myself, not for his approval. For the sake of keeping the peace at Lark's rehearsal dinner, I try not to let my resentment show, but on the inside, I'm seething.

How dare he ambush my mom like this. What is his problem?

Over my dad's shoulder, I lock eyes with my mom. She knocks back a champagne flute and steals another from Aunt Sharon, who obliviously chirps about how lovely it is to have a family reunion. Nothing rips the scabs off old wounds like seeing your lost love in the flesh. I should know. I can only imagine how Mom feels. Dad checked out emotionally long before he and Mom finally split up. His distance sent Mom into a spiraling depression that threatened to swallow me up, too.

"Uncle Gustavo actually RSVP'd 'no,'" Lark says, her tone light. "So I did a spit take when he walked in three minutes ago. But hey! The more the merrier."

My dad walks with me back to the only available seat, which is sandwiched between him and Aidan, right across from my mom. Aidan's brows knit together as he tries to gauge my mental state. He's always been much better at smoothing out social interactions than I have.

"Maybe if we saw each other more, you'd know I hate surprises," I tell my dad pointedly. "Just like Mom."

It's one of the few things we have in common. We like to be in control and to manage expectations. The last thing I expected tonight was having to explain this to the man who was married to her for twenty years.

Dad rears back a little. "I know it's been a while since we've seen each other—"

My chair wobbles in the grass as I scoot toward the table with a little more force than necessary.

"You're the one who chose to study abroad, Cielito," he gently reminds me in the lightly accented, patient tone I remember from my childhood. Hearing my childhood nickname makes my eyes sting.

"Of all people, you're the last one who should be trying to make me feel guilty for thinking of my career first."

Hurt crosses his face before it shutters. He quickly manufactures a generic smile. "Lark, I was so happy to hear about your engagement, and even happier to receive an invitation to the big day."

Get it together, girl. I mess with the array of silverware in front of me, adjusting the salad fork so that it's aligned with the bread knife just so. My dad starts making small talk with another guest.

Aidan leans close. "You good?" he whispers under his breath.

"Not really," I admit.

His hand finds mine under the table. Countless hours picking and strumming have calloused his fingertips. I'd asked Aidan to be discreet about our history, but honestly, I need this small gesture of comfort. Their familiarity is exactly what I need.

The third course comes and everything is delicious. It's a shame I can't fully appreciate it since my attention is pulled between my parents and Aidan's grounding touch.

My mom picks at her food with disinterest. I remember the headache medicine I'd left to retrieve and pass her the bottle.

"That should help," I say. She nods mechanically.

"Tracy," my dad says. "Everything okay?"

"She's fine," I answer curtly. He wasn't concerned with her well-being when he decided to show up without notice. "Mom, let's call it an early night."

After we each give Lark a hug, I escort my mom to her room in silence. We both pretend like I can't see her chin waver as she slips off her shoes.

"Try to get some rest," I tell her in my best "caring physician" tone. My bedside manner still might need some work, though, because she responds with a faraway, "Yeah, good night."

I slip into the hallway and her door clicks shut behind me. Going back to the garden and facing my dad again sounds awful. Is it too rude to simply grab my dessert and hide in my room?

On my way back, I dig my phone out of my clutch and notice the screen is covered in notifications. Aidan had tried to warn me before I stepped into the garden. So had Lark. The realization makes my heart lurch in my chest. Footsteps thump down the hallway. I jerk my head up, anticipating another conversation with my dad that I simply don't have the bandwidth for right now.

But it's Aidan. A tiny sigh of relief passes my lips.

"I just saw your texts," I say softly.

"The second you stepped into that garden, I could tell you hadn't read them yet."

"You tried. And I appreciate it."

Aidan leans down and examines my face. I self-consciously swipe at the moisture collecting in the corner of my eye.

He stuffs his hands in his pockets. "That was quite the ambush for you and your mam."

"Yeah, I just walked her to her room. She doesn't feel well."

"And you? Are you okay? Hell of a move from him, showing up like this."

"I'm okay. I'm upset for my mom," I answer automatically, despite the long-suppressed emotions roaring back to life since dinner began. Protective. Jagged. Hurt. Abandoned. "He tried to talk to her during dinner and I had to run interference—"

Aidan's brow furrows. "Why not let them sort it? Protect yourself."

The question catches me off guard.

"I just don't want her to feel trapped into talking with her ex when she doesn't want to." I look at him pointedly, though I know the comparison isn't really fair.

"You've managed it," he says.

"I didn't want it to ruin her weekend. Seeing your ex can bring up lots of feelings. I'm sure it's worse to do it at a wedding when you have memories of marrying them."

"I'd imagine so," Aidan agrees. "But I know he didn't just hurt your mam."

My teeth grind.

"Put out your hand." Aidan pulls something from his pocket and holds out his fist.

My only movement is a lifted brow.

"I'm not an eight-year-old trying to surprise you with a frog."

"I dunno. You were fully dressed in a creek earlier today. A frog in your pocket wouldn't be completely out of left field."

"Give me your hand, Lo."

I hold a palm out, and he fills it with . . . a crumpled, already opened Skittles bag. My mouth twists in confusion as I stare at it. "Uh . . . Thanks?"

"You left before pudding, and I know you inhale those things when you're stressed."

Suddenly, the piece of trash in my hand becomes almost precious. I had been craving something sugary and planned on scrounging around the caterer's table after getting my mom settled, so she couldn't judge me for it. I smile up at him. If only they'd been sealed.

"Thanks," I repeat. I dump a few into my palm and examine the colorful candies. Something is missing. I peer into the bag and don't find them there, either. "Did they discontinue those nasty purple ones?"

Aidan looks away. "I picked them all out. After I washed my hands, of course."

If anyone else's grubby paws had been all over my candy, I'd throw the whole bag away. But Aidan remembered my fondness for Skittles, all except those disgusting purple ones—and also how neurotic I am about food contamination.

"But why?"

"Because you hate the European ones that taste like black currant," he says, as if this is totally normal. "You don't mind the American ones that taste like grape. Although I don't see how you can taste the difference."

I stuff a handful in my mouth and watch a smug little smile bloom under his auburn beard while I chew. They're sticky and artificial and perfect.

"That was very sweet of you," I say around another mouthful. "To anticipate my family-based neurosis. Or should I be offended?"

"I remember your coping mechanisms and my family drives me mad sometimes, too." He tucks his hands into his pockets, flirty as he adds, "No need to read more into it than that, unless you want to have another row tonight?"

I sweep a playful gaze up and down his body. "Why do I have a feeling you'd kinda like that?"

His focus sharpens, hot like a magnifying glass concentrating light. "Because you remember me, too."

The air between us is suddenly electric. I think about the way he studied me practicing knots. The sweet insistence of his mouth when we kissed at the creek. The memory of his melodic voice begging for mercy the last time we made love. Some people are just compatible.

Aidan was the first guy I felt comfortable enough with to experiment in new ways. He'd let me explore my desire for control and I discovered that sex could be more than physical release. It was empowering and exhilarating to be in charge of his pleasure, to tease him until his desire built so intensely. To be trusted. I allowed Aidan into my deepest fantasies, and he met them with open enthusiasm. Allowing someone else to see that side of me helped me experience my body as a vessel of sensuality, rather than something that caused me pain. I'll always be thankful to Aidan for that bit of self-discovery.

He scratches at his neck. "So, I have good news and bad news. Which do you want first?"

"Bad. Always give me the bad first."

"While you were walking your mom to her room, Lark told your dad he could take one of the rooms in the castle. He was yawning and looked so tired—"

"I figured he'd stay here." I scrape together the last of my emotional fortitude, then train my eyes on Aidan again. "She was just trying to be a polite hostess. I'm not mad at her."

"How about some good news?" he asks. I nod and offer him the homely bag of sweets. He puts up a hand in refusal. "No, thanks. I ate all the purple ones and now I'm ready to be sick." I start to frown, wondering if he really is nauseated, before he dips a hand into the bag with a small smile. He tosses a few candies into his mouth and sucks for a moment. "Well, the good news is your dad opened a trapdoor looking for his room and promptly fell into the moat."

Despite myself, I snort. There is no moat here.

"An alligator got him. My condolences." Aidan smiles. "He's still in the garden. But I thought that mental image would make you laugh."

I pop a few more Skittles into my mouth. "So there is no good news?"

"Nope. Unless you count more opportunity for reconciliation and bonding with your old man."

I pull a face. "What if I'd asked you to lead with the good news?"

"You wouldn't," he says confidently.

I open my mouth to object, but he is right. Loath as I am to admit it, Aidan is not only thoughtful, he's observant. And he remembers. Two years later, it seems he still knows me. Maybe he's not so fake, after all.

"Hey," Aidan says, "would you like to go for a swim with me? Right now, in the creek?"

CHAPTER 15

Aidan

CIELO STARES AT me like I've grown a second head. "A swim? Now?"

"Right now." Laps in her gym's indoor pool always helped her recalibrate. And I'm not ready to say good night yet.

Her eyes narrow. "What for?"

"Old times' sake."

"I just can't believe you're already nostalgic about falling into the creek. That was only a couple hours ago. Don't you remember how cold it was?"

"Come on." I gently brush her arm. "Let's sneak out. The rehearsal dinner is already over."

"It's dark outside," she says, but she's smiling a little. She wants to be talked into it. I can do that.

The hall window reveals a pale moon rising in a late September sky. I gesture to the pristine garden beyond. The tables of the wedding party are illuminated by string lights, but the guests are filing out. Shafts of pale light stream through the fruit trees, and the flower blossoms are pinched closed for the night. "Tomorrow is a full moon. There's plenty of light to see."

Lo steps closer to the window—and me—to get a better look. Moonlight spills across her cheekbones and she is divine. "It is pretty out there."

I grab her hand. "Come with me."

She doesn't jerk out of my grasp. "I didn't bring a bathing suit."

"It's practically pitch-black out there. I won't see a thing." I wink.

She laughs and I can feel some of the tension leave her.

After a quick detour to my room to grab bath towels, we are on our way. Most of the guests have settled into their rooms for the evening. We slip past the courtyard and it takes a moment for my vision to acclimate, but once it does the sparkle in Lo's eyes is enough to rival any star.

She hasn't looked at me in this way in so long. I keep my big mouth shut on the walk there so I don't mess this up. The back of Cielo's hand nearly brushes mine again as our arms naturally swing with an unrushed pace. My fingers itch to reach out and wrap around hers.

Lush grass releases its fresh, heady scent under our feet with each step. Frogs croak around us as we amble in silence, filled with wonder at the beautiful night. From here, the castle is impressively lit, spotlights on each majestic ash tree along the grand entrance; it looks like something from a storybook. But now that we've turned off the lit footpath to follow the creek itself, everything is darker and a little less refined.

Clusters of reeds grow thickly, and it takes some time to find an easier route to the water's edge. I've no idea if the creek is deep enough for a proper swim but that doesn't seem to matter now. I'd splash around in a paddling pool just for a few more minutes with her.

Cielo pauses when we reach a gap in the reeds, giving me a sidelong glance. "Is this whole thing a ploy to get me undressed?"

"Don't worry, I can't see you in the dark, anyway."

This earns me a flash of her teeth because obviously we can see each other just fine. Lo wrings her towel in her hands, either dreading a dip into the freezing water or hesitant to get her kit off in front of me. Definitely the latter. Murmuring water is the only sound for a few moments.

A low branch close to the water's edge is a good place for the towels. I hang mine over it and whip my shirt off, tossing it over a bush.

"Are we going the full monty?" I ask, unfastening my belt.

"Does it really matter in pitch-black darkness?" Now she gives me a sarcastic wink and I can't help but laugh.

"Suppose not."

For a second, it looks like Lo will lose her nerve, but she pulls her dress over her head. The navel ring at the center of her soft belly glints in the light, and I'm reminded of her telling me about piercing it as her first small act of rebellion when she turned eighteen. A lacy bra I don't recognize cups her full breasts. Of course she's bought new underwear since we were together. I squash the possessive jealousy that flares through me. I've no right, though it doesn't stop the feeling. This is a racy one, made to be enjoyed with the eyes, touched by the hands, stripped off by teeth. God, I want to do all those things. Though I've always had a soft spot for her simple cotton knickers that hugged her round arse just so.

"You okay?" she asks.

I suddenly realize that I've been standing here with my belt in my hand, just watching her strip, but can anyone blame me? She's a vision. I quickly push my trousers down and then notice that I'm still wearing my shoes. I step out of them and only remember my socks when they squish against the moist soil. "Grand."

Lo tosses her dress over a handy bush and kicks her sandals near it. She considers me for a moment. A greedy part of me hopes she'll undress further. She doesn't. This is enough. More than enough, more than I expected or deserve.

She steps toward the water in her knickers, and I reach my hand out to help her along the murky bank. A hiss escapes her lips when she dips her foot into the chilled water, then a bubbling laugh that breaks the tension. This is ridiculous. Two adults sneaking out in the night to wade in a little creek. Yet I'm almost as excited as I was when I performed as a headliner for the first time.

"Ahh, that's cold!" I bark when it hits me. My dick practically inverts by the time the water is waist-height. Stones shift under our feet and make it a slow journey, which is fine by me— I want this moment to last. Cielo's hand in mine, a smile on her face, the silver moon watching overhead.

Beside a boulder that peeks out from the surface and breaks the flow, we find a swath of water that moves a bit slower. Lo sinks into it until she's underwater. That's how she handles life— a complete submersion into everything she does. No half-assed attempts or lukewarm commitments. There's where I'd messed up: I hadn't proven to her that I was all in.

Lo pops out of the water. Already, she's more relaxed. Moonlight shimmers on the water droplets stuck to the strands of hair that cling to her face. We float on our backs and cast our gazes up at the stars. Heavy light pollution in London means I don't see them much anymore. Now there's one blazing right in front of me. Brilliantly mesmerizing and slightly volatile.

"What are you thinking about?" I venture after a few moments of restorative silence.

"Wondering if it's going to rain tomorrow."

I chuckle, because the answer is obvious. "You do realize we're in Ireland? I can count on one hand the number of days it *hasn't* rained since I was ten. What difference would it make anyway?"

"Some people think it's bad luck on a wedding day."

"Well, we don't. Or no one here would ever do it."

"I just want things to go well. Today, I had to get after the linen company because they brought these weirdly yellow-tinted tablecloths that didn't match the sample Lark and Callum chose."

"Isn't the wedding planner supposed to handle that?"

"Pfft." She shakes her head. "It's faster if I just take care of it myself, rather than trying to get ahold of her and explain the situation and wait for a resolution."

This is worse than I thought. "So you didn't even give her a chance to handle it?"

Cielo frowns. "I'm not trying to take credit or anything. I didn't even tell Lark it happened because I'm trying not to add more stress. Getting remarried is a loaded issue for her. I don't want to give her any reason to get anxious about this. She loves Callum, they're the perfect match."

"Exactly. They can handle ivory tablecloths without it derailing their relationship."

"Making things easier for her is what being the maid of honor is all about. I'm smoothing out potential drama, not creating it."

"So, you're gonna control the weather and do other people's jobs without even giving them a chance to step up? Maybe people would surprise you if you let them."

Lo blinks at me, and suddenly I'm very aware I'm not just talking about Lark's wedding. She never gave me a chance to prove the feasibility of a healthy relationship while I traveled and toured. But we can set up standing video-chat dates. I can commit to a frequent schedule of flying home to visit. Whatever she needs—but first, I need to convince her I deserve a chance.

"I'm pretty good at predicting how things are gonna go. Curse of being a realist. Just doing my best to prepare."

"You don't need to do that. Things will be okay even if everything doesn't go exactly as you planned."

"I just want my cousin to enjoy her wedding."

"She will! But it's not only about that. It's the way you approach school and life and everything. This hyper-independence. Like you have to excel in everything all the time and try to take care of everyone else out of some weird sense of guilt."

Cielo scoffs. "What am I guilty of?"

"I don't know, but don't tell me it's not guilt. I'm Catholic, I recognize guilt when I see it, okay?"

"I . . . well, yeah, I mean . . ." Lo's expression drops. "My parents' marriage fell apart because I got sick. I would hope something positive came out of the experience."

"It already has." I softly smile to reassure her, but my heart breaks. On some level she really believes her parents' divorce is her fault. "You're here today and that is the best possible out-come. That little girl grew up to be a phenomenal woman and will be a phenomenal doctor. But you don't need to be perfect to deserve good things in life."

Cielo's floating on her back, but she pauses, turns completely to look at me. Even in the dark, it's clear there is more than cynicism in her eyes. "Thank you."

She's even closer now, lazily treading water.

"I get it, though," I say. "Wanting to protect the people you care about from unnecessary distress. Make things easier on them. It's noble. It's one of the things I—" I stop myself before I scare her off. "Well, you can't go fighting rain clouds."

Cielo hums and closes her eyes.

I'd close mine, but this moment is too beautiful. Every detail perfect. Water pools in the dip between her collarbones and her lips gently part as she relaxes her jaw. I want to memorize every detail and immortalize them in lyrics, set them to the strum of a guitar and hold up a mirror for Lo in song. Try to show her how it makes me feel to be with her right now. I want to play music for Lo again. I crave her praise, yes, but more than that: I want her to understand how I feel and it's somehow easier to play than to speak.

Water gently swishes around Lo as she slowly waves her arms to stay above the surface. Smooth stones are only inches under our feet, but the dark water and murky sky feel merged thanks to the sensation of weightlessness.

"I've been a real bitch lately," she says, regret in her voice.

I stay quiet, waiting for her to continue.

She huffs playfully. "Don't rush to argue with me, now."

"There's no use fighting someone who's always right."

She splashes me and I yelp when the cold water hits my face. "Gah! You witch!"

Lo grins widely. My cheeks hurt from doing the same. God, I love her sense of humor.

"Come here," I say, pulling her closer. Her arm is freezing under my hand. I should get her out of this water soon. "I was just waiting for you to go on, you know. Why do you say that about yourself?"

"Because I've been treating you like crap. Aidan, I'm sorry."

Our foreheads press together. Lo is close enough to kiss. All I have to do is give in to the gravitational pull between us.

I lower my voice. "This hasn't been easy for me, either. I'm afraid I don't know how to talk to you anymore and I never know if I'm making it worse between us."

"You're not."

Earlier today, in this very creek, she'd said it was a bad idea for us to kiss. But I want to soothe away every worry in her heart. Warm her in my arms.

"Remember what I said about your name when we met?" I ask.

The memory softens her features. "'Oh, Cielo? That means "heaven" in Spanish, right?'" she says in a horrible mimic of my accent. Not that I can do an American one well.

"Then you told me that you're actually a hellacious bitch."

"Figured it was only fair to warn you. The name really doesn't suit me."

"Yes, it does." She's radiant and untouchable. She is heavenly to me. "I've missed you," I admit, cupping her jaw.

Our mouths are so close I can sense the warmth. Cielo's absence has been like a phantom limb. When I got terribly lost while visiting Brussels or wanted feedback on lyrics in progress . . . my instinct was to call Lo. "But it feels inadequate to say. It's not enough."

Her eyes lock onto mine. "I missed you, too."

She needs to know that I want to rekindle what we once had. She needs to hear that I'm sorry.

"Lo, I have to tell you—"

Something catches her attention. "Hang on, you've got a leaf on your neck." Lo reaches to brush it off then recoils in horror. "Oh, hell no."

"What?" On its own accord, my hand rises to touch whatever it is, because I can't feel anything.

"Don't!"

"You're freaking me out. What is on me?"

Something sends her into a full-body gag, and she flails her arms like she's trying to shake something off.

"It's a fecking leech, isn't it?"

"I know I have to be detached about things like this on the job, but right now my skin is crawling." It's not often you get to see something rattle Lo, but she doesn't deal with anything that creeps or slithers.

"Okay. I can handle this," she says, pulling herself together. "We need to break the suction first. If you just rip it off, the mouth pieces could get stuck in the wound and cause an infection."

The thought of pieces of leech being caught in my neck makes me go green. "Go on, then."

"I'd rather do it where I can see properly. And I'll need something to stop the bleeding then anyway."

"How do you know so much about this?"

"One of my first patients chopped two of his fingers off reaching under a lawn mower to free a jammed stick."

One moment, I'm holding Cielo's wet, nearly nude body against me. The next, I'm being feasted on by a parasite and discussing dismemberment. I wince but fail to see the connection.

"Medicinal leeches are helpful when we have a replantation of the digits," Lo explains. "They help the swelling. It sounds like something from another century, but when other methods fail, applying leeches to the healing site can mean the difference between keeping your fingers or not. Pretty revolting, though."

In different circumstances, I might find that fascinating. Lo's perpetual curiosity has rubbed off on me before. Currently, however, I just want this bloodsucker off me.

Towels wrapped around ourselves, we sprint back to the castle. She borrows a first aid kit from reception, leaving a dripping trail through the lobby as she leads me to her room. It's decorated in the same decadent, historically inspired style as mine, and as pristine as it was upon check-in.

We set our clothes on a chair and rush to the bathroom sink. Lo's face barely contorts when she sees the leech writhe against my skin. I think it's because she knows I can see her clearly now. She's the picture of professionalism, neatly arranging the first aid kit on the counter before we begin: tweezers, tongue depressor, a small tube of hemostatic powder, saline, ointment, plasters.

"So much for a night swim being relaxing for you," I say. She'd always gravitated to the water to blow off steam, so it sounded like a good idea to me. "Now you're back to work."

"No, no. It was just what I needed."

We smile at each other a moment, still damp and dripping under the vanity light. I'd let myself get covered in these retched things if it meant Lo's happiness. Then she arms herself with a set of tweezers in one hand and a wooden tongue depressor in the other and my anxiety spikes.

"Wait."

"Don't worry. It won't hurt. There's also an analgesic in their saliva," she tells me. "So you probably won't feel anything at all."

"Before you start, I should check you for leeches."

"Stop stalling."

"Just let me check. I know you don't want one of these on you."

Cielo had been so concerned about me that she hadn't thought to do a quick scan of herself. Her expression wavers between revulsion and hesitation. "Okay. But this isn't some strip-tease."

I ought to school my expression, but when she opens the white towel to reveal the lovely expanse of lace and light brown skin, I can't help what my face does.

"You're enjoying this parasite check far too much."

"Guilty. Turn around so I can check your back."

Lo holds the towel in front of her and slowly turns. Those lace knickers form a little triangle at her sacrum, drawing my eye to her deliciously wide hips and round ass. I do not have the willpower for this.

"All clear."

She draws the towel back around her and tucks it under her arms. "Now you."

"Me?"

"You might have one in a place other than your neck."

"You're awfully keen to get a look at my arse."

She pretends to be scandalized. "I'm a healthcare professional performing a duty here."

"Only fair, I guess, after you showed me yours." My towel drops and her pupils dilate as they skim over the ink on my chest and the wet briefs clinging to me. Her gaze hovers a little too long to be purely clinical.

"Just the one," Cielo says. "Now if you're done showing off, let's take care of it."

The terrycloth wrapped around her torso slips a little when she presses against my neck to break the suction.

"Quit staring," she whispers in playful admonishment.

"Some bedside manner, Dr. Valdez." Worried about causing more damage, I try to keep still. My voice softens. "I bet you have repeat offenders coming through the A&E just for the chance of getting stitched up by you."

She shakes her head like that's a ridiculous notion, but I'm only half kidding.

"In the future, when you're taking care of the little ones, you'll be their favorite."

"You really think so?"

"Mark my words."

I feel a pinch, and a splat in the sink catches my attention. The leech squirms in the elegant porcelain bowl. Lo and I shout in unison, a duet of disgust. We've grabbed each other for support, my palms firm on her shoulders, hers wrapped around my biceps. Our eyes meet.

"Kill it! Kill it with fire!" she shouts.

I snatch the tweezers and grab the slimy bastard. Lo flips the toilet seat up. I fling it into the bowl and send it to hell with a flush.

Lo dry heaves again. "Ugh. I need to clean you up. Hold still."

She's ready with saline rinse and a tube of powder to clean the bite. She dusts it on and I flinch. "Sorry," she murmurs.

"Lo, don't apologize. I'm just glad it bit me and not you."

She presses the plaster against my neck, gently rubbing her thumb along the edges so the corners don't peel.

As the eldest child in my family, I've always been the one to care for Fionn and Marie, to help my parents in tight spots, especially when they moved to Galway. We never had much ourselves, but I learned to care for others. Until Lo, I hadn't ever felt the warmth that blooms, the absolute magic of having someone, someone as gorgeous and capable as Lo no less, tuning in to your needs. Not out of obligation or duty or familial love, but because she wanted to take care of me. Now that I've made a name for myself, people want a piece of me for their own reasons.

It feels good to simply be cared for by Lo.

"You had something to tell me earlier," she says. "Don't think I forgot about that."

My gaze drifts to my hands, but I force myself to look her in the eye. She deserves as much. "I've been wanting to say I'm sorry for the way we ended things. For the way I talked to you that night."

Silence forms around us, heavy as a morning fog. I lean an elbow against the cold stone countertop.

"You were so happy about the record deal and I brought the hammer down on your joy before you could even celebrate. That wasn't fair to you." She rests a hand on my arm. "You deserved far better than the way I reacted. I'm sorry, too."

"I only wanted to celebrate together."

"I know. So why didn't you fight for me?"

"How could I when you slammed that door closed? You didn't even want to attempt long distance."

"Of course I didn't want you gone, I wanted you here and close to me."

Does she still want that, somewhere deep down?

"But . . . I blew up and drove you away instead." Lo busies herself with gathering the first aid supplies. "I guess I needed to know that you'd put in the energy to make it work when things got tough. I know I should have communicated that back then—that's on me—but if you would've insisted, I would've given it a try."

Instead of doing that, I'd called her a hypocrite and told her that if she were in my position she'd make the same choice as me, a hundred times. She had already left her family behind to pursue her dreams. I'd been furious that she lashed out at me for doing the same. And not only for myself, but for my family when they needed it most.

"It broke my heart when you gave up on us so easily." Cielo closes the first aid kit and her hands finally still. "I expected you to tell me all the ways we'd be able to make it work, but instead you just accepted it immediately and walked away."

"Because I took you at your word that your mind was made up."

"It was immature and toxic and selfish of me," Lo admits. "I should've just told you exactly how I felt. I'm sorry. When you said you needed to leave for your career, it reminded me of my dad and I reacted all wrong."

How had I not realized that the undercurrent of her reaction was one of fear and hurt? I hoist myself up to sit on the vanity.

"I'm sorry for calling you a hypocrite."

"You were right, though. Even if I didn't want to hear it." Lo steps forward, standing between my knees. "I never wanted to make you choose between me and your future. I'd break it off before I held you back."

How could she think such a thing when she was the reason for my success? From encouraging me to perform original songs to recording video and helping me expand my online presence, Lo had helped my dreams come true. I just want to support her as she works toward her goals, too.

"You didn't need to cut me out of your life completely."

Her lovely hazel eyes drift across my face. We lost so much time together.

"Aidan, it was the only way I could let that wound heal. If we'd kept in touch, if I'd let myself listen to your music, it would rip the scab off every time and dump salt over it. I had to quit you cold turkey. It doesn't mean I didn't miss you."

That's a lot to take in, but my brain snags on one detail. "You've never listened to the album?"

"Only what I couldn't avoid. I blocked you on Spotify," she confesses, looking down at the counter instead of my face.

When people wrong Cielo, they are excised from her life like a malignancy. She protects her heart with clinical detachment and ruthless precision. When a tumor is removed, the surgeon cuts around the growth, all the way to the healthy tissue. They sacrifice a chunk of good with the bad, as a preventative measure. My songs were cut out right alongside me.

Hurt shines in her eyes when they finally meet mine. "Whether it was about us or someone new, it would break my heart."

I lean down, pressing my forehead against hers until we share our breath, steadying us both.

"The whole album is about you, Lo. Every song. Why do you think it's called *Heaven-Bound*?"

The title track isn't about being bound for heaven as some destination. It's about being bound to her.

Lo is the only woman who inspires me to find the ugly beautiful truth, songwriting pulled from the depths of heartache and the heights of adoration. It's plain as day that I'm still in love with her. How she feels about me remains murky. Not so long ago, she asked that we treat each other as strangers, but we know each other better than anyone. We've exposed too much of our souls to the other to pretend this bond doesn't exist.

"Our lives aren't any less complicated now," Lo says. "If anything, it's worse. You're on your way to becoming a household name and touring. I still have my residency to focus on."

I lean back to see her whole face. "So that's it?"

Lo sighs. "My parents loved each other, they really did. But my dad worked so hard to provide for us. Long hours and constant business trips. My mother would treasure the expensive gifts he brought home as an apology for being away, but I knew damn well that she didn't care about material things: She just wanted her husband home. It was inevitable that they grew apart, but they were in denial and drew it out for years. She resented him for being gone; he couldn't get over the physical and emotional distance. He'd come home and it felt like he was a distant relative just visiting, not my dad who technically still lived with us."

"You don't believe you can have it all," I surmise. The idea breaks my heart.

"That's nothing but a fairy tale. Sooner or later, reality will come crashing in. My mother didn't want to wake up to an empty bed that was supposed to be full anymore. She was lonely, overextended because she was still doing it all on her own, even if my dad kept us in financial comfort. Caring for a sick kid, running the household. I can't blame her: Why feel lonely when you're in a relationship? Splitting up was the natural conclusion."

No wonder Cielo felt so pessimistic. She'd seen her parents' marriage dissolve, and in some way, she felt responsible because her dad only left so they could afford her treatment. And because he was scared.

"My dad sacrificed being close to his family in Oaxaca to come to the States so he could pursue a better life. Everything he did was to give me a brighter future, even when it meant not being there for me and my mom. Even when it led to them getting divorced. I have to focus on my residency, or it was all for nothing."

From what I understand, it sounds like the classic "first-generation kid" pressure, to make their immigrant parents' sacrifices worthwhile and uplift their community. My heart goes out to her for being put under that unique kind of stress.

"Lo, you put so much pressure on yourself and somehow you can't see how remarkable you are. You're brilliant and disciplined and you work your arse off—and you deserve something good just for yourself. Not for validation of your parents' struggles, or for the betterment of mankind. Just for you. Take a breather and enjoy an indulgence every now and then."

Lo slides both hands up my thighs and my bloodstream ignites with desire. Although her fingers smooth gently over the towel that covers me, I can sense desperation in her touch. "When I do treat myself, it's only temporary."

Temporary is an opening. Her thinking may not have changed, but mine has. And I'm determined to make her see that we're worth trying for.

I frame her face with my hands. "Then let it be temporary. Let me remind you how to feel good."

"How long? The wedding?"

That's not nearly long enough.

"If that's how long I get, I'll take it."

CHAPTER 16

Lo

LET IT BE temporary, Aidan said. I can do that. What other choice do I have, with him living in another country? I do deserve to feel good.

Aidan's muscular thighs bracket me close to him. I slowly run my palms up them. They tense and his breath grows shaky. I can't help but feel like the sweetness of being close to him now is worth the eventual sting I'll feel later.

His eyes do that crinkly thing at the corners.

"What?" I ask.

"Just thinking about that questionable mnemonic device about butts I came up with for you."

A shocked laugh bursts from me. It's not what I expected him to say at such a charged moment. "Some say marry money, but my brother says big butts matter more," I recite. That one was to help recall which cranial nerves are for either sensory or motor function, or both. The idea was that the more ridiculous the mnemonic device, the more likely the information was to stick in your mind.

Aidan's grip on my ass is possessive as he draws me close enough to feel the heat of him against my stomach. "I'd marry you for that doctor money, too. Either way, it's a win."

He's obviously kidding, but my heart still constricts at the word. This whole weekend is about two people promising to be there for each other. Forever. I can't think about that right now. Aidan keeps bringing up the past, but I want to be in this moment.

His piercing blue eyes stay riveted to me as I caress up his bare thighs, skimming past his towel-draped hips, sliding up his sternum, until they rest on his chest. The scent of fresh water and grass still clings to his warm, tattooed skin. He leans in, stopping just before our lips brush to let his eyes drift closed.

Our kiss is tentative at first, but I revel in a give-and-take both exquisite and excruciating. Soon, any hesitation gives way to insistence. Aidan reclaims my mouth and my body. He's possessive. Indulgent. Passionate. Aidan's always made it so easy to turn off the relentless chatter inside my mind and tune in to sensory pleasure.

Somehow, I've carried a flame for him all this time. It's burned on, the last glowing embers of emotion privately tended in the deepest recesses of my heart, even after I'd promised myself to smother it and stamp out the ashes. I'd been so afraid that flame would consume me, but still I hadn't extinguished it completely. Couldn't.

Temporary, I remind myself.

"Can I make a confession?" he asks. "Watching you tie knots is all I've been thinking about."

Artfully binding him has consumed my thoughts, too. And my internet search history has gotten much more interesting.

Mutual respect and communication always gave us the confidence to explore together. Discover new things about ourselves and each other. I want to re-learn everything about Aidan, starting with how gorgeous he looks bound and debauched. Fulfilling Aidan's fantasies of light domination always made me feel powerful. His raw desire is palpable when I control his pleasure and my own. It's intoxicating.

"I touched myself thinking about it. About you, helpless and submissive for me . . ."

Mischief glimmers in his eye. "Think this castle has a dungeon?"

"Don't get ahead of yourself."

The four-post bed in the center of the room is perfect for this scenario. I walk over to it, letting my towel fall to the bathroom floor before I cross into the bedroom. Aidan groans and hops off the vanity, tossing his towel aside before following me.

"There are some rolls of ribbon and scissors in my bag," I tell him. "And a condom in the side pocket."

"Bossy," Aidan scoffs, but his rapid breathing betrays him as he fetches it.

"I'm going to remind you who's the boss tonight." I pluck the ribbon from his hands, but he holds on to the foil wrapper. I'd packed the wide, white satin ribbon to decorate Lark and Callum's car for photos, but it can be multipurpose.

Strands of tousled auburn hair slide through my fingers as I gently tug to direct him to sit on to the bed beside me. He scatters kisses up my neck, lowering me into the mattress until he's climbing over me. His weight is familiar and comforting, but not what this moment needs. With a hand on Aidan's arm, I hook his foot with mine, then jerk to the side. We tumble across the bed and I pin him beneath me. Bewildered lust colors his expression as he looks up at me. His abject awe makes me feel invincible.

"Did I just get manhandled?"

"Is it still manhandling if a woman does it?"

"Either way," he says, "that was super hot."

My fingertips trace up the underside of Aidan's forearms, appreciating the softer skin and veins that run under their inked surfaces. He squirms and swallows hard, resisting the teasing tickle. I stop at his wrists, bracing them on either side of his head close to the bedposts.

With the insides of his arms exposed, I get a good look at the tattoo that so distracted me on the boat. A wickedly sharp pair of shears prepares to sever a piece of traditional Celtic knot-work. The image faces toward his heart, mostly unseen by others. Now that I'm up close, I notice a new detail. The crux of the scissors bears a *C.* My heart flips at the sight.

I regret how sharp I was to Aidan in our last conversation as a couple. Ending things cleanly felt like the humane thing to do at the time, even if his optimism was snuffed out alongside our future together.

I gently trace the curve of my initial. "This is for me?"

Aidan trembles at the maddening sensation but doesn't pull away. He whispers, "It's always for you."

Deep down, I knew that. The songs he sings, the tattoo marking him. What must have been going through his mind as he made my initial a part of his body after we broke up? Was it anger, devotion, or obsession, or simply an act of denial? "Why?"

"I was in Amsterdam and my bass player was getting something at this little tattoo shop. One of my songs started playing and it felt like a sign."

"I cut off something meant to go on forever?" I ask softly.

"Do you see any strings cut?"

It takes some effort to tear myself from the earnestness on Aidan's face and get another look at the ink. He's right: All the strings remain intact. The scissors haven't followed through on their threat. Now I'm not sure how to interpret the image. Is the point that the thread between us hasn't been severed?

Keeping his wrists pinned, I lean down and gently lick the outline of the ink. A soft breath of air on the streak of moisture earns me his gasp, a buck of his hips. I let myself straddle him then claim his mouth. Our kiss is a charged conversation. Hot and emotion-filled and desperate.

I tie the ribbon loosely around the post and his wrist with a sailor's knot I learned that day on the boat. The white satin isn't ideal, but this knot shouldn't tighten as he pulls, and I can release it with one yank. I diligently snip the length of ribbon with the scissors and repeat on the other side. As I lean over him to tie the knots, he nuzzles his face into my breasts through my bra. The drag of his beard and the heat of his tongue has me gasping for air. I push a pillow under him to raise his chest, so it's about level with his wrists. Dexterity is so important to his music—his career, his soul—and I refuse to risk nerve damage.

"Too snug?" I ask, taking the condom from his grasp. "Tell me if you can't feel your fingers."

Aidan leans closer to kiss me, and just to tease him, I pull out of reach. Slowly, I drag fingertips along his jaw, his chest, his stomach, as he squirms. Now that I have the chance, I'm giving

Aidan a taste of the frustration I felt when his music was all around me but he was too far away to touch.

I slide one strap of my bra down and toy with it while he looks on, anguished. The other strap. I comb my fingers through my damp hair and shake it out, buying some time to tease him.

"You're hell-bent on torturing me, aren't you?"

"And we didn't even have to visit the dungeon," I say, unhooking my bra. My chest drops and Aidan's eyes flash. Being so close to him but not touching is painful for me, too. I slip off my panties and climb over him.

"Smother me with those tits."

They're heavy and aching to be touched. He sucks a nipple into his hot mouth. I cry out at how sensitized they already are. He flicks his tongue against it, nibbling and teasing until I'm delirious.

"I could do anything I want with you," I remind him.

Flashing a challenging smirk, he jerks against the ribbon, testing its hold. "Then do it."

Our eyes lock as my fingers curl around his waistband. I tug his underwear off and discard them on the floor. Aidan sucks in a quick gasp as I give him a couple long strokes.

I pull away and reach for the protection, rolling it on quickly. The need, the ache is so intense. I need him now.

"Use me to get yourself off, Lo," Aidan says, voice ragged with want. "Show me what you've missed."

Something snaps in me. The culmination of two years of longing, of remembering, of resenting. All the nights I cried over him, all the nights I fantasized over our memories. I grab his thighs, push them up until he's bent at the knees, and climb on top of him.

"What are you—" he starts to ask, but the words shrink in his throat. I reach down to notch his length against me and mount him kneeling, Amazon style. The unconventional position, with his legs spread wider than mine, throws him off, but there's an undeniable current of excitement. We've never tried this before.

Aidan looks deep into my eyes as I sink down. There's a bit of resistance, and then such fullness that I moan out his name. He's a dream under me. All flushed cheeks and mussed hair. Vulnerable and exposed.

"You're gonna break me in half," he groans.

"Exactly." I sink deeper, accepting him inch by inch.

He throws his head back, exposing his throat as he vocalizes his bliss. "Oh god, you feel amazing. So gorgeous for me."

Amazing doesn't begin to describe it. Not even close. There's a familiar, slight sting as he stretches me but my memories did not do it justice. We lock eyes and I feel like the vulnerable one. Because despite everything I tell myself, I still can't resist him. Aidan must see this. It's intense, the unflinching stare and the way my body slowly accommodates his. Finally, he's fully inside. He tries to buck his hips, but I hold his knees up. I want him passive.

Aidan's forearms flex as he uselessly jerks against the ribbons. The contrast of smooth white satin pinning down his inked muscle is striking. He's grinning as if this is all he's ever wanted in bed. And I realize, I'm grinning, too. Because this— trust, compatibility, connection with him—*is* all I've wanted.

"Don't move."

Aidan's brow quirks. "Then you need to move, *babe*."

He knows that'll get a rise out of me. Rolling my hips, I

brace myself against his thighs. "Still. Not. Your. Babe." With each syllable, I grind against him and pleasure ripples through every cell of my body.

"Yes, you are," he repeats in that lilting accent. "You're gonna make a mess all over this cock because you're mine and I'm yours."

Pink streaks bloom against his black tattoos where I gently rake my nails down his chest. I've certainly marked him as my own.

He might not have much physical control right now, but he always knows which buttons to push. Pouring my yearning and years-old anger into each thrust, I move into a squatting position. My thighs burn with the workout. It feels dominating, even though I'm the one being penetrated. Aidan's eyes roll shut, mouth quirked in a beatific smile. That's exactly what he likes about it.

Frustrated because he doesn't have leverage to piston his hips, he groans. Damn, I might have to bind his ankles and his wrists for round two, because this is too much fun.

"Keep riding me . . . Let me feel that tight little cunt drip." Aidan's voice cracks in desperation.

Tension builds deep in my stomach, propelling me toward climax. I chase that feeling, increasing my pace despite the burning of my hamstrings.

"That's it, Lo, take it all," he mumbles against my breasts. "I know you missed the way I fill you up."

That's what sends me over the edge: his voice. Pleasure eclipses everything else, warm and white in my vision. But Aidan's not quite there yet and I need him to feel this with me.

"What do you need?" I manage to ask between strokes. He's so close, I can feel the tension.

"*You.* I just need you."

He's on the brink of bliss, gently thrashing against his binds as I ride him harder. Just perfect, flushed cheeks and blue eyes heavy-lidded with lust. Aidan moans as he goes over the edge and I swear I feel it in every cell of my body.

My hands tenderly frame his face, dragging along his soft beard as our hips slow. "Aidan . . ."

When his softening length slips out of me, he whimpers at the loss. *Whimpers.*

I pull at one knot so that it comes undone. Satin ribbon loosens around his wrist. I rub the red area with my thumb, drop a kiss into the center of his palm, then tug free the ribbon binding him to the opposite post.

"So beautiful, so good for me," I praise as his hands smooth over my curves. Beads of sweat on his inked chest glimmer in the lamplight as his breathing recovers. I cuddle in close and sling a leg across his torso. He needs to know I don't *really* just want to use him to get myself off. "It's always been so good between us."

"Every minute. Every time," he answers, stealing a kiss.

God, I never thought that would happen again. I don't want to return to the reality outside this bed. Not to the family drama nor the reality of his stardom or the stress of rounds at the hospital. Aidan's arms feel safe. They always have—but I can't stay in them all night. This arrangement has a time limit. I'll give it fifteen more minutes until I send him back to his own room.

"Saoirse said you'd eat my head afterward like a praying mantis if this happened again," he says, chuckling.

I lift my head up and look him in the eye. "I am kinda hungry."

He laughs harder and squeezes me closer.

CHAPTER 17

Aidan

AFTER CIELO SENT me back to my own room, I lay awake most of the night. Some of that was dedicated to writing down lyrics thanks to the sudden flow of inspiration.

Falling asleep in a hotel is never easy for me and trying to rest after what had just happened felt impossible. I should be in bed with her right now, the comforting weight of her thigh slung across my body and the steady rhythm of her breath reassuring in my ear. Instead, I'm alone, plotting how I can possibly make the leap from *temporary* to *forever*.

I can't let Lo slip through my fingers again. Over the course of the day, I have to fulfill my duties as best man, run interference with Cielo's parents, and figure out how to keep her. I should've gotten more sleep, but I don't regret an instant of our time together.

Cielo still feels like home. On the road, I'd tried to convince myself I was just a little homesick, but it's so obvious now that I've been heartsick.

By the time the bedside clock reads 5:34, I decide to cut my losses and start my day. Mist casts a soft haze across the formal garden as the sun begins to peek over the horizon. As I walk, I pull the folded best man speech from my pocket.

Speaking in front of a crowd has never bothered me—I've always enjoyed being the center of attention—but today's performance comes with added pressure. I repeat my carefully chosen words under my breath, trying to make sure I won't need to rely on my notes. Engrossed in rehearsing the speech, I look up and realize I've reached the end of the garden. There's movement near the garage.

Cielo kneels next to Callum's black Peugeot, fixing white streamers to the back bumper. She's not in her bridesmaid garb yet, just a tee and shorts that hug her gorgeous ass. My heart races at the memory of last night, the desperation in her eyes as she bound my wrists.

"Ready for round two?" I ask, gesturing to the roll of ribbon in her hand.

She jerks upright and gasps at the sound of my voice.

"Sorry to startle you."

Lo breathes deeply, hand against her chest. "It's okay."

"Canned peas? They're serving breakfast inside later, you know," I tease, grabbing the aluminum can off the boot of the car. Half a dozen cans are stripped of their labels and tied to the bumper by white ribbons.

"We should move the car. I kind of want the decoration to be a surprise. They're not doing the whole 'ride off into the sunset' thing at the end of the night to start their honeymoon, but I know Lark wanted some cute pictures anyway. I also have those bubbles for everyone during the send-off."

"You're not bad at this maid of honor thing."

Cielo rips the paper label off the peas and fixes the can to a length of ribbon. "What has you up so early?"

Wondering how to turn one weekend into a relationship. I hold up the folded paper. "Practicing my big speech. I always have a hard time sleeping somewhere new."

"Oh. I didn't know that."

"Neither did I before I went on tour." Before then, when I'd spent the night in a strange bed, I usually wasn't trying to sleep. By the time I'd spent the night with Lo enough times to want to rest, it had felt familiar. She had felt familiar.

"How does that work while you're on the road?"

"Eventually I got used to the tour bus," I answer. "Hotels are roomier and private, but I toss and turn the whole night." *It gives me lots of time to think of you,* I want to tell her. Not in a sexual way—although I've done plenty of that, too—but in the reflective yearning that seems to happen best in the quiet hours. The only remedy was to perform myself to exhaustion night after night and sink into the unfamiliar beds after a couple nightcaps. Just one more reason I was relieved to be on a hiatus for a while.

"Other than the rest, how's it been? Getting kind of famous, I mean?" Lo hooks her hair behind her ear.

"Most days, it's a dream come true." Do I tell her the line I give in interviews? Or the unabridged version? With everyone else in my life, it feels taboo to be too honest. Considering how many people would kill to be in my position, anything that acknowledges the darker side of it all feels ungrateful for my extreme luck in a brutal industry. You don't want a reputation for ingratitude spreading among fans, fellow performers, or record company executives. But Lo isn't just anyone. And she's also always been a realist. "Some days, there is so much pressure, I don't even want to pick up a guitar. That's never happened to me since I started playing."

I haven't admitted that to anyone, not even my own mam, who sees my career as a fairy tale. Shattering that for her just feels wrong.

Cielo's brows knit. "Burnout is bound to happen if you're giving it your all, all the time."

She would know. She never stops, never takes shortcuts, never compromises.

"My manager hated the last few demos I made. I hated them, too, although not for the same reason. I thought they weren't deep enough lyrically, but he thought they weren't commercial enough."

Anger flashes in her topaz eyes. "He doesn't like your music?"

"I haven't even liked my music lately. The label wants me to move away from the singer-songwriter direction, at least for singles."

"What? The folkier sound is what makes you special. Sure, you can evolve as a musician, but it should come organically."

"I'm under contract for the next album and they want to start recording by the end of next month. I might have to take their direction," I admit, rolling an empty can between my palms. My future hasn't truly felt self-driven since I signed with the label. A loss of creative autonomy has been the price of financial security.

Lo stares in shock. "Think about it hard before you do anything that threatens your artistic integrity. There's got to be a compromise."

"They also want to lock in an album and a tour each year for the next five. Five albums guaranteed to be produced and re-leased is a rare bit of career stability for this industry."

"You don't want some assholes dictating what you can and can't do for half a decade of *your* life."

"This isn't just about what I want. There's a fan base and executives to satisfy now and I've got to be honest: It's . . . a lot of money they're offering. With careful management, I could make sure my family is comfortable for the rest of their lives."

"You need to be comfortable with the music you'll be performing for the rest of yours. Do you want your name associated with music you don't care about?"

Trust Lo to give it to me straight.

"What does it say about me that I haven't been able to write a decent song in months?"

"That surrounding yourself with dicks makes you question your creative vision and sucks the joy out of it. Screw that. I always believed you'd make it big one day if people just heard you. The *real* you. And it's been true. Don't let them convince you that you're suddenly not good enough."

A cautious smile lifts the corner of my mouth.

Lo leans back to admire her work on the Peugeot's decorated bumper. "Okay, I'm gonna park this closer to the garden."

I step back to give her some room. She turns over the engine, but there's only a whirring sound.

Black smoke billows from under the bonnet. Shite. I motion for Lo to pop it and take a peek at the engine to confirm that this thing isn't going anywhere without a tow truck.

Lo waves a hand through the cloud and coughs. "What happened?"

"Looks like the starter is banjaxed."

"Do you think we can push it somewhere scenic and then roll it back when they're done with the photos?"

Fine morning mist shrouds the surrounding grassy hills. "It would be fine one direction, a pain in the arse in the other."

We call every mechanic in a half-hour radius, but most are closed for the weekend. Every one of them says that car isn't getting back on the road tonight.

"It's fine," I tell Lo. "We can decorate my car for photos. Cover it in fondant and make it look like a cake on wheels for all I care."

"Would that seem weird? Someone else's random car?" she asks. "It's too bad they only have the one vehicle."

"No, they don't."

"Lark wouldn't want to drag her Cinderella dress from a Lambretta. It would get filthy."

"I'm talking about the *other* vehicle."

Mischief flashes across her face. "Not the hearse!"

"'Just married' rhymes with 'just buried,' after all."

Lo shakes her head. "Lark might prefer her dress getting ruined."

"Hey, weddings aren't only for the bride. You've gotta think of what the groom wants as well."

"Well, Callum got his own cake. And it wasn't red velvet and armadillo shaped."

Despite dating a Texan, I will never understand Texas. "Armadillo? For Callum? What, is he not allowed to have any of the big cake?"

"It's a *Steel Magnolias* reference. Lark has made me watch that movie like five times." Cielo bats away my confusion. "Anyway, he can have plenty. Ugly groom's cakes are a tradition in the States, in addition to the giant ganache monstrosity. It's just something for the groom that the bride can't veto."

Wedding rules are lost on me. In the past, I'd only paid attention to the receptions afterward, but I want to be present for Callum and Lark. Cielo is much better at the role of maid of honor than I am at playing best man. "What did he choose?"

"It's a surprise."

"So," I reason, "the groom's cake isn't because a ganache monstrosity isn't enough. It's so the man can see his taste or interests reflected somewhere at his own party?"

Lo nods. "Basically. Everything else is all about the bride."

"Then we've gotta do it. Decorate the hearse, I mean. Callum deserves to have some of his personality in this day. Equality, babe."

Hand on her hip, Cielo gives me a look. "Not your babe. And Lark might be so mad that I'll need a lift in a hearse when she's done with me."

"If she hates it, we'll pop the Peugeot in neutral and push it out of the garage for their getaway photos," I say. "How will we nick his keys, though?"

"I keep a spare to their place. Callum hangs the hearse keys in their kitchen."

"Then it's settled. We do it for gender equity."

"You make stealing a hearse sound so noble."

"Borrow," I correct. "I intend to earn my 'best man' badge back after losing the ring—"

"Nearly losing the ring. It's safe, and it wasn't your fault."

Our eyes linger on each other until she pulls her phone out

and consults what I assume is her scheduling app. She shows me the screen. The wedding preparations and festivities fill almost the entire day, but we're in the slim empty portion right now.

"Want me to come with you to pick up the hearse?" Lo asks. "So you won't have to leave your car at their place? But I'm not driving the ghoul wagon through Galway."

"You'd do that for me?"

"It's not a big deal. We'll make it back before breakfast."

A few guests mill around the lobby of the castle, anxious for the morning buffet, as I wait for Lo to grab her keys.

"So how long do we have?" I ask as we walk to her car.

"Until about nine. That's when we'll start getting ready. We'll have enough time, it's only thirty minutes to their place," she tells me as the fob chirps, and she opens the passenger door. I double-check my watch. It's seven-thirty.

Sunlight spills through the cloud cover in brilliant patches, making the mist on the surrounding hills almost glow. It's beautiful, but when I glance at Lo in the driver's seat with the light haloing her, it's that sight that makes my heart skip. The scent of her rosemary shampoo fills the enclosed space and a Mitski song plays on the stereo. I gently twirl her hair around my finger. It's just long enough to wrap around my palm.

"I like your hair like this."

"I like your beard." She leans closer and adds, "But I miss the dimples."

I'm torn between going full lumberjack and shaving it off completely. I let my knuckle graze the skin of her shoulder. Her eyes flutter, not quite closing as she soaks in the tiny caress.

"Stop distracting me," she lightly admonishes, eyes on the road.

I rest a hand on Lo's thigh like I've done a hundred times before. The chemistry between us is palpable. If anything, it's even hotter than before.

We pull up to Willow Haven funeral home and Lo uses her spare to get inside and grab the hearse's key. She spins the ring around her index finger victoriously. "See? Plenty of time to get back by breakfast."

CHAPTER 18

Lo

AS I FOLLOW the hearse back to Castle Teachan, a blur of white fills the road ahead, like a cumulus cloud floated down to earth.

As we head downhill, the flock of sheep comes into view. Woolly bodies pack into the narrow space between the stone walls lining the street, and Aidan slows the hearse to a stop as the animals are seemingly in no rush to vacate the only path. He taps the horn a few times, but they are unfazed.

Immediately, my light mood darkens with anxiety. I glance at my phone. Lark is gonna freak out if both the maid of honor and best man are missing. Not to mention my mom will notice if I'm not there for breakfast with the rest of the ladies in the bridal party. On instinct, I reach into my purse and pull out the crumpled bag of purple-free Skittles Aidan gave me.

Aidan steps out of the hearse and waves his arms at the sheep, but they remain unmoved.

My car door swings open with a squeak, and I hop out. "Want me to help chase them off?"

Ewes make up most of the herd, but a few rams carry their

twisted horns high. I jog toward them, expecting them to scatter, but they just look annoyed and chew their cud right in the roadway. One bleats in defiance. "Come on! We have a wedding to get to," I shout—not that they care about our plans, but maybe the noise will scare them off. But as soon as a few of them slowly disperse, the rest of the herd quickly refill the gap. This is going nowhere.

"Shoo! Shoo! Go on, now." I throw up my arms as Aidan tries and fails to hold back a smile. Lord, that smile of his. "This is useless."

"We're still making good time. It's only eight."

"What if my mom needs me? Or Lark? What if we're stuck here and late—"

"Hey, they'll be okay for now. And the sheep will move. Eventually."

A low stone wall lines one side of the narrow road, the other side is a steep, wildflower-studded hill. Where did the sheep even come from? I don't see anyone here. "Usually there's a farmer or something around, right?"

Aidan tilts his chin. "A shepherd?"

"Whatever, Mr. Sheep Whisperer. I'm just saying, don't they have dogs for this?"

"Maybe they'll listen if we say 'woof.'"

This is getting ridiculous. Enough is enough. Throwing my arms up, I run at the herd one last time. "Get outta here, you woolly little shits!"

It's working. The sheep begin to part—but only because an angry ram is making his way through the herd. His low bellow sends my heart rate spiking. Out of instinct, I step back. "Uh, nice sheep . . ."

With a snort, he charges toward me. Aidan dashes in front of me with his arms held out protectively.

"Aidan!"

"Go," he shouts, running toward the cars.

I hop into my car and he follows on the passenger's side, slamming the door shut.

The ram circles the vehicle, feinting a couple times before he waits next to the door.

"Why do all the animals hate you?" I demand.

"That ram was clearly after you!"

Aidan had protected me without a second thought. Again. Outside the window, the ram continues to huff with indignation.

"Aren't they supposed to be docile?" I ask.

"To be fair, you called them 'woolly little shits' first." Aidan lifts himself off the seat and recovers the bag of Skittles he sat on. "Sorry. Surprised you didn't finish those off last night."

I grab the bag and lift a red one to my mouth, but don't place it on my tongue.

"Nah. I took care of stress another way."

Right now, we're both panting a little from exertion and I can't deny that it gives me . . . thoughts.

"Is that right?" he asks, far too nonchalantly.

The chilly press of his lips against mine in the creek echoes in my mind. The way he stared into my eyes as I rode him. The sweet release of my climax.

"Mmm-hmmm." I toss the candy into my mouth and the shell gives under my molars with a satisfying crunch. "I have plenty of self-discipline."

Propping his arm on the dash, he stares at me. "Meanwhile, I'm already on my last shred of it."

I dip my fingers back into the bag, extract a couple colorful pieces, and hold them close to Aidan's lips. Without breaking eye contact, he opens slowly. I carefully place the candies on his tongue, feeling the heat of his breath fan across my knuckles.

Maybe it would be smart to keep last night a one-off event, but he's too tempting.

Aidan follows my finger as I pull it away, nipping playfully. I laugh and jerk my hand back, but he's already captured my wrist. He sucks at my pulse, his mouth warm against the sensitive skin. Channeling his internal Gomez Addams, he kisses a trail up my inner forearm as I squeal and pretend to fight it. It feels so good to laugh and lean into Aidan's natural silliness, especially when I'm stressed.

"Still taste good," he murmurs against my forearm. "Still ticklish."

"Don't you dare. I'll flail around until I accidentally break your nose!" I warn through a grin. "And I'd hate to give the best man a shiner hours before the ceremony. Lark really would kill me."

"Not if I eat you alive first." He tugs me closer. When I look into his eyes, I can tell it's more than a saucy little threat. It's a promise.

Outside the car, the sheep gently bleat and shuffle around. No shepherd in sight.

I give in to my impulse to softly drag my nails along the edge of his jaw, enjoying the new texture. The caress earns me a sexy moan. I'm instantly ablaze with the sound of his pleasure. There is way too much space between us right now. I let my hand drop from his jaw, down his chest, until my wrist hits the gear shifter. "Sorry. Tight space."

Aidan's eyes dance with amusement.

"Do not say a word."

He grins and raises his hands. "Let the record show I didn't say anything."

"I know how your dirty brain works."

"No. Your brain went there." Aidan tilts his head and I follow his line of sight. "My brain went there."

The hearse. The three-alarm fire in my shorts immediately downgrades to the flicker of a single matchstick.

"You can't be serious."

His warm hand skims my leg, and I don't want him to break contact. "I'm serious. Dead serious." Outside the window, I notice the ram is done posturing and back to grazing.

"In a hearse, Aidan? You're a very sick man."

"I'm the best man," he corrects.

We stare at each other for a beat. It's such a cheesy joke that I can't help but smile.

"We won't get another chance till after the reception." He's right. Once we're back at Castle Teachan, I'll be busy making sure the ceremony is on time, the wedding party is in their places, and the reception events are on schedule. And he'll be . . . other than holding on to the rings and giving an embarrassing speech at the reception, I'm not sure what else he's responsible for. His hand slips higher. He drags a thumb up the seam of my shorts, just enough pressure that he must feel the heat there. Now it's hard to think at all. "Already thinking about my mouth on you, aren't you?"

Weakly, I nod.

Aidan leans closer, dropping his voice. "I'm hungry now."

That silky voice makes me shudder with want. It's just the confirmation he needs.

Aidan opens the car door and walks to the back of the hearse. I follow. With a quirked brow, he opens the hatch and sweeps his arm in a welcoming gesture.

"Look, if it's rank in there, we'll bail. But there are curtains on the windows for privacy and plenty of room. We're stuck here either way."

The sheep around us are at a standstill.

I crawl in behind him, keeping my head low. Rose scent lingers in the enclosed, upholstered space. No suspect stains or odor. The door swings shut behind us and I laugh at how ridiculous this is.

"Aren't you claustrophobic?" I ask.

He crawls closer on his hands and knees. "Guess you'll just have to distract me, so." Nimble fingers wrap around my bare ankles, slowly moving up my calves, my thighs. Then he pushes them apart and tilts his head. Enjoying the view.

Breathless, I ask, "Weren't you just saying something about eating me alive?"

"I don't want to waste any more time, babe."

"Not your babe," I shoot back. "And you're pretty bold to push my buttons, when I'm about to unfasten yours."

"Force of habit." A devilish grin spreads across Aidan's face.

Carpet covers the floor, but something cold presses against my hip. Metal bars studded with wheels are embedded along the floor. Casters to smoothly roll coffins in.

This is messed up, but I don't care. We're alone. When he's touching me, everything else fades away.

"Let me fuck you with my tongue till you're delirious."

I swear, I could get off on his filthy Irish lilt alone. I get to work unbuttoning my shorts. Aidan's breaths come rapidly as he watches me sit up and toss them aside, then pull my panties down.

"Bra, too," Aidan says. "I need to touch all of you."

"You don't get to make demands. Ask nicely," I remind him.

"Please, Lo." His voice is softer now. "Let me play with your gorgeous tits while I lick you. Please . . ."

"Mmm. Much better." I take my bra off and toss it aside, leaving my top on.

Aidan draws in a shaky breath when I seize his zipper and pull it down one millimeter at a time. The anticipation of first touch is delicious; I think I might be trembling from the adrenaline alone. He's flushed, eyes hooded and chest heaving.

I turn, swinging my leg over his chest before I settle down to sit on his jaw. My hands reach down and wrap around him. Aidan is ready—no, more than that, he's eager. His arms hook around my thighs, the reverse position giving him even better access to my clit. He hums, a vibration felt in the very core of my body.

Ravenously, he laps and sucks at the most sensitive part of me while his hands reach up blindly to pinch and roll my nipples. Pleasure mingles with pain. I smooth my palms over the backs of his hands, reminding him to be gentle. He takes direction well.

"I feckin' love it, babe." His voice comes out a bit hoarse.

"I'm. Not." I arch my back, sliding against his lips as I cut him off. He makes a muffled noise that doesn't sound like a protest. "Your. Babe."

Aidan breaks contact with a wet sound. "You are while I'm inside you."

His breath is hot against me.

"While I'm kissing you, while I'm touching you, while I'm licking you . . . While I'm inside you, you're mine."

I can't argue with that, so I put my own mouth to better use around him. Aidan makes up for lost time, pulsing his tongue until I squirm and sigh. He moans as I grind against his jaw, trying to maintain my composure enough to pleasure him at the same time. I don't want this to be one-sided, but I can barely focus when his face is buried between my thighs.

Soon, Aidan is gently thrusting in time with my movements. Dragging a hand through my hair, pulling his mouth away only to whimper, "Lo, please . . . I'm so close."

He squeezes my thighs and the taste of his release hits my tongue. I swallow it down until he's writhing with sensitivity.

You're mine.

I turn around, needing to be face-to-face with him again. He brushes my bangs off my forehead, and we let the weight of the moment settle between us: I just sixty-nined my ex in a hearse.

On-again, off-again relationships sound startlingly close to that famous quote about the definition of insanity. I've never been able to understand why someone would let themselves get wrapped up in a relationship when it's already been proven not to work. But with Aidan and the phantomlike aftershocks still coursing between my legs, I get it now. Doing the same thing over and over isn't a bad thing when this is the result.

Lips pressed to my shoulder, Aidan wraps a dewy arm around me. His heartbeat thumps against my back. I've enjoyed hookups since our breakup—if not quite this intensely—but cuddling has been strictly off-limits. I let myself luxuriate now in the tenderness.

"I've gotta say, a hearse is the most creative place we've done this," he says. "I can honestly say I'd never considered it."

"You're a horrible influence."

Aidan kisses me deeply once more. Reluctantly, I shimmy back into my shorts and find my bra while he stuffs himself back into his pants. All I want is to stay here in the afterglow, but we've already been reckless with our time.

Pulling aside the curtain, I peek out the fogged window. Only a few sheep linger nearby. "The herd is gone."

Aidan's shoulders drop in mock disappointment. "Are you sure? I swore there was a stampede."

"We've really gotta get back to Teachan. We have breakfast, hair, makeup. Saoirse might need help with a last-minute floral installation . . ."

His hands hold mine. "Trust the professionals. Everything is going to be grand."

Aidan must have the charisma of a cult leader because I believe him. His optimism threatens my cynical tarnish, gently buffing away layers of resentment until he reveals a soft glow. I feel exposed, a raw nerve. I worry the pain is going to sneak up on me like a cavity, but I try to savor his sweetness, anyway.

I lean in for one more slow kiss and reach for the door handle.

But nothing happens. It's not connected to a mechanism, simply a handhold to close the back hatch.

"Oh. Oh crap. This . . . isn't a handle."

"What do mean it's not a—" Aidan reaches for it, waiting

for the telltale click of a latch that doesn't come. My eyes dart back to the glass partition between the cargo area and the cab, but there is no hole or gap to snake my hand through. And no obvious button on the dash to release the back door. Aidan's phone is sitting in the cupholder, so close but out of reach.

"We'll just call Callum. Sure, it would ruin the surprise, but he'll tell us how to open it." I reach for my phone, only to realize it's still on the front seat of my car. "Okay. So that's not an option."

"We're trapped!" Panic rises in his voice. Suddenly, the humidity of our bodies is too much. "It only opens from the outside. Oh my god. We have to break a window."

After going out of our way to deliver the hearse to the castle for their photos, we were going to damage it. Fantastic. And I don't even want to know the cost of replacing one of these wide, etched windows. Maybe we can kick through the barrier instead.

Aidan's breath comes in shallow pants.

I steady his shoulders. "You're okay. We're gonna be okay, like you just said."

"We aren't. I'm full of shite."

I get it: Being trapped in a hearse is one step removed from being buried alive. At least this option has windows. He shuffles along the floor and peers through one. I follow, shoulder to shoulder next to him. A few straggling sheep are on the move. And there's a shepherd. An older man.

"Hey!" Aidan cries, beating a fist against the etched glass. "In here!"

"What are you doing?"

His eyes widen. "Calling for help."

"We can handle it," I assure him. We don't need this guy asking questions. "There's got to be a way to pop a window out or something."

Poor Aidan is sweating again. "Over here! We're locked in!"

The hearse gently rocks as Aidan knocks on the window to get the shepherd's attention. I run my hand along the door's seams, searching blindly for an emergency lever.

"Hey, he sees me." Aidan looks over his shoulder, eyes full of hope, then bangs on the window again. "Come on, help us. Open the door!"

I poke my head through the curtain and find the elderly man making the sign of the cross. Laughter bursts out of me. He's in no hurry to investigate a moaning, rocking hearse with frantic hands beating on the windows to escape.

"We're not dead!" I shout, even though it's doubtful he can hear us. He takes a step closer, removing his cap as he squints at the vehicle. "And we're not undead!"

Aidan cocks his head. "That's not suspicious at all. You might as well be shouting, 'Braaaains.'"

"You were the one moaning."

My fingertip grazes something cool when I go back to searching for an emergency handle, and I pause. The little nub of metal is the size of a door lock, and I yank up on it.

"Do me a favor and push—"

With a squeak the back door of the hearse swings open. Aidan grabs me by the waist before I go toppling out straight onto my face.

It's only then that I remember my hair is wild from Aidan's hands. We'd gotten so preoccupied with the prospect of being trapped that I hadn't really cleaned myself up, just slipped my bra back on and patted down the worst of my frizz. What we were doing back there is painfully obvious.

I climb out and give the bewildered man a jaunty salute. I've never done that in my entire life, but my body is on humiliation autopilot.

Aidan climbs out of the back door. His ginger waves could be considered "artfully tousled." The sexy disheveled look works for him, whereas I will certainly need the help of the hair and makeup artists Lark hired.

I crook a finger at him. "You'd better not write a song about this."

He bites back a grin, probably already mentally writing his next summer hit. "But I have the perfect name: 'Last Ride.'"

CHAPTER 19

Aidan

LO AND I tie white ribbons around the hearse's bumper. They look so innocent, although I can't help but associate them with being bound to her bed. Our hands brush as we both reach for the same old tin can. Lo's gold-flecked eyes snap to mine. It's odd, the rush I get from the accidental contact. Less than an hour ago, we were wrapped around each other. Her face still glows a little, her smile coming easier after releasing that pent-up tension. God, she's radiant.

Saoirse fixes a large garland of sunflowers and roses across the windshield and another across the back hatch. When Lo and I pulled up together, she gave me a knowing look.

Lo glances at her scheduling app and gives a satisfied nod to the hearse.

"Time to get ready," she says. "I'll see you later, Aidan."

If she hadn't asked for discretion, I'd pull her into a kiss. Instead, my attention drops to her mouth. While she's having her makeup done, I want her to relive those moments when we steamed up the windows. I want the memory of my kiss to burn on her lips. Cielo lingers for a moment before she leaves, and I know it does.

So far I'd gotten on my knees—more or less—but I still have a way to go toward true atonement. After the ceremony, she could decide to make another clean break. Tonight might be my last chance to win her back.

I rip my gaze away from her and collect the window marker and leftover bolts of ribbon. "Saoirse, need any help?"

"My assistant is working on setting up the garden arch."

My jaw drops when we enter the reception hall. What a gorgeous transformation. Burgundy and ivory linens cover tables laid with mountains of rustic florals. Roses fill the space with a sweet scent and willow branches rise high above the tables, offering ambiance as well as space for conversation. I can only imagine how lovely it will be bathed in flickering candlelight.

"This one still needs to be hung." She gestures to a huge willow centerpiece. Moss and tiny fairy lights wrap around the gnarled branches, supporting an array of tapered candles.

"Wow. You're getting really good at this."

Pride beams on Saoirse's face as she adjusts the ivory roses on one arrangement. "It was nice to have some creative license this time. Lark asked for something that told their story and let me run with it. Would you mind giving me a hand? There are screws in the beam over the head table."

"No problem," I assure her. The staff at the castle have already put out a ladder. I climb it and attach a cable to the eyelet, letting the excess hang all the way to the floor. Then I move the ladder and repeat the process.

Saoirse threads the cable through fasteners on the willow branches and starts to hoist the left half of it into the air.

Tapered candles affixed to each branch weigh it down more than we anticipated, and it swings suddenly. One of the candles falls out and we hear an *ouch*.

Rubbing at the crown of his head, a tall, long-haired man using forearm crutches scowls up at me. While the staff has been working around the property all day, he wasn't there a moment ago.

"Oh!" Saoirse cries. "I'm so sorry!"

His scowl evaporates. "Nice aim." Maybe one of Lark's guests?

"It was an accident," she insists, her eyes going wide when theirs meet. Saoirse's tall, but he's built like a grizzly bear.

"Someone like you should be used to taking compliments."

"What?" Flustered, Saoirse swipes her bangs out of her face. "I—well, I'm no—no."

He awkwardly bends to pick up the candle, juggling the crutches and a clipboard, just as Saoirse reaches for it. Their hands brush and she flinches with a giggle I've never heard come out of her before. Apparently, she has a thing for long-haired men with big, dark eyes. Maybe I should look away, but honestly, this isn't bad fodder for songwriting.

"I'm Gabe." He hands her the candle. "Nice to meet you, Miss . . ."

"Saoirse Delany."

They smile at each other for a beat. I can't wait to tease Saoirse about how red her ears get when she blushes.

"Sorry, I'd help you hang that ugly thing up"—Gabe glances at the sleek crutches helping to prop him upright—"but ladders and I don't get along."

Saoirse stiffens. "Ugly?"

Uh-oh.

"I have to wonder if the bride or the florist was responsible for that idea. Vision doesn't always equal taste."

Saoirse tilts her head.

Gabe pulls a business card from the clipboard he's carrying and hands it to her with a roguish smile. The lad has no idea of the danger he's in. "If you're looking for a real professional, I do event design."

"Gabriel Maguire, huh? You're an arsehole." Saoirse rejects the card.

He blinks a couple times before his expression falls. "Oh . . . Oh no. *You're* the florist."

"I guess I'm not a 'real professional' like you."

"I'm so sorry, I was just trying to say that I wouldn't have paired sunflowers with—"

"I don't care." Saoirse shoves the taper back into place on a branch a little too forcefully for it to *not* be a message.

"I thought you worked for the castle!"

"I thought *you* worked for the castle." Saoirse seems to remember me, still up on the ladder, watching this entire interaction. "I don't need help, Mr. Maguire. Thank you. Aidan, let's get this ugly thing hung so I can finish setting up this amateur design."

Gabe's attention snaps to me, and God help me, I pity the man. He doesn't even say anything, just gazes at Saoirse in consternation. Then there's the sound of his crutches against the stone floor of the reception hall as he retreats.

Tossing her head, Saoirse marches over to the second cable holding the branch. She never allows herself to be proud of her achievements, like successfully running the flower shop or playing a fiddle solo on a hit song, but as we entered this decadent space, I could feel her sense of accomplishment. Then one careless comment dashed it all.

"You've done a fine job, Saoirse. It's beautiful and Lark loves it. Ignore that twat," I say, readying my length of cable. Together, we smoothly pull the branch and secure each side.

"I should expect it. Things get cutthroat in the wedding world, especially when you start getting booked for custom installations in venues like this."

"He's clearly threatened by you, then."

Saoirse smiles. "He should be."

AS THE TIME of the ceremony draws near, I busy myself with last-minute tasks. A mechanic arrives to pick up Callum's car and after that's squared away, I head to the bar. A toast with the groom is in order. Callum doesn't do well with a lot of attention and a nip of whisky might ease his anxiety. There's a quick exchange—the barkeep already knew to expect me—and I thank him for the bottle. Whisky acquired.

Cielo's father, Gustavo, is seated in a leather chair in the lobby, tapping away on a laptop. Lo must have inherited her tireless work ethic from him.

"Mr. Valdez. Good morning."

"You're Lo's friend."

Friend.

"Aidan. Best man," I supply, extending my free hand. Of course, being spotted at a bar just after breakfast doesn't give the best impression. He's businesslike, especially in that impeccable suit. Cielo told me he rarely cuts loose. Holidays, mostly, which is why she loved their family's annual Nochebuena celebration. It was a glimpse into the more carefree version of the man who raised her.

His eyes are trained on the bottle clutched in my hand.

"I'm, erm, just picking up something to calm the groom's nerves," I explain.

Gustavo's smile warms slightly. "Been there."

My family bickers and then makes amends minutes later. Lo's communication with her parents feels like it's in breakdown by comparison, but I can't force things between them. Lark, Cielo, and their mothers enjoyed a private breakfast to avoid the bad luck of the bride and groom seeing each other before the ceremony. It made sense that Lo's father wouldn't be invited, but I feel for the man.

"About what happened at the rehearsal—Lo is just protective of her mom."

"Well, I'm not here to cause trouble," Gustavo says. "I'm just here to support my niece and spend a little time with my daughter. But she doesn't seem to want anything to do with me."

There's hurt and guilt in his eyes. I understand because I've been there, regretting the decisions I made with Lo. "Yeah, she'll push you away at first, but she's worth the trouble. Don't give up on her because she's stubborn."

"Sounds like you speak from experience."

"She doesn't hate you," I say. "She'll just act like she does for a while."

"Okay, you're definitely speaking from experience," Gustavo says then lightly laughs.

I crack a cautious smile. "Maybe."

As I head upstairs to meet Callum, I replay the interaction in my head. My time with Cielo is so limited that I want to soak in every moment of her company, but this could also be the opportunity to start healing the rift between her and her father. It seems like he's genuinely trying, but Lo refuses to recognize his effort. Too little too late, perhaps.

When I reach Callum's suite, he greets me from under a layer of shaving cream and ushers me inside.

"Thought you could use a bit of liquid courage. How are you feeling about the vows?"

Relief blooms on his face when he gets a look at the bottle in my hand. "B-b-better already."

I lean against the doorframe of the bathroom as he goes back to the sink.

His eyes meet mine in the mirror and he pauses. "I just want this to be perfect for Lark. What if I go mute? It happens sometimes when I'm emotional."

"No one here will judge you. Lark wants you just as you are."

"I can't understand how you manage it." Callum watches his reflection as he carefully guides the razor across his jaw. "Performing in front of a crowd."

A memory flashes of watching Cielo in the audience as I played onstage. Covers and trad staples came naturally, but performing new original songs for the first time always sent me into a bout of nerves. Locking eyes with Lo as I sang brought out the best in me. Her unabashed enthusiasm for my music, the way she'd mouth the lyrics, whistling and clapping after every tune. I know Lark's presence offers Callum the same comfort.

"You can't think about it that way," I say. "Your vows aren't a performance. They're a promise. Just focus on Lark. Let the rest of it fade away."

Maybe that's how I need to reframe my songwriting process: follow the message within each lyric, rather than concern myself with the judgment of the audience. That worked for the first album, but since then, I've been wrapped up in the pressure of the business. It keeps me in my head and stops me from writing with my whole heart.

Callum drags a towel across his face and reveals a smile.

"What's that look about?" I ask.

"When Lo is in the room, you can't take your eyes off her."

"Am I that obvious?" I pull his freshly pressed shirt from the hanger and hand it over. "I've really missed her. Tomorrow morning this bubble we're in with the wedding is going to pop. Tonight might be my last chance."

"Remember the time Lark and I split up?" He reaches for his waistcoat. "I was so worried about holding on to her, I proposed to her before she was ready and nearly lost her over it."

"You think I need to wait?"

"You need to listen. Cielo has probably already told you what she needs."

Although he says it simply, it feels anything but. My music career hinges on being away, and Lo refused to abide by that. She needs a reason to trust that we wouldn't grow apart when separated by distance, but I'm still not sure how I can prove that to her if she won't give me a chance.

"You've got the ring?" Callum asks.

"Of course I've got it."

Thanks to Lo, that is. She never gave up and because of that tenacity, something beautiful was saved that would have been lost forever.

A series of knocks interrupts our conversation.

I answer the door, and Saoirse and Deirdre peek their heads in. A burgundy bridesmaid gown swishes around Saoirse's legs and a sprig of baby's breath contrasts against her dark bun, while Deirdre is in a more conservative dress. "Hey, it's almost time."

"Come in. We were just about to toast."

"Callum!" Deirdre beams at him. "You're looking extra dapper."

"I'm so thrilled for you two," Saoirse adds.

"Are you ready?" I ask as I pour three measures.

He gives his spectacles one final polish. "I've been ready to marry Lark since we met."

I raise a tiny glass and they follow suit. "To the ones worth waiting for, then."

"Sláinte," we say in unison before downing the whisky.

Saoirse grimaces. Deirdre smacks her lips.

"Thank you," Callum says earnestly. "Making friends has never been easy for me. It means a lot that you're here. I love you all."

"Now who's being dramatic?" I clap him on the back and pull them both into a hug.

"Have we got a few minutes to spare?" I ask Saoirse.

"We don't want to leave the bride waiting. Why?"

"I've an idea of how to show Lo that I've been listening."

CHAPTER 20

Lo

BONG.

Aunt Sharon whacks the mallet against the crystal singing bowl again. With every strike, the makeup artist flinches. I hiss in pain as the eyeliner pencil jabs into my eyeball for the second time.

"Sorry!"

"It's all right," I assure her.

I cut a sidelong glare at Aunt Sharon, obliviously parading the thing around the room as the bridal party gets ready. This new age singing bowl ritual wouldn't be so bad if she kept circling the rim of the quartz vessel with her mallet, but she insists on "banishing the negative vibes" every few minutes with a few random whacks. And it's been going on for twenty minutes. Not to mention her headache-inducing cloud of patchouli. No wonder Rory and Anvi fled in search of champagne, and my mom slipped out to grill the caterer about their organic ingredients.

I'm *this* close to snatching that mallet away from Sharon and beating her with it.

The wide curlers in Lark's bangs bounce a little as we make

eye contact. My cousin's never been great at confrontation, and this is an emotional time for her and her mother, so no one wants to start an argument.

"Hey, Aunt Sharon," I say casually as the makeup artist swipes some eyeshadow across my lids. "Have you cleared out the garden's energy yet?"

She gasps and halts the mallet. The sound continues to reverberate. "I'll be right back."

Aunt Sharon dashes through the bridal suite, crystal singing bowl in hand. Lark smiles at me in gratitude.

The hairstylist starts to unfurl the Velcro rollers. Her hair will be down in loose curls, while mine is half-up, dusting my shoulders but pinned away from my face by a rose-covered comb.

"She means well," Lark says with a shrug. "Even if she is a bit . . . misguided."

"I know." There's a lot to unpack here, but I leave it at that. This is Lark's day. "Check-in time: How are you feeling?"

She's absolutely glowing. Taking my hand, she says, "I never thought I'd find love again after losing Reese. But I'm ready, you know? I'm crazy about Cal."

Emotions swell in my chest.

"Callum's a good one," I tell her, squeezing her palm. "You deserve this."

Lark gingerly dabs at a tear. "I sure hope this is waterproof."

The makeup artist snaps her case shut and rises to leave. "Don't you worry, that face is bulletproof."

With a final blast of industrial-strength hair spray for each of us, the stylist offers Lark congratulations before also leaving. Now that it's just the two of us, we decide to tackle getting Lark into the dress.

"How are you holding up with Aidan around?" She steps into a petticoat. "And your parents?"

"Surprisingly, Aidan's not the problem."

At least not yet.

"I noticed you two spending some time together . . ." As if that hadn't been carefully orchestrated by the bride herself.

"He's been really understanding about the whole mess with my dad."

Of course, Lark can sense what's left unsaid. "You have no idea how invested I am right now. Tell me everything."

Everything? The scissors tattoo on Aidan's arm flashes through my mind's eye. Which makes me think of ribbon fastening his wrists to the headboard and the wrecked lust in his voice.

Her mouth forms an O shape. "Okay, we need to discuss whatever just went through your mind because that's the perviest grin I've ever seen in my life."

Back when I was an undergrad in Austin, Lark and I would laugh over my sordid tales and memories of her college days. But it's always been different with Aidan. I suddenly understood why she didn't share any intimate details about her and Callum.

"Oh my god, chill!" I can't help the smile that creeps up my mouth as I tighten the corset-style bodice. "It's just . . . felt natural between us. I didn't think that Aidan and I would fall into old patterns again, but we have and I can't even be upset about it."

Hope glimmers in her eyes. "You've forgiven him for leaving?"

I chew on my lip before I remember the expensive gloss on them. "We both have regrets about the way things ended. I pushed him away and he left without a fight."

"I told you; you can't keep holding grudges, Lo."

"You might be right."

"Now, back to your dad—"

"One piece of psychological trauma at a time, please."

Lark catches her reflection in the mirror and goes mute. Ivory satin straps drape off her shoulders and the full skirt contrasts with the cinched waist, creating a timelessly romantic silhouette. Glamorous blonde waves studded with baby's breath and fresh mini roses tumble over her clavicle. She didn't have a big wedding the first time around, just a dress she already owned and a trip to the courthouse. So much has changed in both our lives since I stood by her side as maid of honor back then.

"You're stunning."

Joyful tears well in her eyes. We embrace and I remind her that she deserves to be happy and that Callum is one lucky man.

There's a knock at the door. It's Anvi and Rory. Anvi carries an ice bucket cooling a bottle of champagne, and Rory has a tray of strawberry-rimmed flutes. Anvi and I match, the streamlined bridesmaids' dresses a flattering burgundy that works beautifully against our rich skin tones. Rory sports a suit in a matching shade. Both squeal when they see Lark in all her bridal glory, which gets her squealing.

I am not the squealing type and never will be, but I smile wide.

We pop the cork and Rory pours.

"When I came to Ireland," Lark begins, looking into our eyes one by one as she speaks from the heart, "I never thought my life would change quite this—"

Aunt Sharon bursts back into the suite waving sprigs of juniper and a lighter. "I almost forgot! I read about this Celtic smoke-cleansing practice called 'saining.' The parallels between it and Native American sage smudging are fascinating—"

"Whoa, whoa, whoa." I throw a hand up to halt her before she can step farther inside. First she barges in, interrupting Lark's toast. Now she wants to light things on fire? "Put down the Zippo and back away from the tulle."

Her brows furrow. "Really?"

I place a hand on my hip. The universal signal for *try me*. No way was I about to let Lark's wedding dress go up in flames moments before the ceremony thanks to some dubiously appropriated ritual.

My mom is in the doorway behind Aunt Sharon, watching this unfold without helping me try to reason with her sister. Probably because she knows how infuriating it feels.

"It's fine. Right, Lark?" Sharon asks over my shoulder.

The rest of the bridal party looks uncomfortable. Lark says, "I think this is a non-smoking room."

"How would they know?"

"Perhaps the smell of smoke," Anvi replies.

Aunt Sharon bats the idea away with a wave of her hand.

"Come on, Aunt Sharon. Didn't you clear the bad juju away already?"

She scoffs and holds the juniper aloft. "Lark, you obviously need an energy cleanse in here, with your cousin around."

She flicks the lighter and I reach to snatch it from her hands, when I feel a soft *whoosh*.

Sharon freezes. I smell nasty burning and realize it's not the juniper—it's me.

My hair is on fire.

I'm not a squealer, but under the right circumstances anything goes. Screaming fills the bridal suite. The poor bride, her airhead of a mother, and the smoke alarm. Me. All screaming.

Anvi tosses a throw blanket over my head and smothers the fire.

Sputtering in horror, I reach for the hot, now-brittle ends of my hair and feel them crumble between my fingertips. The alarm continues to blare. Rory stands on a chair, waving a pocket square in front of the sensor to clear away the smoke and bitter smell of burnt hair.

Saoirse stands in the doorway Sharon left open, mouth agape as she takes in the chaos. "The groom is, uh, ready for you, Lark."

CHAPTER 21

Aidan

WE'VE BEEN WAITING to start the ceremony for fifteen minutes. Long enough for Callum to begin pacing around the formal garden where all the guests are already anxiously murmuring.

"Everything is grand." I straighten his boutonniere. It's the only bit of color in his black-on-black ensemble. "But let me text Saoirse to see what's going on."

Footsteps and hushed voices grab our attention. Callum turns away, not wanting to catch an accidental peek at his bride before the big moment.

"Sorry to make you wait, Callum. Minor wardrobe malfunction," Saoirse explains. "Lark is on her way now."

His shoulders sag in relief, and I pat him on the back. "See, told you."

The rest of the bridesmaids enter the hallway leading to the gardens in their burgundy dresses that match my suit.

Cielo is a stunner no matter what she wears, but today she looks divine. Sprigs of baby's breath peek out from her pinned-up hair, and her gown gives her a classic elegance. A healthy glow lingers on her cheeks that didn't come from the makeup artist, proof that she's no angel, but damn does she look like one.

"You're a vision," I say.

She traces my freshly shaven jaw and dips a fingertip into one of my dimples. Tenderness in her eyes, she whispers, "I missed these dimples."

It's a lot to hope for just from a shave, but I want Lo to see that under the trappings of fame, I'm still the man she used to love. Still the man who loves her. Martin says it's important to keep a distinct image, and that the beard tested well with the record label's focus group. But it'll grow back before the festival in New York.

"Thought I'd tidy up a bit for the wedding. Honestly, though, the suit makes me feel a bit like Beetlejuice."

Lo smiles, but she doesn't refute the resemblance.

Something acrid crinkles my nose. I lean closer and sniff her. "What's that smell?"

"My aunt lit me on fire fifteen minutes ago."

"She—What?"

Cielo shakes her head, quickly recounting the events that led to hiding the burnt ends of her hair in a flower-covered bun. Apparently, she was the picture of chaos only minutes earlier.

"I'd never know. You look perfect to me. You always do."

At that, she blushes.

The wedding planner wrangles the group, reminds us of our places. Delicate notes fill the air as the harpist begins plucking out "Rockin' Years" by Dolly Parton. With a final nod to us, Callum opens the garden door to the outdoor ceremony space. It's an explosion of autumnal colors, rows of golden tones of sunflowers flanking the burgundy aisle leading to an arch fashioned of willow branches, sunflowers, and roses. Matching fabric covers the guest seats, fixed with bows and even more florals. The palette is warm and welcoming against a bright sky.

Lark's mother heads down the aisle first. The planner waves for Lo and me to go next, and I offer my arm. We wait in the doorway.

She looks a bit frazzled as she counts out the beats of the song. "All right. Step out on my count."

"Stop bossing me around, Lo," I murmur. "You'll get me hard."

She tries not to laugh, but it earns me a smile anyway. Much better. "Three, two, go."

The flirtatious heat between us intensifies as we begin our procession. It's a wonder I can walk in a straight line. Her smile lights up the most shadowed places of my heart. Where I wonder if I'm good enough. Talented enough. Where I doubt that people like me for me. The places that have felt incomplete since that fateful night two years ago. It feels right to walk by her side.

Saoirse and Deirdre walk together, followed by Rory and Anvi.

All eyes turn to the end of the aisle as the harpist plays the first strains of the "Bridal Chorus." Lark is lovely in a classic gown, blonde locks loose under a soft veil. She meets Lo's eyes and they exchange a giddy grin.

Then Lark and Callum gaze at each other, and it feels almost invasive to watch such a tender moment. Instead, my eyes meet Lo's across the aisle as the officiant speaks about being brave enough to love. Even though he is alluding to Lark finding happiness with Callum after losing her first husband, I can't help but think of Lo and me. The mistakes I've made, the magnetic draw back to her. I nearly forget to present the rings.

The couple holds hands, and the officiant lays a braided cord over them. As he speaks, he wraps it around their wrists. "May this knot remain tied for as long as love shall last. May the vows you have spoken never grow bitter in your mouths. Hold tight to each other through good times and bad and watch as your strength grows. In the joining of hands and the fashion of a knot, so are your lives now bound, one to another."

Lo's eyes shimmer with moisture. She looks up at me and it nearly splits my heart in two. So much is still unsaid between us, but when she'd bound me to the bed, we both knew it was about more than kink. Will she allow herself to be bound by me? Will she ever trust me as I've trusted her? We never talked about marriage, but she craves stability. Something that I might never be able to give her.

Callum's attention drifts over the attendees before they land on me. I offer a nod of encouragement. *Focus on her. Let the rest fade away.*

Lark and Callum exchange personal vows in Irish. She must've studied hard; even my grasp of it is tenuous. Callum stutters as expected, but he doesn't let it distract him from his patiently smiling bride. The couple kisses—really kisses, with hands cupping each other's jaws and a dip that sends the guests chuckling when Lark yelps in delight—and slides off the knotted cord before raising it in the air together. My parents still have theirs hanging over the corner of their wedding portrait on the mantel. We clap, and I let out a whoop that startles a giggle out of Lo.

I offer her my arm and Lo looks up at me with emotion-misted eyes. She's gorgeous and relaxed. This weekend isn't enough. I want to see that open expression of joy on her face again and again. I want to be the one to put it there.

We head back down the flower-lined aisle inside. Sunflowers and willow branches seem to wrap around every surface of the medieval reception hall, vibrant arrangements blooming up doorframes and chandeliers. Taper candles on branches suspended above banquet tables cast the guests in a flattering glow.

Lark squeezes Saoirse's hand to acknowledge her beautiful work. "It looks like a dream."

Then we're swept up in a whirlwind of photos and handshaking before finding our seats at the head table. Time for my best man speech. Someone hands me a mic and I pull out my notes just in case I get tripped up.

"My name is Aidan O'Toole, I'm a friend of the lovely couple. The first time I met Callum, I was actually on a date with Lark."

Murmurs ripple through the guests and a few sit up straighter at the prospect of a scandalizing story.

"Don't get too excited; we were never an item. I never even got a kiss." I lean an elbow on the table and bounce an eyebrow at the bride. "Unless . . . ?"

"Feck off!" Callum shouts, slinging an arm around his wife's shoulders.

Lo laughs, and immediately, I'm looser.

The mic is a comfortable weight in my hand, my voice steady. "It was a first date. A double date. Callum was there with someone else, in fact." I cast a quick look at Saoirse. Nothing happened between them, either. "The whole time I was dancing with Lark, doing my best to be charming, these two only had eyes for each other. We ended up switching dance partners, and today, I'm so happy to see you take your first steps together as husband and wife.

"Sometimes," I continue, instinctively looking down at Cielo grinning beside me, "the right person is standing directly in front of you. It might not be how or when or who you expect, but when it's right, you feel it."

I stare into Lo's eyes, my heart in my throat, then tear my gaze away and raise my glass. "Callum, Lark, congratulations. Sláinte!"

Drinks raised to our lips, Lo and I watch each other over the rims of our glasses. I know she can feel it, the same way I do. Time hasn't tarnished the unique connection between us.

After the toast, I sit back down and tuck my chair in.

"Nice speech." Lo adjusts my tie without asking and my heart beats faster from that bit of intimacy than it did from public speaking.

CHAPTER 22

Lo

NO ONE IS more beautiful than a bride on her wedding day, but Aidan is a close second. His suit stretches distractingly across his toned shoulders and those killer dimples are back on full display. I can't keep my eyes off him during dinner.

The only thing that could distract me from the magnetic pull between us is accidentally eavesdropping on my parents at the next table over. They're close enough to catch my dad mingling with Deirdre while my mom miserably picks at her salmon.

Aidan follows my gaze to their table and frowns. "Does your mam need help?"

It's sweet that he is concerned about her, but I don't know what I could do, other than invite her to the head table with us. And, well, I'm feeling guarded over my limited time with Aidan. I don't really want to let her into this space. "Maybe it's best if I stay out of it."

From my place at the head table, I hear Aunt Sharon start to tell my mom about how Reiki would release my heart chakra, and I've never been so relieved for a band to call guests to the dance floor. I snatch Aidan's hand and he sprints out with me.

The wedding couple's eclectic music tastes make for a whiplash-inducing set list of Irish trad, old-school alternative covers, and country classics, even a little disco. The band was a bit starstruck by Aidan's presence but tried their best to play it cool. I can tell he's doing his best to keep out of the limelight and center Callum and Lark tonight.

When they break into Steve Earle's "The Galway Girl," changing the hair color of the song's heroine to match the bride's blonde locks, Aidan spins me. Laughter shakes his chest as he looks at me with such affection. His toast echoes in my mind: *It might not be how you expect, but when it's right, you feel it.* Staring into his face, smooth-shaven and dimpled once more, has me feeling weightless. This is *my* Aidan and being in his arms again is right. I feel it.

He slows, turns his head, and I realize he's speaking to my dad. Immediately, that bubbly sensation is replaced by a lead weight in my stomach. Aidan squeezes my hand as he gives my dad permission to cut in, then excuses himself to peruse the dessert table.

"Lovely wedding," my dad says, bringing me into a formal dance hold. "Lark looks so happy."

Salt and pepper threads through his dark hair and a tasteful Italian suit rests on his shoulders.

"Mmm-hmmm," I hum.

"Why are you so cold to me?"

"Sorry, but it's kind of hard for me to pretend to be a big, happy family."

"I'm trying here, mija. You can meet me halfway."

"Don't you think it's a little late for that?"

"I'm still a part of this family. And Lark invited me."

"And you RSVP'd no, only to pop up here anyway because you feel lonely or bored or worried about who will take care of you when you're old. Where were you when Mom needed taking care of? Or for her fiftieth? My sweet sixteen? Hell, my last chemo infusion?" Hurt flashes across his face alongside the flecks of light from the disco ball overhead, but I power on. "How do you think Mom felt, doing it all on her own while you traveled the country? How do you think she feels seeing you at a wedding, of all places, after you broke her heart?"

"Someone had to provide for you. That's all I could do," he says, pulling away. "It's true that I wasn't a perfect father or a perfect husband, but I did my best. I was alone through it also."

Part of me wants to shout that the isolation was his fault and all he had to do was talk, but that's not fair. He was raised different. My abuelos were stoic and old-school, and male emotional vulnerability can be seen as weakness where my dad grew up. Just admitting that he was powerless is probably a huge deal for him. But I need more.

I wish he'd absolve me of my guilt that my sickness broke our family. My guilt for resenting the very job that enabled us to afford my treatment and a portion of my tuition. I've thanked him for helping me many times, but it's easier to prove my gratitude by excelling in school than to articulate those complicated feelings. My teeth grind at the effort it takes to swallow that down. "This isn't the appropriate time, okay? We can talk about it tomorrow, but just let me enjoy the reception."

I push past my dad and dodge dancers on my march to the dessert table, where I find Aidan. Towers of gold-leafed macarons rise high above ice-filled steel tubs of water bottles. Votive candles and lush blossoms snake through the tablescape and hang suspended overhead. Callum's "Havarti and Plague Rat" groom's cake steals the spotlight: a round white mouse in a bridal veil and a dark rat in a waistcoat. Lark had based the now-iconic characters on her and Callum.

Aidan leans close. "Are you sure you don't need to spend time with your parents?"

"Maybe later." I grab a bottle of water and take a swig.

"Just let me know, all right? All I want is to dance with you, touch you, but I also don't want to monopolize your whole night."

"I want to spend it with you." The look on his face is the greatest reward. I'm two wine spritzers in at this point and determined to make my cousin's wedding—and my limited time with Aidan—a positive memory. "Come on. Let's have some fun."

When the band finishes the song, Lark gets up in front of the stage and lifts the hem of her dress to reveal pink boots. A string wraps around her ankle, leading to a balloon. Filled with air instead of helium, it rolls and bounces along the floor at her feet. Callum lifts his foot to reveal a balloon around his ankle, too.

"Okay y'all, we're going to play balloon stomp," she announces. "Rules are simple: Keep your balloon on and intact. Last balloon standing wins."

I grab a tray filled with uninflated balloons, lengths of string, and pass them out to each reveler. Guests are puffy-cheeked as they blow up their balloons, laughing and making threats. I get to Aidan, flushed pink and already a little undone.

"You're going down, Valdez," he murmurs as he selects a balloon.

"We'll see about that, O'Toole."

I set the tray down and get to work inflating my balloon. I tie the string around my ankle just above a strappy heel. They're killing my feet, but the outfit is simply not right without them. Besides, the sharp heel will make a marvelous balloon-popping weapon. Aunt Sharon better stay the hell out of my way.

When all the guests have their balloons secured, I give the thumbs-up to Callum and Lark that we're ready to begin.

"What's the prize?" Anvi asks.

"B-b-bragging rights," Callum answers.

Aidan loosens his tie. "Good enough for me."

After a countdown, the band plays a feverish reel—the signal to begin. Colored lights strobe in time with the thumping drum and energetic fiddle. Chaos erupts around us, with Rory and Saoirse chasing each other while my mom and aunt shout and shriek but refuse to get close enough to risk it.

I charge toward Aidan, grabbing him by the arm to steady myself. He pivots to avoid his balloon being popped, sending me careening into the macaron table directly behind him. Damn heels.

A few confections wobble on a three-tiered display as the surface shakes.

"Shite!" He steadies me with a hand cupped to my elbow. "You all right?"

"Yeah. Yeah, I'm fine."

With a steady hand, he brushes a rogue lock of hair from my face. Gentle knuckles graze my cheek and my knees liquefy.

Ugh, the effect this man has on me. Intensity burns in the depths of his eyes as they lock with mine. He leans in.

Then he stomps.

A loud pop fills my ears and I flinch. Aidan has the most infuriating expression on his face when my eyes open. Cocky and playful. It ignites my competitive side and my libido at once.

"You. Bastard."

A smirk spreads across his mouth. "No mercy, babe."

"I am not your babe." With that, his balloon bursts under my heel. "But if I'm going down, you're coming down with me."

Aidan's palm curls around the nape of my neck and he pulls me into a possessive kiss. My stomach careens as I melt into it. *While I'm kissing you, while I'm inside you, you're mine.*

Pops and laughter fill the air, reminding me where we are—on a dance floor, surrounded by guests, including my family. I muster the willpower to pull away from Aidan's kiss. I'm teetering on the brink of admitting that I like it when he calls me "babe." My swallow is comically audible.

"Did I do something wrong?" he asks. "Oh god, your parents. I forgot."

There will likely be fallout when my mom gets over her depression stupor and goes back to her micromanaging ways, but she'll be back in Austin soon.

"Right. Plus, it's just impolite to suck on your tongue on the dance floor. Imagine us dry humping in the background of these wedding pictures for all eternity."

"We don't have to imagine . . ." he jokes, but a note of unease lingers in his tone.

I straighten my dress and run my finger along my lipliner. "Let's get some fresh air."

Saoirse comes out victorious in the balloon melee, raising her arms in the air. We congratulate her and discreetly slip out the large arched doors leading back to the manicured garden and the impressive willow wedding arch.

Up-lights along the stone path highlight the last of the fall leaves. A perimeter of fruit trees mutes the notes of fiddle and tin whistle coming from the reception hall, but I can still make out the band's rendition of "Boys Don't Cry."

"Did you do this?" I ask.

"No, but that would've been pretty smooth, huh?"

"Lark must've seen that kiss, because it's unlikely that this track was on their wedding playlist. My cousin loves meddling."

The song has me sentimental. Blame the spritzers. Aidan hooks a hand around the small of my back and pulls me into a dance. Closing my eyes, I rest my cheek on his shoulder.

It's much cooler in the garden than in the reception hall and I shiver. Even with his body heat, I can feel goosebumps rise along my arms. Aidan removes his suit jacket to wrap it around my shoulders. Sandalwood and his body heat envelop me.

I touch his hand with a grateful, if sad, smile. "Why'd you play this song when you saw me at the pub?"

"To remind you how good it felt back when we were to-gether. I'm my happiest when I'm with you."

Memories from our time together are filled with so much joy. Passion, yes, but also patience and generosity and an ease I don't experience with anyone else. We'll never know what would've happened in the last two years because I wasn't brave enough to face the uncertainty of a long-distance relationship. We can't regain that lost time, but we have this moment. I want to sink into it, temporary and imperfect and complicated as it is.

I swallow hard. "What if I told you that becoming a stranger to you has been the hardest thing I've ever gone through? Tougher than chemo and med school put together?"

"You're no stranger to me. Not when every love song I sing is about you." Aidan cups my cheek. Sincerity imbues his words. "The truth is, I love performing. But some days, all I look forward to is climbing into bed because there's a chance I might dream of you."

I draw in a shaky breath, but a response doesn't quite form.

"Fans sing along to songs I wrote about loving you. They shout along to lyrics born out of us. And it feels almost invasive to reopen that wound every night and bleed onto the stage, because I can't help but think of you when I sing and relive everything I did wrong."

"God, I had no idea you still felt that way. I thought it was easy for you to move on. With your glamorous new life."

A mirthless huff comes out of him. "It's been a nightmare and a blessing to come from such an emotional place. I've hated that my career is tied to our relationship. In interviews, they always ask about my muse and I let them speculate because I've already spilled enough of my heart out to the public."

I lean closer. "It's taken you a long time to spill it to me, though."

"To be fair, you're far more intimidating than a venue full of screaming fans."

We spot a stone bench overlooking a reflection pond and walk toward it. I sit. "Sorry. These shoes hurt."

"Take them off."

"No, it'll ruin the whole outfit."

"Hey. You don't need to be perfect all the time. You can be barefoot and messy and real. I like you like that."

Aidan drops to my feet, not breaking eye contact. He tugs at the tiny buckle of my ankle strap and slips off one heel, then presses his thumb into the arch until I let out an involuntary moan. Heat flares in his eyes. He gently removes my other heel, repeats the firm, soothing slide.

Either he's taken massage classes since we broke up, or I'm so touch-starved and plagued by plantar fasciitis that he might as well be a touch savant. He gently kneads the arch of each foot with a thumb. "That's . . . really nice, A."

He smiles up at me. "You haven't called me that in a long time."

"I'll call you anything you like, if you just keep going."

It feels wonderful. Confident and not at all ticklish. Aidan folds forward, planting his palms on either side of my feet, and kisses the top of one then the other.

"I'm trying to apologize for making you feel like you weren't worth fighting for. You are. I was an eejit who didn't understand what you needed back then, but I'm listening now."

His eyes flit up to mine as he kneels at my feet. He's not often humbled, but damn does it look good on him. Aidan could have his pick of women, and yet here he is on his knees for me.

"Holy shit. Did you just . . . grovel?"

"Don't you dare tell your cousin I kissed your feet. I'll deny that one even if she waterboards me."

I cross my heart, then run a hand through his hair. "Aidan, I forgive you. But I think you're a little bad for doing this out in the open."

A rare bashfulness comes over him and he takes one of my feet, kneading it slowly. His knuckle runs along my insole and I'm melting. "There's little I wouldn't do for you."

He kisses each of my knees as if he's asking for entry between them. "God, I've missed you," he whispers into the inside of one knee while holding eye contact, his breath hot on my skin. His palms glide up the sides of my satin-covered thighs. I resist the urge to pull up my dress, spread my knees wide. "All of you."

"I've missed you, too," I breathlessly admit. It's been sweet torture being so close to him all day.

"What are you gonna do about it?"

I tap my chin theatrically. "I don't know. I kinda like you here, kneeling."

"Some things never change, do they?"

But they do. I've learned that I can yearn for someone more than I ever thought possible. I've learned that I was wrong about Aidan.

"You wanna get off your knees before someone sees us and people start to talk?"

"Let 'em." He rests his hands on my lap, one on top of the other and drops his chin on them. He's a sight to behold. Large aquamarine eyes twinkling with mischief and cheeks flushed from dance, drink, and a dash of subjugation.

I grip his undone collar to ensure his full attention. "Meet me in my room in five minutes. Don't make me wait."

"Yes, ma'am." Aidan lifts his fingers to his temple in the same mortifyingly dorky salute I gave the shepherd, and I roll my eyes.

My body thrums with anticipation as I sneak away from the

reception and upstairs to my room. I pull the flowers from my hair and rake my fingers through it, frowning at the singed ends.

The candle-like sconces bathe the historically inspired room in a soft amber light. It's a far more romantic environment than the hearse. I prop the door and leave my bridesmaid dress on, leaning back on my elbows on the bed as I breathlessly wait for Aidan's knock.

It's not long until it comes.

The door clicks shut behind Aidan and he leans against it, hugging a champagne bucket to his chest with an expression of pure trouble. "Hey."

He sets the ice bucket on the nightstand and picks up the ribbon there.

"I was thinking . . ." Aidan's dimples deepen as he rolls the bolt back and forth between his palms. "It feels good to let someone else take the reins for a bit. You might like it."

I sit up straight. "Are you asking to tie me up?"

"Yes. Let me take care of you. Let go."

Allowing myself to be passive goes against my every instinct—but ever since this wedding began, I've spent so much energy worrying over the smallest things just to feel like I have some control. And what has it really accomplished?

"I don't know if I can let go," I admit. "Even the thought of doing bondage 'wrong' makes me anxious. What if I feel trapped? What if I panic?"

"We'll stop. I don't want to do anything you're not into," Aidan says. "Think you can you trust me enough to try?"

"I do." The words come out before I realize, and I feel the truth of them. I do trust Aidan. I rise from the bed and stand in front of him. "I want to try."

An understanding passes between us. My mouth goes dry as his nimble fingers deftly undo the buttons of his shirt. Inked skin on display in the low lamplight, he lays it across a chair and slips off his dress shoes.

Satin slides across my skin as Aidan brushes the straps of my gown off my shoulders. I draw in a shaky gasp as he slowly pulls my zipper down. Strong hands waste no time stripping me of my bra and panties. Cool air hits my skin and pebbles my nipples. Reverence burns in his eyes as he caresses my bare skin with a maddeningly light touch.

He leads me back to the bed and positions me to kneel on the mattress, supported by my knees with hands in front of my sternum in a prayer position. It looks like I'm pleading—I probably will by the time Aidan's done. He grabs the bolt of ribbon and scissors, unspooling it slowly before clipping a length and winding it around my wrists. "Is this still okay?"

I nod.

"Close your eyes, Lo. Tell me what you feel." Aidan's voice is smooth and composed as he crisscrosses the strip of satin back and forth and tightens the ends.

I swallow and let my eyes drift shut. "Pressure . . ."

"What else?" His index finger gently tucks my hair behind my ear and lingers at my temple. "Tell me what's going on up here?"

"Vulnerability . . . anticipation."

"Perfect." Warm breath fans across my ear.

I gasp and my eyes snap open to find Aidan's hand on an ice cube pressed to my neck.

Dimples bracket his mouth as he watches my response. Oh, he's going to torture me. I should've seen this coming.

A sharp hiss escapes my lips as he presses the melting ice cube to my chest and sucks the drips off. The juxtaposition of his hot tongue and the ice water sets my senses alight. I squirm as he pulls my nipple into his mouth with a groan. Everything feels heightened.

Aidan eases me down onto my back, stretching my arms and bound wrists overhead.

"Need me to cut you loose? Or do you want to keep going?"

Heat radiates off his skin, close enough to sense, but I need the full weight of him on me. My answer comes out breathier than I intend. "Keep going . . ."

"You're desperate for me to devour that juicy little cunt, aren't you?"

"Jesus, Aidan—"

"Yes or no." The authoritative edge to his voice makes me shiver. That's new.

"Yes." I can't seem to keep still. My hips seek the friction he's so cruelly withholding. "I want your mouth on me."

A dark smile creeps across his face as he spreads my thighs. "Be careful what you wish for, babe."

CHAPTER 23

Aidan

I FEATHER OVER Lo's clit, looking up over her soft belly. Her tits are on full display in this position, wrists held over her head. Those generous curves look even better tied up like a gift just for me. I lean back for a moment, enjoying the view and the heady scent of her arousal.

Cielo is making me delirious. I can't imagine wanting someone more than this. I don't want to.

Tonight, Lo is all mine. Including her trust. Just binding her wrists is a big deal.

Keeping my promise, I flip her over onto her stomach with her head down, bound wrists in front of her, and perfect bottom high in the air. I move to the foot of the bed, tracing the round swell with my palm. Even the gentle contact crackles with raw sexual energy.

I can't resist giving her a little spank to remind her that I'm in charge now.

Lo jumps. "Oh!"

Again, I give her a crisp smack. Her arse and thighs jiggle in a way that makes my cock lurch, and a red mark begins to bloom.

While she's still gasping, I pluck another ice cube from the champagne bucket and place it at the small of her back. Flinching at the cold, Lo sucks in a breath but doesn't protest. She's trusting me.

Slowly, I slide the ice cube in circles, then I draw it down her spine, between her cheeks. Drips of water form an abstract pattern on her searing skin. My fingertips tingle with the cold.

Lo squirms and curls her toes when it grazes her. I pull it away and descend on her with my tongue to soothe the cold. She's delicious. I seek her pleasure as if it's my own, because it is. Hooking my arms around her thick thighs, I lavish Lo with all the attention she deserves. Probing, sucking, moaning, teasing her with the melting remains of the ice cube. The alternating sensations have her overstimulated, gasping and kicking her legs. I'm making good on my threat. Staying right here until she's writhing. Tugging against her ribbon restraint. Panting. Begging. Cuming.

"Aidan—ohmygod, yes—" The cry she makes as she presses against my face will echo in my memory forever.

"All those little noises you make drive me wild." My voice is ragged as I wipe my chin.

Lo's arse is still on erotic display as she turns to look at my face. "I love it when you moan against me. Your voice alone could probably make me come."

"I accept that challenge."

"You want to hear it, don't you?" A devious smile curls her mouth. "You want me to ask for it."

"You're usually the more demanding type," I reply, skimming an index finger up and down her slit. Lo's back arches as I gently push in. She's bound and presented to me like a feast, still wet and quivering with aftershocks. But I want her to want it just as badly as I do. "Ask me."

"Aidan." Cielo's voice trembles. She's always the collected one and I'm the whimpering mess. Hearing her like this has me at the edge of my control. "Please give it to me."

"Come here."

Cielo's eyes flash with defiance. Submission doesn't come naturally to her, but tonight, she wants a taste. I give her a stern look and point to the floor in front of me.

She hesitates, biting her bottom lip.

"Get over here now."

She rises from the bed and stands before me, hazel eyes glittering with excitement, but she's holding back. Still grasping at control. I tenderly run my hand along her jaw and kiss her. It's deep, emotional, hot. I'm telling her to let go and trust me. That it's okay to let someone else take the wheel sometimes. That it's even possible to enjoy it.

She breathes against my lips. "What do you want?"

I sit on the edge of the bed. "Get on your knees. I want to fuck those pretty tits first."

There's a darkness in Lo's eyes as she positions herself on her knees between my legs, wrists still bound. Her full tits look amazing like this. My hands follow her arms, skimming her rib cage until I cup them. Lo trembles as I roll her nipples between my fingers.

Looking directly into my eyes, she licks the head of my cock. A little reminder of the power she'll always wield over me.

Pushing her breasts together, I slide between them. So soft, so luscious.

"Aidan . . ." Her voice is a greedy whine. "I can't wait any longer. I need you."

I need you. That's what I wanted to hear. I pull away, reaching for the condoms in the nightstand and put one on as fast as humanly possible.

"How do you want me?" she asks.

All the ways. Every way. Forever. Instead of saying any of that, I untie her. As the ribbon falls away, I can see understanding in her eyes. It's just a prop. Cielo eases down onto the bed and I climb over her.

"One more time, babe," I coax. "Say it."

"I need you."

I can't resist that. I finally push into her and we're lost in each other.

THE FIRST RAYS of the morning sun slant through the window. I hike the duvet up my shoulder, wanting to sink back into the memory of Cielo, when I realize this bed is in her room. And although it was a personal fantasy come to life, last night wasn't a dream.

After we were both spent, Lo told me to stay. So I did. I almost expect her to be gone when I crack one eye open, but she's beside me in bed, laptop open.

"Nice . . . erm, rash," I mumble. PowerPoint slides of what appear to be infectious diseases light up the screen. A rude contrast to her sweet-smelling shampoo.

"Good morning to you, too."

A rust-colored University of Texas sweater hangs off her shoulder. She hands me a steaming Castle Teachan–branded mug.

Propping myself up on an elbow, I take a sip and begin to resurrect. "I think I've said this before, but you're my dream girl." My nose crinkles as she clicks on the trackpad to bring up a photo of something oozing. "I could do without seeing that first thing in the morning, though."

Lo closes the laptop with an apologetic grimace and sets it on the nightstand. "Sorry. I have a research paper due soon."

I set the mug down on my nightstand and throw an arm around her. I've missed our quiet morning talks deeply. They feel different than nighttime talks, somehow. Vulnerability feels different in the light of day. The intimacy is sober, intentional. "What do you have planned for today?"

"Afternoon with my mom and aunt while they're in town. They wanted to check out Eyre Square."

I think back to Gustavo's heavy eyes when he said he wanted to spend time with Lo. "And your da?"

"We're having dinner before he flies out. I think it'll be easier to talk to him without my mom involved. Maybe."

"It's probably going to be awkward either way," I agree. "But it's a start."

"I was thinking about what you said, that no one can pleasantly surprise me if I don't give them a chance." Lo gives a little shrug. "Well, you did. So maybe my dad will surprise me, too."

Just being around him makes her feel defensive. Agreeing to spend time alone with her dad is a major step, but she won't like it if I make a big deal out of it.

Cielo's eyes drift across my face deliberately, like she's committing it to memory. "When are you going back to London?"

"I'll be in town a bit longer yet," I say. The festival in New York isn't for another week and a half, which at least gives me some time to develop the new material. And more time to spend with Lo.

"Have you ever thought of moving back to Galway?"

My cautious heart leaps at her question. Living here would calm Lo's worries more than regular visits and nightly phone calls. It's where I want to be.

"I know your family wants you close. And I bet London doesn't have spice bags that come close to the ones from your favorite place."

What always made the greasy little chipper special was Cielo snatching mine away after she'd said she didn't want any.

"I thought this town wasn't big enough for both of us."

We talked about this being temporary, but what if these past few days have shown Lo what I've known all along: that we could work, if we try. I'm willing to, if she is.

"I wouldn't mind sharing it, maybe."

"You want me to move back?"

She rolls her eyes affectionately. "Yes, A. That's a yes."

Professional connections might be in London, but my heart is here in Galway. My muse. My friends. My family. Screw where the label wants me to live—I'll find a way to make it work.

"That's all I need to hear," I tell her.

My overpriced flat is devoid of life most of the year; I really won't miss it. Lo, on the other hand? I've pined for her every day for the last two years. There's no contest, just logistics to settle.

Martin insists that living in London lends me credibility and ease of networking, so he won't like this decision—especially since he doesn't want me romantically linked to anyone without some pop culture notoriety.

"You know . . ." She glances at the bedside clock then nuzzles back against my chest. "There's an hour before the breakfast buffet opens. We can spare fifteen more minutes."

CHAPTER 24

Lo

AIDAN PULLS ON his suit trousers from last night. "Are we still playing it cool around your mom? Because after last night, she probably suspects something."

"We can sit together. Maybe we'll head to breakfast separately, though?"

He's not leaving town immediately, but he hasn't committed to living in Galway full-time again, either. Maybe there's a way forward for us, if he wasn't just humoring me earlier when I asked. The idea of him being away for months at a time touring still puts me on edge, but now I know what it feels like to have none of him for years, and I'm willing to try if he is. Still, I'd rather not give this a label or make it "Mom official" until there's concrete evidence of him relocating back to Galway. A signed lease, a moving date, something. Before Aidan leaves to change his clothes, I pull him into one last, lingering kiss, knowing they're the final moments before we each go back to our everyday lives. This fragile, unnamed thing between us has to survive in the real world. The conviction and honesty in his kiss tell me that it has a fighting chance.

Alone for now, I take a quick look at my email while the shower water heats up. There's a message from my doctor's office saying new paperwork has been added to my patient portal. Nice. My mom wanted the full update from my latest annual checkup, and I'll be able to relay the all clear in person over a couple omelets.

I follow the link and sniff at the body wash as the page loads.

It's the bloodwork panel.

Elevated lymph levels. Elevated white blood cell count. What? This can't be right.

It's my name and date of birth at the top, but this has to be a mistake. If anything is amiss, the patient's records are not supposed to be updated in the portal. A human being from the office is supposed to break the news; you're not meant to find out that you probably have cancer from a cold set of numbers on a website. When I toggle back to my email, I find it was time-stamped for midnight. It must have automatically updated and sent to me by mistake. Right when I'd been dancing with Aidan.

Three treatment cycles of chemo were needed to go into remission before. Hours a day tethered to an IV full of powerful drugs for six weeks at a time. Constant nausea, brain fog, crushing fatigue. Steroids gave me mood swings and a puffy face. Could I endure months of that while vying for a top spot in my class to impress the attending physician, and with the uncertainty of whatever is between me and Aidan? I've never been one to shy away from a challenge, but last time, chemo gave me the energy of a slug.

The stress of being a third-year has already been taking its toll. I'm constantly tired, my appetite has dwindled, and I'll realize at the end of a frantic day that I've barely eaten. Medical school is designed to be grueling, so I'd written off those symptoms as typical stress from being challenged every day in the hospital. But now, I can't ignore that they look like evidence the leukemia is back. My breathing becomes shallow as fear threatens to overtake me. This was not the plan. This cannot be happening. I take a deep breath and then another. I force myself to focus on what I know.

Results like these mean following up with a bone marrow aspiration and biopsy. It will be straightforward enough: local anesthetic, a special needle that twists into the hip to remove a small section of the solid bone and marrow, dressing the wound. The whole procedure will take around twenty-five minutes and then I can go about my day.

Condensation collects on the phone screen, making me aware of the steam now filling the bathroom. How long have I been staring at these results? Shit. Now I only have a few minutes to meet my mom downstairs before she comes up here looking for me again. Instead of the shower I need, I turn off the water and put up my hair to hide the singed ends. I'm not ready to face either of my parents on any terms but my own right now. At this rate, I'll start losing my hair from stress before I even start chemo.

Another round of treatment would derail my academic career, right when I'm finally spending time in clinical rotations with real patients; when I can finally start making a difference. I've carried the weight of my parents' impossible expectations and the responsibility to advocate for my own community since

I was a kid. Everything I've worked for: striving for salutatorian in my graduating class, earning a bachelor's in biology from University of Texas at Austin, scoring a 514 on my MCAT . . . could be for nothing if I withdraw from the program.

And Aidan . . .

Deep breaths. I need to compartmentalize this new information and get through breakfast. Then the rest of the day. Then the next couple weeks. Just take it one hour at a time. Then I can brace myself for the biopsy. Until then, it's Schrödinger's test results: both false alarm and utterly life-changing.

My phone buzzes and I expect it to be Aidan, but it's my mom demanding to know why I'm not downstairs. The buffet hasn't even officially opened yet. It's like she can sense the bad news. She already hates that I decided to study abroad, and I don't want to give her any reason to insist I return stateside.

Gathering myself, I head to the banquet hall. Aidan is sat with my mom and dad, who are on opposite ends of the table with a spot for me in the middle. Their eyes all snap to me at the same time.

"Good morning," I greet the table as cheerfully as I can manage.

An attending once told me that physicians also need to be actors. Hold neutral poker faces when patients present in the A&E with various objects lodged in their colons. Mustering patience when a combative patient is on your last nerve. A pleasant demeanor for the next case, after you've just given a family horrible news about their loved one. I've never been one to hide my feelings—about anything but Aidan, I guess—but bedside manner is an important part of the job. I try to take that approach now: This is for their sake, not mine.

"Why are you late?" my mom asks before I even have a chance to sit. A few of the other guests at the table swing their necks toward me at the question.

"The burnt ends of my hair aren't easy to style." I pat my brunette bob self-consciously. It's in desperate need of a trim to even out the patch that singed.

At the end of the table, my dad's face brightens in a smile. "Morning."

"Hey, Dad." We have to talk soon, but right now, I'm just trying to get through this meal without breaking down.

Concern shades Aidan's face when I take the chair beside him. My mom pushes a plate with a veggie omelet my way. "Here, you need something nutritious after drinking last night."

"She's allowed to have some fun at a wedding, Tracy," my dad says lightly.

I clench my jaw and Aidan pats my leg reassuringly under the table. The small touch offers me so much strength. "Thanks, Mom."

Aidan nods, eager to keep things smooth. "I'm so glad you could all be here to celebrate the happy couple. The reception was gas."

"Cielo really shouldn't be drinking." No matter what I do, my mom will see a cancer recurrence as my fault. I didn't eat clean enough. Didn't get enough sleep. Used a microwave too often. Burned the wrong candle. She wanted so desperately to know why I got sick to begin with, but the truth is that sometimes it just happens. I still don't think she's accepted that.

Anxiety has zapped my appetite, but I dig in anyway because if I don't eat, the whole table will get an earful about overindulgence.

Aidan makes small talk with my mom and a few other guests who have joined us, chatting about the history of the castle, but periodically his gaze lands on me. When the others split off into a side conversation, he whispers, "Are you all right?"

Of course he's sensed the energy shift since he left to take a shower.

"It's just been a long weekend."

"Too bad we couldn't sleep in."

I can't help but think back to my first serious boyfriend. I convinced my mom to let me return to public high school for senior year using a PowerPoint presentation explaining the advantages of in-person advanced placement courses and extra curriculars on my college transcript. After being kept on a short leash while homeschooled, I immediately fell for a boy at school. We dated for a few months before prom and I wanted that night to be my first time. Seventeen-year-old me was determined to finally get some pleasure out of a body that knew the insides of MRI machines before it knew intimacy.

Then I got a cold that developed into pneumonia and spent prom night in the hospital as a precautionary measure. My first love ended up going with someone else and publicly cheated on me in front of the whole school. I was devastated, but I learned a lesson: Guys don't want to be with someone sick.

One of the many depressing facts I learned in class about cancer is that it nearly doubles the divorce rate—but only when the patient is a woman in a relationship with a healthy man. When the roles are reversed and the man is the one diagnosed, it plummets to a fraction of the typical separation rate. It didn't surprise me that it sent guys packing: It happened to me.

Aidan isn't the dirtbag seventeen-year-old who cheated on

me while I was hospitalized. Not by a long shot. But his life does resemble my dad's. Work takes him away, and his work is what gives him purpose.

Something about this thought process must show on my face, because he sets his fork down and pivots in his seat to face me. "What's wrong?"

I fidget with my napkin. "It's not you."

"I'm here, okay? I'm right here if you need me."

Yes, he's here now, but he won't always be. Is it better to protect myself from that pain now or wait until I'm in deep with him again?

Lark and Callum thank everyone for joining them. Her eyes train on me, slightly watery, her smile filled with love and gratitude. I hate keeping secrets from Lark, but I can't tell her about the test results now. It would hover over her romantic Spanish honeymoon like a dark cloud. For her sake, I grin widely and pass out the bubble favors that Aidan and I made.

Everyone heads outside, bubbles in hand, for the honeymoon send-off. Aidan's eyes glimmer with anticipation as we follow Callum and Lark toward their Peugeot, only to find the hearse, decorated in streamers and flower garlands instead.

"Who's responsible for this?" Callum laughs. Lark shakes her head in amusement, but delicately touches the sunflowers and acknowledges Saoirse in the crowd.

I grab Aidan's hand and raise it for him. "It was all this guy's idea."

"Look," Lark cries, "the garland on the back window!"

I affectionately nudge Aidan. "You did good."

"I had a little help."

After a flurry of photos, bubbles, and more tearful hugs,

Lark and Callum ride into the countryside as husband and wife. The official end to the weekend's festivities feels bittersweet. Some guests linger and chat while others head to checkout.

"I have a lot of packing," I tell Aidan with a reluctant smile. "A bunch of Lark's stuff she's not taking on their trip, plus my own bag."

"Ring me and I'll give you a hand to the car when you're ready."

Every cell in my body aches to kiss him, but my mom pouncing on my love life is the last thing I need. I call on my sense of self-discipline and pull away. Will I ultimately need to do the same to protect my heart?

Before I can unlock my room, my dad corners me in the tapestry-lined hallway. "Cielito, what were you thinking for dinner? Someone told me they have amazing seafood at this waterfront bistro. I remember how you love that."

"I don't know," I say, letting the exhaustion come through in my voice. "Whatever."

I've masked it for my mom. For Lark. For Aidan. But I'm tired and scared and agitated, and my dad's presence isn't helping. Those test results brought all those ugly, helpless feelings right back to the surface, but worse: They reminded me that he couldn't handle me sick. Why should I bother protecting his feelings when he couldn't put mine before his own comfort when I was just a sick kid? And I'm sure this new attempt at spending time together will come to a swift end the moment I get sick again.

"Are you all right?"

"Yeah," I snap. He backs into the hallway. "Seafood is fine. Pick whatever you want."

"Stop this resentment, Lo. Ever since you were little, you've held on to your anger so tightly. I can't change the past, and I'm sorry for it, but I want to know the woman my own daughter has grown into. You've practically cut me out of your life—"

"Oh," I scoff incredulously. "You feel hurt that I'm cutting you out of my life? You cut me out when you couldn't handle what *I* was going through."

"I felt like a failure. I couldn't even donate marrow to you. The only time I felt useful was when I was working, so that's what I did."

"Why have you waited so long to say any of this?"

"How can I ever start to make it right if you won't give me a chance?"

"Just give me some space, please? You're usually pretty good at leaving me alone when I'm emotional."

My dad's mouth pops open, but he doesn't have a rebuttal. We both know I'm right. Guilt prickles in my chest, but if anyone is going to be the target of my ire, it's him.

Blowing up at my mom would only set off her internal alarms that something is wrong, sending her into Helicopter Parent DEFCON 1. Lark doesn't deserve any of my negativity to begin her marriage. And I've just started to test out forgiveness when it comes to Aidan. I don't want to go backward with him. Although, if I had to pick a runner-up for my dad, I wouldn't mind smashing one of Aunt Sharon's crystal bowls to banish some of my *bad vibes*.

Fuming, I jam the keycard into the lock and shove the door open. It shuts as my dad says something—I can't make out his words, but it doesn't matter. He leaves. He always leaves. So he might as well do it again, now that I want him gone.

Packing up the bridal suite to an "auditory Xanax" playlist takes longer than I expected. It's all right. Making myself useful to someone else without actually being *around* anyone else is exactly what I need right now. I pore over the checklist of items, ensuring nothing gets left behind in Lark's haste to make their flight to Barcelona.

The door of the bridal suite clicks shut behind me as I lug the duffel bag over my shoulder and roll Lark's suitcase behind me with my overnight bag balanced on top. I press the elevator button and hear Aidan's soft admonishment.

"Hey, hey, you said you'd text me to help with these, then I look up and see you buried in luggage from the lobby." He's a little breathless, having rushed up the stairs to alleviate my burden.

"I got it," comes out of my mouth even as I reluctantly release my death grip on the strap.

The elevator arrives with a ding and we step inside.

"Just because you can do it doesn't mean I'm cool with you doing it on your own. You can accept help, you know." Aidan smooths a hand over my bare arm. "What happened?"

"Where to begin?" I mutter. I'm furious. This health scare couldn't have come at a worse time. I'm under a ton of pressure in my clinical rounds. Surrounded by family members who send my blood pressure skyward. My fear of abandonment is rearing its head, warring with my newfound hope that a future with Aidan is possible.

I should never have been given access to those results without the guidance of my doctor, either. Add it to the list.

Aidan's arms curl around me. I feel so brittle. I tell him what I feel able to share.

"I don't know if I can ever forgive my dad. He left me when

I needed him. I understand he wanted to provide for us, but he made it a point to be away, even when it interfered with big events. It makes it really hard to play nice with him now. He's only back at his own convenience, to assuage his own conscience about my childhood. He's only here because he thinks I don't need him."

And I hear what I said at the end of the outburst. "I don't," I quickly correct myself. "I don't need him. I don't need anyone."

Aidan's arms tense slightly, but he knows it's true. Other than Lark and Oisín, I'm not close with many people. I could get by on my own. But Aidan, here in this enclosed space with me, encumbered by luggage, forces me to acknowledge that sometimes, you find someone you can trust to share some of your burden.

Aidan swallows thickly. "Lo. There are people in your life who don't want you to do it all on your own because they love and respect you."

Before the elevator opens, I run my hand along his stubbled jaw and give him a soft kiss.

I spent the last of my energy lashing out at my dad. The spike of adrenaline from the discovery of my lab results wore off long ago, leaving nothing but a simmering sense of dread. If my mom and Aunt Sharon hadn't already made plans, I'd be tempted to hang a DO NOT DISTURB sign on the door and hide under the covers of that four-poster bed with Aidan. Instead, we lug the suitcases out to the parking lot together.

A porter from the castle is assisting my mom and Aunt Sharon with bringing their bags down to my car. My mom looks Aidan up and down. Of course, she's been giving him the stink eye ever since she noticed his tattoos. Never mind the fact that

Aidan has been nothing but polite in her presence. He stuffs Lark's luggage and my bag into the trunk and lingers after it slams shut.

"I'll call you later," I say.

"I've heard that before," he replies. Fair point.

Kissing in front of my mom isn't going to happen, but I step into Aidan's arms for a hug. I greedily inhale his sandalwood warmth, but I remind myself that this isn't a final goodbye. Not yet. He'll be in town for a while longer. He might even decide to stay. I move out of his arms far sooner than I feel prepared for. I wait until our eyes meet before softly reassuring him, "I'll call. Promise."

He's going to stand there and wave as we drive away, isn't he?

"You know him well?" my mom asks the instant I shut the driver's door. She didn't even wait until I'm buckled in and the car is in motion before starting the inquisition.

Aunt Sharon lowers her sunglasses on her nose. "He's got a great aura."

Eew. "Please stop looking at Aidan's aura."

My mom scowls at him through the mirror. And yep, he's waving all right. "What does he do for a living, again?"

She remembers. She grilled him about his work history like he was interviewing for a job. Aidan described himself as a recording artist.

"He's a professional musician."

"I don't know Irish Gaelic, but 'musician' universally translates to 'unemployed.'"

"He was nominated for a big music award a few months ago, Mom."

"You're awfully defensive over this man."

"Yeah, well, he hasn't done anything worth attacking."

Thank god I never told her the truth about us. She'd never forgive Aidan if she knew how badly he'd shattered my heart.

Aunt Sharon takes out her phone and starts rattling off the itinerary. I simply don't have it in me. For weeks, I've been feeling run-down during my rotations, which I now know may be the cancer coming back. In this instant I'm exhausted on a spiritual level. This morning's email was a wake-up call, imploring me to listen to my body. When we arrive at Eyre Square, where she wanted to begin, I inhale through my teeth as we pull into a parking spot near the iconic display of colorful tribal flags.

"Listen, Mom, I'm not feeling so great. I'm kinda sensitive to all that patchouli, remember?"

"We'll be out in the fresh air," she counters. Her tone is sharp, but the disappointment on her face is unmistakable.

"Sorry. I need to lie down for a while. I can meet you for dinner after you do a little exploring by yourselves?"

Now that I've run my dad off, my night is free.

CHAPTER 25

Aidan

A SKEIN OF yarn rolls to a stop at my feet when I let myself into my parents' house. I pick it up and gently toss it at my mam, seated on the couch and working on another piece. The braided rope commemorating my parents' handfasting ceremony thirty-odd years earlier hangs from the mantel, just like always. This house is far nicer than the one we left behind in Cork, but my parents brought along the best parts—well, except Da's ugly chair, where Mam stacks the yarn balls in a teetering pyramid. A Saint Brigid's cross fashioned of rushes still hangs over the main doorway year-round and awkward school photos litter these walls, too. By comparison, my flat in Peckham feels like the sterile showroom of a car dealership.

"How was the wedding?" Mam asks.

"She means, 'How is Cielo,'" Fionn informs me as he comes into the living room holding a carton of milk. How he can chug dairy straight after a football match while he's still in his sweaty GAA gear is beyond me.

"I do mean, 'How is Cielo,'" Mam agrees without looking

up from her needles. "And stop drinking from the carton, you heathen."

"So?" Fionn prompts. As if he's gonna get any salacious details about this weekend. I only kiss and tell in the form of lyrics.

"Oh, you know. Handfasting. Disco. Whisky. All the classic wedding activities. Food was class."

Something in my glib tone makes Mam look up from her needles. "Fionn, you're rank. Put that milk away and hose yourself off."

The look on his face tells me he'll badger me about this again later, when Mam's not making a—is that a baby sweater?—and saunters off to the bathroom.

"What happened?" Mam asks, point-blank.

"I realized I need to move back to Galway."

Needles still in hand, she hops off the couch and bolts toward me. "Watch it with those yokes. You'll put my eye out." I laugh as she engulfs me with a hug. The more I think about it, the more excitement begins to infuse my soul.

"This has been a long time coming. Let me have my moment. Your da will be so happy."

The thought of brightening his day with the news makes me smile wider. "Cielo and I got to talking, and she wants me here."

"How lovely to have you two back together!"

The proverbial record scratches at that. What exactly had we decided by the end of it? Lo had said she wanted me here, but we didn't talk further about me relocating full-time or the implication of officially dating again.

"We're as good as back together," I say, my stomach pinching at the memory of Lo pulling me into a hug instead of kissing me. I understand she was emotional after the fight with her da, but it would've been nice if Lo had been confident enough to kiss me in front of her mother.

"I'll never understand you young people, but I'm happy if you are. I'd love to have Lo over for supper soon."

I take a seat on the couch next to her. "I am. Mam, I feel like things might be finally falling into place. I thought London was where I needed to be, and it's great, but these last few weeks have made me realize that it's not where I *want* to be."

The pressure of a second album still weighs heavily on me. My contract comes with legal consequences and a steep financial penalty if I fail to deliver something the label deems marketable by the end of October. I can't simply shop around for a new deal when there's a twelve-month non-compete clause and they own the master recordings of every song I've released.

Things are looking up, though, between the festival and the rekindling of romance between me and Lo. Lyrics and melodies have been scrolling through my mind all weekend. Her company alone gets my creativity buzzing, and that's what I need going into Harvest in the Park: inspired new material. With any luck, these songs will help me win back my artistic freedom.

"Well, your da and sister will be happy to hear when they get home from shopping."

Fionn stands in the hallway, wet hair dripping on to the carpet with a towel slung around his waist. "Hear what? What did I miss?"

"Your brother says he wants to move back here."

Fionn is nothing if not his mother's son. With a shout, he lunges for me with his arms outstretched. And the towel drops.

CHAPTER 26

Lo

I NEVER THOUGHT I'd say this but thank god for Aunt Sharon. I'm convinced it was her influence that kept my mom from hounding me over my attitude on Sunday. Sharon probably just wanted to spend some time with her sister abroad while avoiding my "low vibrational frequencies" and pitch-black aura, but I'll take it. In all their busyness experiencing the quaint sights of Galway, my mom apparently forgot about my last doctor's visit.

Last night, I dropped them off at the airport in Shannon and breathed a sigh of relief. The longer they were here, the more I'd feared being found out. The receptionist from the cancer center had even called to discuss my lab work while I was showing them around Shop Street, but I'd sent it to voicemail. I already know how to interpret the results, even if I'm far from being able to make a conclusive self-diagnosis. A biopsy is needed for any solid answer, and I'm just not ready to learn for sure that the cancer is back.

If Lark's conflict-avoidance makes her an ostrich with her head in the sand, I'm usually a rhinoceros charging straight at anything that makes me uncomfortable. But for the first time, I'm not sure I feel strong enough to face the challenge. Denial isn't the wisest way to handle potential cancer—believe me, I know this.

Somehow, the annual visits always felt like a formality. I never expected them to turn up anything concerning. A little more time is all I need to get my bearings.

Aidan encouraged me to spend time with my mom before she left town, visiting his own family and working on a "top-secret" cache of new songs with the help of Saoirse and Fionn. According to him, Ruth has asked what I've wanted for supper every one of the four nights since the wedding and will continue to do so until I grace his family's new home with a visit.

Lark's been updating me from her sun-drenched Barcelona honeymoon, including photos of paella, colorful street art, and Callum's tour of old-world cemeteries full of hauntingly beautiful statues.

And I've been working rotations in the A&E, making up for the lost time.

We lost a patient today and I could do nothing. A team rushed in with a crash cart as a nurse did compressions. A flurry of chaos, and then somber silence. Oisín wasn't on rotation, so I ugly cried in the supply room for ten minutes before I managed to pull myself together, dabbing Visine on my reddened eyes and powder on my nose to regain some semblance of composure for the next patient. It just hit too hard, especially after the lab results. The last thing I needed was the reminder that even a room full of medical professionals can't change fate when it's truly your time.

As soon as I'm home from my shift, I give Aidan a call.

"Lo?" His voice saying my name is like homemade caldo de pollo to my soul. Comforting and familiar. "Lo, are you there?"

My throat spasms, but I manage to croak out, "Are you busy right now?"

"What's going on?"

"I just . . . I had a horrible day. Is this a bad time?"

"No, I'm at my parents' gaff. Want to come over? My mam is fixing stew."

"Another time. I just need you right now."

"I can be at yours in ten minutes."

True to his word, Aidan pulls into the driveway a few minutes later. Ginger-flecked stubble chafes my cheek when he greets me with a tender kiss. His presence already feels like a weight's been lifted from my chest. I don't have to feel this alone. He takes me to the Long Walk, where the famous row of simple, colorful houses reflect in the shimmering water of the bay. He doesn't prod, patiently waiting for me to speak when I'm ready.

"I lost a patient today. I keep replaying it in my head over and over."

Aidan stops and wraps me in his arms. "I'm so sorry."

I bury my nose in his neck and breathe deep. "Logically, I know there is nothing more that could've been done for the guy. I just—I thought I was ready for it. That I could stay emotionally detached. I had no problem with the cadaver lab. It doesn't bother me going into the funeral home."

"Of course this is different. You can't beat yourself up for being affected. You're only human." He strokes my hair as he speaks.

"How am I supposed to deal with losing a patient in pediatrics? This was an adult and I can barely cope."

"I can only imagine how hard it is for the people who work

with children. They're angels, really, but it's not a job for everyone," Aidan says.

"What if I'm not cut out to be a doctor? I can't wash out after all this hard work—"

"Hey." Aidan grasps my shoulders and looks into my face—my soul. How can eyes the color of the bay feel so grounding? "You're capable of doing something meaningful. Even if it's not on the front lines."

"But I want to be there," I protest.

"I know you do. Plus, it would be a shame to deprive the world of how hot you look in a white coat and rubber clogs."

I crack a weak smile at his ill-timed attempt to hit on me. "There she is," he says, gently brushing my cheek. "You'll change lives. Save lives. I've never doubted you for an instant."

We're so close that I can feel the heat of his chest through our sweaters. I don't even know who made the approach. It doesn't matter. Aidan's gravity pulls me toward him every time we're together, and tonight I'm powerless against it . . . but somehow, he manages to make me feel like it's okay to let my guard down, just for a little while.

"I'm not joking," he insists. "I'll take those clogs over stilettos any day. They're deadly."

This time, I breathe out a self-deprecating laugh. "Stop teasing me."

"Not a chance. I'm still making up for lost time."

His mouth is right there, sweet and distracting. I contemplate kissing him but step back and look out at the view instead. Headlights glow in the distance, and the autumn sky is painted in rich indigo. When I turn back to Aidan, his eyes are shadowed but I can feel their tenderness.

I'm afraid to trust my own voice. "Thanks for coming."

"Thanks for sharing this with me." The secret I've been carrying all week threatens to claw its way up my throat. Our hands find each other, and his warm palm squeezes mine. "Tell me something good."

"Well. I got lucky with two spots at Harvest in the Park next week. Nigel Culpepper is supposed to be there. He—"

"Worked on four of your top five favorite albums."

Aidan's eyes widen.

I nudge him affectionately. "You never shut up about his genius."

His modest smile widens now, too.

"Sorry to interrupt. Go on."

"Nigel is making his first public appearance in years. He's usually untouchable, unreachable. Real desert-island stuff. But here's my chance to meet him. Maybe I can convince him to produce my next album. He records out of London, so that would work out well before I come back to Galway."

Sharing a stage with his heroes, bringing a crowd to their feet, rubbing elbows with the most talented musicians of our time. It sounds like his dream come true, even before the possibility of working with the famed producer.

"I need to make a good impression, but I'll probably forget the words to my own songs if he's watching."

This isn't the right time to tell Aidan about the sketchy lab results and the tiny hole that will be drilled into my hip for a biopsy. He needs to focus. If it is cancer, I'll decide when to tell him once I've come to grips with it.

I've always known that having a boyfriend would be distracting as a med student. I'd never thought about the toll a partner could take on a performer. No matter what he's feeling inside, he plays what the crowd wants to hear. Even if it doesn't fit the soundtrack of his heart. As it is, he worries about his family and his friends and the kids at the hospital. My inconclusive test results would only add to the mix—and for what? Anxiety isn't going to help him. Or me.

"Lo?" His smile drops slightly. "Did I lose you?"

My thoughts must've shown on my face. "It's just been a long day. But this is important to you, so it's important to me. I want to know. Why does it matter so much to get him right now?"

I take his hand, tracing from the ends of his fingertips to the creases in his palm. Aidan has the most beautiful hands, made even more beautiful by the music he creates with them.

"I have to get this second album recorded by the end of October and I'm afraid of disappointing everyone. What if I've only got one decent one in me?"

"Your talent isn't finite. But even musical geniuses can't please everyone."

"Did you just call me a genius?"

"All you can do is make something genuine. Same as you've been doing all this time."

"If only it was that easy." Aidan sighs. "The label hasn't been impressed with my newer stuff. The last demo I sent was better than anything I've written in two years, but they've already decided they want to go in a new direction. Getting someone like Nigel on board would restore their faith in me."

"A 'new direction'? What does that mean?"

Grimacing, he keeps his eye on the bay. "Ever heard of Neon Joy? They're set to produce."

The pop band isn't bad, but I don't see the connection between their dance anthems and Aidan's intimate ballads. "Tell those record company people to forget it."

"I can't refuse without consequence. I'd be penalized for breach of contract, on top of recoupment on the advance and what they've invested in me. Meaning I'd be stuck with massive debt and a non-compete clause that prevents me from releasing anything for a year. And they'll still own all the master recordings."

I deflate. With Aidan's background in law, I believe him if he says the contract is airtight.

He points to his bared teeth. "Speaking of genuine: I'm sure you noticed. My manager and the label insisted."

"It looks nice." It's true. What had unsettled me about the perfect row of white teeth was their unfamiliarity, reinforcing my misconception of Aidan. But I was wrong. He's still the same man. "There was nothing wrong with your smile before. It's always been beautiful. But do you feel better now? That's what's important."

He shrugs. "Fionn used to say 'mind the gap' and other shite, as brothers do, but I didn't really care about it either way. Now there's a team of people concerned about my image. They even asked me to go out with that actress Emma Kinnane to stoke rumors, make a point to be seen in the posh side of London nightlife. I'm sure she's lovely, but . . ."

I don't love the idea of a PR stunt with a beautiful actress, either.

"It's never been about fame," Aidan says. "I just want to write songs that make people feel something. I don't need anyone sending me a pre-selected wardrobe and scheduling spray tans."

"I knew it!"

Aidan extends his arm. The color's back to normal now. "Christ. Is it that obvious?"

"You don't look like a tangerine. It was only obvious to me because I know exactly how blindingly pale your ginger ass is."

"What I'm hearing is, you think I'm a genius with a great arse . . ." He waggles his brows.

"I said no such thing."

His flirtation gives way to something more serious. "Tell me the truth. Do you think I'm a sellout?"

"No. You're an artist up against a corporation that has an entire legal division."

"I haven't admitted that to anyone."

"The spray tans? It's not a big deal . . ." I try for a little levity, but I know what he really means. Aidan rolls his eyes. "Those record company executives see the potential for you to blow up, but you don't need a makeover or a celebrity girlfriend to do that. All you need is a label that'll show you some respect."

"If I can just get the right producer—someone I like who is also proven to sell—they'll back off me. My poor da worked two jobs when Mam had to homeschool Marie. They've done so much to provide for us. If this next record is a success, I can pay off their house. Help them retire. The label knows how to make hit albums, Lo."

With such a modest upbringing, it makes sense that Aidan's idea of success is directly linked to how well he can take care of his family. I always admired that about him.

"*You* know how to make a hit album," I remind him. "You've already done it once. Your music is special because it's real, not because a stylist bought you leather pants to wear onstage."

"Where are you getting this idea that I perform in assless chaps?"

I raise a brow. "If the spiked collar fits."

"Now I'm starting to believe it's wishful thinking."

"Aidan, you can't control how well your album will do. You just control how well you make it. Fight for it. Don't let them pressure you into creating something that doesn't feel right. Your family wouldn't want that on their account."

I've been better about remembering that not everything is in our control lately. For better or worse. The timing of our re-connection isn't what I would have chosen, had I any say. Aidan is performing again in New York, so soon after he'd declared he was taking a break. And he's courting his dream producer, aim-ing to record his next album in London. He'll have to tour to promote it. Even if we lived in the same city, he might not phys-ically be around enough to make this work.

If the leukemia is back, I may not be able to stay in school, and if that happens, my educational visa will be pulled. Moving back to the States would be the end of us, right when I lose my health, my purpose, my new home.

Still, my sense of hope flies in the face of the odds. I can't bear to really consider the possibility that just as Aidan walks back into my life, the rest of it might detonate around us.

"It feels good to be here." He watches the reflections from the houses and streetlights dance upon the choppy waves, then his focus settles on me. "Home."

"Nice to have you back."

This is gonna really hurt if I have to let go again.

CHAPTER 27

Aidan

"COME ON, WHEN was the last time you had a real meal?" I ask Lo during our lunch call. Our heart-to-heart at the Long Walk was only the night before last, but I can't wait to see her again. Today she's in class, not twelve hours of clinicals, and that feels like the perfect excuse to feed her a proper supper.

"Let's just say, yesterday I fought Oisín over a beat-up granola bar he found in his coat pocket."

"How was it?"

"You know, it's really sexy how you assume I won."

I move the mobile to my other ear as I rake the garden. Leaves fell around me all morning when I'd worked on songs under the yellowing canopy of a tree. "It's settled, then. I'll pick you up after your lecture. Oh, and my mam only serves fish on Fridays, is that all right?"

"Reminds me of home." Nostalgia tinges her voice.

We haven't talked about her father, other than my asking if she'd spoken to him since their argument. I couldn't help but feel like her anger at him mirrored the anger she held for me. Lo's afraid of abandonment. Understandably so.

At the end of our conversations, *I love you* stays lodged in my throat. We're not there yet. A pause rests in its place where we can both feel its absence. It feels like an unfinished song.

My mobile vibrates in my hand again before I even put it down.

Martin's rapid-fire voice comes through the line. "Aidan, how are you? I wanted to see if you need anything before the festival."

"Can you please schedule some practice with the touring band? The new songs are really shaping up." Fionn's been providing a steady beat on the bodhrán while I experiment with different arrangements. Lyrics have been coming easier, too. I filled up my notebook and had to run to Dunnes for another.

"None of that sad bastard shit, right?"

"I think you'll like them." Why did the label even sign a singer-songwriter if they wanted to control what I wrote? I bet Glen Hansard never had to deal with this.

"We don't have time to waste on something that won't sell."

I bristle at the idea that song crafting is ever a waste of time. Even if the song is never recorded or performed, the act of creation itself matters.

Nevertheless, I promise to record what I have so far and send it to him.

Breaking Lo's heart got me to the top of the charts, and I've avoided writing a song about it for two years. Mostly because I didn't want to end up regularly performing something that would force me to confront my guilt. I'm finally getting over my cowardice enough to articulate just how much regret I feel.

For the rest of the afternoon, until it's time to pick up Lo, I work on a new song, tentatively titled "Apology Tour."

———

DA PRACTICALLY LEAPS out of his battered La-Z-Boy when I bring Cielo home.

"Glad you're here, love."

"Thanks for the invitation to dinner, Mr. O'Toole," she answers with a kiss on his cheek.

"James," he insists. "I keep telling you."

The smell of freshly baked bread, smoked fish, and garlic fill the house. Lo inhales deeply. "I literally just started salivating."

"My mam's trying to impress you." I appreciate the sentiment; I want Lo to stick around, too.

"I've been thinking about her seafood chowder for the past two years."

We turn the corner into the kitchen. Mam's rapping a spoon against the shells of mussels gathered on the chopping board. They pinch closed except for one, which she puts atop a heap of potato peels.

"Oh my goodness. Cielo!" She pulls her into a hug that nearly crushes the autumnal bouquet she brought from Saoirse's shop. Cielo isn't a big hugger, but she can't escape my mam. "These are brilliant."

"Thanks for having me, Ruth; this smells incredible. Can I give you any help?"

Mam rummages through a cupboard until she finds a vase and drops Lo's flowers into it. "You're sweet, but I can manage the last few minutes on my own," she assures Lo. "Aidan, will you hand me the dill, please? It's in the press behind you. Then go tell Marie and Fionn supper's almost ready."

Distracted by the relaxed smile on Lo's face and the way her shoulders have dropped, I reach into the press. If only she felt the same ease around her own family. When I turn to find the bottle of dried dill, soulless painted eyes stare back at me from among the spices and pantry staples. I recoil with a yawp.

One more ventriloquist dummy scare and I'll need to be fitted for a pacemaker.

Mam chuckles heartily and Lo collapses in laughter. A lovely flush paints her cheeks. Marie pops into the doorway with a cackle worthy of a cinema villain.

"You're a menace!" I yank the dummy from the press by its neck and shove it toward my sister. Mam's outfitted it in its own Fair Isle jumper.

Batting her lashes, Marie cradles it in her arms like a baby and stretches her mouth into a sinister smile. "He just wants to be your friend."

"Stop being creepy."

Cielo throws an arm around her and examines the dummy. "I think he's kinda cute. Maybe you can teach me how to throw my voice?"

Marie's eyes light up. "Of course!"

"And he'll sit next to me for dinner," Lo jokes.

"No ventriloquism at the table," I plead. "At least put that horrible thing in your room while we eat. Or better yet, the bin."

We sit, my da taking the helm of the table. Fionn bursts in through the back door and snatches a piece of bread, stuffing it into his mouth with a casual, "Hey, Lo," before Da demands he wash up. I pull out the chair for Lo and our eyes meet. Mam proudly ladles chowder into everyone's bowls. Da says grace, and we dig in.

They ask Cielo about her rotations, Da tells an exaggerated fishing tale, Fionn recounts a story wherein he was the hero in his team's latest match. It's likely more exaggerated than Da's fish story, but Lo is nodding along in between bites all the same. Before long, our spoons clink the bottom of the bowls, and the last of the bread has soaked up the soup.

After Lo thanks my mom for the third time, I can tell she's appreciative of more than home cooking. She attempts to gather the bowls at the end of the meal and my mam shoos her away.

The people I love most, all in one place. Moving back is the right decision—I just hope Cielo still feels the same way.

"I have something for you. Come here." I lead her down the hallway.

She narrows her eyes. "Are you allowed to have girls in your room?"

"Only if I promise to keep the door open."

The guest room is generic, but over the past few weeks, I've gotten comfortable. Old clothes dug out of storage hang in the wardrobe alongside my London clothes. Fionn is right, city folk dress to impress. In Galway, being spotted at the neighborhood pub wearing anything designer will garner "fashion show" jokes and mutters of developing notions. We relish the opportunity to destroy people's confidence.

"Got you this." I hand her an LP inside a paper sleeve, feeling ridiculous. "I know you're a vinyl girl. Figured this would be the best introduction."

She slides out the record to reveal the deluxe edition of *Heaven-Bound*. Gold foil on the title shines as she flips it over to read the track listing. Lo rises up on her toes to peck my cheek. "Thank you. I'm excited to finally give it a proper listen."

Suddenly, I'm feeling shy. "There's something else I wanted you to hear. A new song I'm still fine-tuning."

"Oh my god, yes!" Lo sits at attention on my bed. It's adorable.

I grab my mandolin and sling the woven strap around my shoulder. To warm up my hands, I pluck out a quick chromatic descent, starting on the seventh fret and playing my way down to the first. "Fair warning, it's going to sound better with the rest of the band. The mandolin is really more a melody instrument. It doesn't have the full range for rhythm—"

"Just play the song already."

"I'm trying to woo you here. Let me work up to it."

Playfully impatient, she taps her fingers on my quilt. Sure, I am stalling. But I haven't performed for her in so long and Lo's opinion matters. Perhaps more than anyone else's, considering the subject matter. The advice I'd given to a nervous Callum rings true in this moment, too: It's not a performance. It's a promise.

I keep my attention on the fretboard. Fionn and I have tweaked the arrangement a handful of times and I'm working on developing the muscle memory to play it without focusing so hard. The song is bright like Cielo's intelligent hazel eyes. Energetic to reflect the way my heart kicks my sternum every time she kisses me.

Fierce and battle-ready, yeah
You're gearing up for war
But I kneel at your feet on my apology tour

Every beat, every song
All the times I've done wrong
Now I humble myself to the one who I adore
Our hearts beat in time
When our bodies intertwine
Babe I'm yours forevermore
Begging for forgiveness on the apology tour

When I dare to look up at her during the chorus, Lo is rapt. I can't help but grin right back. She brings out the best in me and I want to offer the same support to her. But first, I have to convince her that we really are better off together—especially when it doesn't match the vision of her five-year plan.

I close out the song and clear my throat. "It's, uh, something like that."

She springs off the bed and throws her arms around my neck.

"I take it you approve?"

"Wooing successful. It's incredible, A."

"Thank you for inspiring me." I press my forehead against hers. "There's one last thing I want to tell you. I gave my landlord notice to vacate today. I'm moving back to Galway. Officially."

Hope flickers on Cielo's face. It's a beautiful, delicate thing worth writing a hundred songs about.

"I know how you feel about long distance," I rush in before she can say anything, "but we aren't your parents. We'll put in the effort when I'm away on tour. We'll make it work. I love you."

"I love you, too, Aidan. Let's prove it to each other this time."

CHAPTER 28

Lo

PEOPLE CAN SURPRISE you—and rarely, it's even possible to surprise yourself. Before Lark's wedding, I was certain that Aidan and I were done forever. But nostalgia and romance are a powerful combination, and spending time together again has only reinforced how much I missed him all along.

My heart nearly burst when Aidan said he loved me. More important, he proved it by taking action. I melted into his arms when he told me he'd found a flat, finally allowing myself to revel in the sense of comfort I've only found in his embrace. His follow-through renewed a sense of hope and light in my life that I hadn't realized was missing.

Things are good now—so good that I'm waiting for the other shoe to drop. The biopsy feels like a steel-toed boot suspended from a frayed shoelace just over my head. I called my doctor and got authorized for the procedure, but haven't actually scheduled it yet. I know it's foolish to wait, but I just want to hold on to this sense of normalcy and happiness for a little while longer.

Lark and Callum are still on their honeymoon, but she screams into the phone when I deliver the news that Aidan and I are officially back together. "I knew it! I knew it would happen before we got back. Cal, you owe me a tenner!"

I laugh. "Glad I can make you some cash."

Oisín was more skeptical when I told him I'm giving Aidan another chance, but he came around when Aidan dropped off lunch for me at the hospital and included a vegan burger especially for him. Of course, Oisín's still giving me crap about my complete one-eighty, but that's what friends are for.

One person who doesn't know yet is my mom. She's got to be suspicious of the upbeat inflection of my voice as I run down the events of my week, and the general lift in my mood since the wedding, but she hasn't asked. Yet. I just want to enjoy Aidan without hearing all the ways this relationship is doomed. Our lives aren't perfect, but now we understand what we lost before. We can make it this time. When Aidan flashes me that crinkle-eye smile that makes my heart swell, it feels right.

I know I'm living in a bubble of my own creation, keeping Lark—and worse, Aidan—in the dark about my lab results. I can't help feeling that once I tell them, once I schedule the biopsy the possibility that the cancer is back will become real. I will face reality . . . soon.

Tomorrow morning, Aidan's parents are driving him to the airport in Shannon. He plans to record demos with his band as part of rehearsals in London before they fly to New York together. He pulls designer pieces that cost more than my rent from the closet of the guest room. Now I know that the image is one constructed for him.

Aidan zips the suitcase shut. "I wish you could be there with me."

"Me, too. But you don't have to feel guilty about it. It's only a week." It's not that I don't trust him to be faithful, or that I can't stand to be apart for any length of time. What makes me nervous is the way distance can become cumulative until eventually you barely know each other.

The bed dips under his weight as he sits beside me. "We'll video chat every night."

"New York's five hours behind, but we can manage."

"I'll set an alarm on my phone so we can talk when you're on lunch." He grabs his phone from the nightstand and programs a reminder. The simple act is reassuring.

"You deserve this, A. I'm excited for you."

"I'm nervous, to be honest."

I take his hands in mine. "Don't be. Everyone's gonna love the new song as much as I do."

Watching Aidan go fills me with equal parts dread and excitement. The opportunity to play the festival alongside household names is too good to pass up, but there's always been something about a packed suitcase that sends my anxiety spiking. But this isn't the beginning of the end. Two years ago, I refused to trust in us, but I've grown since then. I can deal with challenges head-on and trust that Aidan will be here when I need him. He'll come home to me.

To prove it to myself, I call the cancer center and schedule the biopsy.

The receptionist says I'm in luck: They just had a cancellation and have one opening the Monday after the festival ends.

Aidan isn't scheduled to return to Ireland by then, but that's a good thing. Less time to ruminate before the procedure and a little space to process the results by myself before he returns home. More time to figure out what to tell him. Some weight lifts off my chest as I mark the procedure on my calendar. I just hope my luck keeps.

Aidan sends me recordings of their practice sessions in London. The band is excellent, complementing his smooth tenor voice with lively energy. It's a gorgeous track, but I think I'll always be partial to that stripped-down version he played for me in his parents' guest room.

By day, I focus on my infectious disease research paper in between lectures and clinical rotations. Aidan is beyond supportive, but he's also a little distracting. I haven't felt as sharp as usual since my study sessions have been halved by all the time we've spent together.

At night, I allow myself to listen to *Heaven-Bound* on repeat. I turn off the lights to immerse myself in the sound without distractions, the way Aidan and I used to do together. And I break down in tears every time.

Dynamic, raw vocals contrast with the brightness of the mandolin. Candid lyrics tell a story of doomed love, starting with heated infatuation in track one and ending in bitter heartache with "Never Forever." Some of these songs I've heard before, although never with professional production. Others offer new revelations into the depth of Aidan's feelings for me.

If only I'd had the courage to listen to it before. If only I hadn't refused to entertain the possibility of staying together after he was discovered.

On the fourth night of Aidan being gone, when my phone

lights up with his contact photo, I dive toward it and answer eagerly. Simply hearing his voice say hello soothes my frayed nerves. This is even better, a FaceTime call.

"Hey, beautiful."

"You're way prettier than I was after a cross-Atlantic flight. It's so unfair. Did they put you in first class or something?"

Aidan smooths a hand over his beard. "I can assure you, the label is only willing to spring for economy."

"Gotta keep you humble somehow."

"That's what I have you for."

"I've always wanted to go to New York," I say. "My mom hates flying. Even though we could afford it, she never wanted to go anywhere that required air travel when I was a kid, so our family trips were limited to Six Flags, Dallas, or South Padre Island."

Aidan had never left his small village in Cork until he graduated and began busking his way through Cork and Dublin before finding his place in Galway. We used to talk about one day seeing the world together.

"We can visit when you're on Easter break. When Central Park is filled with cherry blossoms."

"Tell me about it," I say, envisioning a setting worthy of a classic rom-com.

"I did a benefit show in New York last spring. Some of these trees turn completely pink and drop huge piles of blossoms. There was a woman walking her dog, and the dog started rolling around in them. It looked so happy with all these petals stuck to its fur."

"We need to visit, if only to re-create that scene."

"Tongue slobbering and all," he clarifies. "I haven't seen

anything outside the venue this time, to be honest. We did a sound check soon after we arrived and now I have some time to kill."

"You're spending it talking to me? Get out there, sight-see like an annoying tourist!"

Aidan laughs. "What can I say? I miss you."

His admission settles between us softly, and I take a beat to let it sink in.

"Tell me what you've missed."

"Your . . . smile." He brings a fist under his chin.

"Nothing else?"

"Your voice."

"Go on."

Aquamarine eyes rove over me knowingly. Even through a screen, they're so intense. "The feel of your soft skin."

How I've missed the protected feeling of being held in Aidan's embrace. I want to reach through the phone now and touch him.

"I've missed you, too, so I've been listening to your record on repeat," I confess.

He straightens. "Do you like it?"

"Of course. Aidan, it's beautiful. I knew it would be. I just . . . didn't know if I could hear it without remembering everything. Getting emotional."

"You'd really rather forget?"

"When it hurt, I wished I could. Didn't you?"

"No. I'd never let those memories go."

" 'For a bit of warmth, I'd hold on to the burning coal. Better to burn through my palm than let go,' " I quote from one of his songs. It had made my chin quiver. When I'd been resenting the love I carried for him, he'd embraced it even when it hurt.

"It's true."

"I love the way your voice sounds in it," I tell him. "Love the bass line of the first track, all heavy and sexy."

He shoots me a mischievous smile. "You still have your speakers?"

"You know I take my hi-fi seriously."

"Will you do me a favor? Just . . . let me try something. I want to touch you."

"You're in New York," I remind him.

"Let me just . . ." Aidan trails off as he moves out of sight of his web camera. He returns with a guitar and his laptop. "There."

"There what? What are you up to?"

He leans toward the camera, filling the screen. "It's an experiment."

"Okay. Consider my interest piqued."

"I knew I could appeal to the scientist in you. Connect to this livestream I'm setting up to your speaker."

I throw him a suspicious look but comply. The sparkle in his eye is too delicious to refuse.

Configuring the Bluetooth takes a minute, then I join his private livestream. "Okay."

"Now straddle it."

My eyes widen. "You want me to hump my speaker?"

He laughs. "Kind of? Yes, I do. Lo, please. I want to see if I can pleasure you from here."

"You know, they make remote vibrators for a reason."

"Where I'm from, we make do with what we have. Good old County Cork ingenuity."

"Oh my god."

"Jaysus, that makes me sound like a right bogger."

"A little bit," I tease.

"Come on, now, I want to make you come with my music."

I gasp at his words. He wants to watch me masturbate to his voice. I have to say, I'm not opposed to an acapella orgasm.

"Isn't the sound going to be muffled by my . . . well, by my muff?" I manage to ask through a snicker. There's no possible way to say that sentence seriously. I squint at the fabric covering the speaker. "I'm putting down a towel."

"Stop making jokes and let me make you come, dammit."

Aidan fusses with a mini amp and small microphone for the output. After a couple strums of his guitar, he nods. I watch him through both my computer and FaceTime, from different angles.

It feels ridiculous, climbing onto a towel-covered speaker on my bed, but Aidan is already enjoying himself. Bossing me around, even from three thousand miles away. I don't mind. The last time Aidan was in charge, I enjoyed turning my brain off and submitting to his desires. It was actually pretty hot to place my trust in him.

Aidan hums a simple melody into his mic then presses a key to loop it on his laptop. I'm rewarded with a gentle buzz between my thighs. It's his vibrating hum, repeated until it becomes a background noise like cicadas on a summer night.

Aidan adjusts a dial, and the vibration shifts into something deeper. My shoulders soften and I lean back.

"How's that?" Reverb multiplies the lustful rumble. Needing more, I arch my back to grind against the speaker.

"Use your words." His smile kicks up. "And your hands. Take off your shirt and touch yourself for me."

"Your voice . . ." I moan, rolling my nipples in between my fingers. "It could get me there by itself."

"Good," he growls in response.

"You'd better add that," I tell him. Right away. He knows what I mean. He drags the microphone closer to his mouth and breathes a guttural sound I feel deep in my core.

I first fell in love with Aidan while he was singing lyrics filled with tragic beauty and dark, ruthless humor. Nimble fingers swept up and down the fretboard of his mandolin as I swayed from the front row at the Hare's Breath. The rest of the pub melted away and it felt like he was singing just to me. Aidan's always had a way of making the rest of the world seem far away.

Aidan's tongue glides across his bottom lip as he fidgets in his seat. His restlessness sends a different flavor of excitement through my bloodstream, desperate moans and whispered requests that fuel my own rising pleasure. I want to make him feel powerful, perfect. The way I see him.

"Don't make me do this alone," I plead. "You love to perform."

"I'll try to get over the stage fright."

Without hesitation, his pulls his shirt off and opens the zipper of his pants. It feels illicit to watch through my phone. He groans as he slowly begins to pump. With the other hand, he makes an adjustment to change the song playing. I recognize it. "All for You."

Pleasure hits me like a shock wave as his voice flows through the speaker. It's so intense, I lift myself off the vibrating surface.

"Get back there," Aidan says, eyes dark.

"It's too much . . ."

"You're just getting started."

"All for You" is propelled by a heavy, sensual bassline. The seductive energy he harnesses inspires unhinged comments on social media when anyone posts videos of him performing it.

His free hand adjusts something on his computer, and I melt into the sensation.

"Stay with me," he says. "Match my pace."

Vibrations follow the beat of the song, my pleasure climbing higher with it. But I can't make out the racy lyrics with the speaker between my thighs.

"Sing for me, Aidan . . . If it's all for me, that includes your voice."

His lips gently part, and what begins as almost a moan becomes a sustained note. He knows his instrument well and lowers the pitch. I watch as he continues to stroke himself. Not too fast. He's trying to keep control of his breathing, but I want to see him lose it.

Driven by the thought of Aidan's own voice making me feel this way, I grind harder. His lovely mouth, the very breath in his chest and the raw emotion in his heart. His lyrics about us. The shamelessness of singing about doing filthy things to me in a venue full of fans.

The next verse is interrupted by a gasp. Aidan's hand is a blur of movement on my screen. Such focus. Such desperation. All for me.

"Cielo . . ." The *o* at the end is pliable and resonant in his skilled mouth.

Whimpering and frantically seeking friction, I start to unravel. My vision goes soft as the climax crashes over me. "Let me hear you," I demand. That's all it takes for Aidan to catch up.

Labored breaths fill my ears. It's almost as beautiful as his singing. Determination and desperation play across his face as he furiously brings himself there. The corners of his mouth turn up as a deep groan escapes it. He finishes onto a T-shirt that was lying on his hotel bed.

Aidan wipes his brow with the back of his hand with a dazed look at me. "Holy shit."

"That was . . ." Different. Exciting.

"Okay." His breath is still ragged. "Good talk. Now how do I exit out of this thing?"

He reaches for the mouse like he's about to close out our video chat and leave me alone with a towel-covered speaker and an empty computer screen.

"Aidan!" If he was here, I'd toss the soiled towel at him and that wicked grin.

"How was that for a private performance?"

"Not bad, rock star." As if it wasn't abundantly obvious. I collapse onto the bed, taking my phone with me. It's probably at a horribly unflattering angle, but right now it doesn't seem to matter. This is the part where we'd jump into the shower to gently lather each other in between drowsy kisses.

Thanks to the distance between us, all we can do is watch each other. My hands scream to comb through his beard and trace that smile on his lips. His last tour was three months long, sending him across Europe. It's only been a handful of days since he left and already my heart aches.

What have I opened myself to? What kind of pain am I potentially bringing into Aidan's life by letting him get close when I might be getting sick again?

"I miss you," I admit. We've been making good on our plans

to communicate via text and phone each day, but I want to lay my head on his chest in moments like this, not watch him through a screen. "Put on a kick-ass show, then come right back."

"I belong to you. Of course I'm coming back."

He's said that I belong to him and that he belongs to me—but what have I done to show him that's true?

"Aidan . . . I'm gonna tell my mom about us. Is that okay?"

A tenderness enters his face. "Yeah, of course. Are you sure?"

"I want her to know that I found someone special."

He's told the whole world about us in song, but I never got around to telling my own mother about him. I'd been thinking of waiting until we'd been together longer, but this feels right. I'm already hiding a piece of potentially life-changing news from my mom. I want to at least be honest about my heart. Aidan is too important to keep hiding.

I just want to curl into his protective arms and tell him about the bloodwork. But this isn't the right time; I want him to land his dream producer, not distract him. When there's something concrete to share, I can tell him in person. Right now, the elevated levels of my labs are concerning, but they're too vague. It'll only endanger one of the biggest shows of his career.

Just a few more days and I'll have answers.

CHAPTER 29

Aidan

ADRENALINE COURSES THROUGH my body as I thank the audience one last time and step offstage. I feel electric. If only I could share this feeling with Cielo, fly her out with me. Cut her a sidelong glance as she listens from the wings, knowing which lyrics are meant for her. A performance of this scale is nothing like playing a pub, and I want her to share in the intense experience.

Sound techs begin shuttling our equipment backstage, and the band is already deep in a lively conversation in the wings. Personal assistants and roadies shuffle back and forth. Backstage can be chaotic, even more so with a tight festival lineup.

I pull out my mobile and bring up the text conversation with Lo. Feck, I miss her. There's a tap at my shoulder before I can even type a check-in message.

"Excuse me," a striking redhead says. A VIP lanyard dangles from her neck over a bohemian outfit. She's familiar, but I can't quite place her. Then it hits me. Emma Kinnane. Usually she's wearing Victorian clothes in a beloved BBC drama. "I just wanted to say that was a great set."

"Oh, erm, hi. Thanks so much."

"Was that last song new? It was amazing!"

Pride balloons in my chest. If she loved it, Nigel might feel the same. Martin didn't want me to introduce any new work tonight, but I added it to the set list anyway. Maybe now that he's seen the audience's response, he'll agree that it's worth fighting for.

"Yeah, tonight was its debut."

"Is it going to be on the next album—sorry, I'm a big fan but I don't mean to interrogate you."

"No, no. It's nice to hear it. I'm not sure about the track lists on the new one yet," I tell her honestly. If I can't strike a compromise with the label, the next album might sound nothing like how I envision it. "I'm a fan of your show. The second season was really powerful."

I know our teams felt being spotted together would be mutually beneficial, but I don't know how Emma felt about it, or if she was offended that I declined. I pray she doesn't bring it up.

The touring bass player claps me on the back. "Is this the girl you were tellin' me about?"

"No, this is Emma Kinnane," I tell him. "But we haven't been formally introduced yet."

She slaps a palm to her face. "Sorry. I should have included that bit of information when I said hello, huh?"

"Oh! Thought I recognized you," he replies. "The *Spinsters* show."

Extending her hand, she greets him by name. She must be a true fan. With a bright smile that probably gets her whatever she wants, she holds up her mobile. "Aidan, I know you're busy, but can I get a quick photo?"

"Of course."

Martin approaches just as Emma is thanking me again and rushing off to watch the next band perform.

"Have I got some news for you," he says.

"Spit it out, man."

"Nigel Culpepper wants to meet."

My stomach tightens. I didn't know if he'd even notice me, much less give me the time of day. "You're a fecking miracle worker, Martin, you know that?"

"I do, but I so love to hear it."

"Okay, yeah, where do I go?" I ask.

Martin shakes his head. "Not so fast. He says he'll have lunch with you on Monday."

"I can do that," I rush. It's the day after the festival ends, and my flight isn't until late that evening. God, I can't wait to tell Cielo.

"Wonderful. I've already confirmed. Now, there are some people I want you to meet," Martin says, leading me farther backstage. "Other bands from the label. They're having an after-party."

CHAPTER 30

Lo

AUNT SHARON'S SOY candles smell like ass. My mom spent a small fortune shipping them all the way from Austin because she couldn't let it go. Even if they smelled wonderful, burning them would feel like a concession to her neurotic grip on my life, so I just glare at the box full of them on my coffee table.

Aidan sent a "good night" text around midnight shortly after his performance finished, but I'd already been fast asleep. It's comforting to know he's thinking of me. Our private livestream was scorching hot, but more important, it gives me hope that we can maintain a sense of physical and emotional intimacy even when miles stretch between us.

My clock reads one P.M., but it's only eight in the morning in New York and he's definitely asleep, so I don't bother with a message that might wake him. Instead, I check tasks off my list after getting home from my lecture, including "turn in infectious disease case study" and "pay the electric bill." One last thing to do: my weekly video chat with my mom to let her know those stinky candles arrived safely.

Changing her ringtone to Godzilla's roar was Lark's idea of a joke, but the monster's battle cry might be more unsettling than humorous. Though switching my mom's avatar to a giant angry iguana was a stroke of genius.

"Hey, Mom. Thanks for the candles." I hold one up and try not to breathe in. "They're cute."

"You're welcome. Make sure to call Aunt Sharon and let her know which one is your favorite."

My mouth stretches into a forced smile. "I'll do that."

"I don't think we ever talked about your annual appointment—"

"Mom, I'm seeing someone." Not the way I wanted to begin this conversation, but I needed an emergency reroute from that subject.

She blinks and I can practically hear the gears in her head turning in the silence that hangs between our phone screens. "Who is it?"

"Aidan. You met him at the wedding."

Her expression darkens. "The musician."

"Yeah, he's a songwriter. A really gifted one, too."

"This isn't a good idea."

"Well, I'm not asking for permission, I'm letting you know."

"I'm sure he's very charismatic, with his guitar and his accent—I get it, I was once young, too—but you're smarter than that. You know how this story ends and it's not with another wedding."

Defensiveness flashes in me. "Don't assume that my relationship is doomed because you and Dad couldn't make it work."

"What's his last name again?" She's already opening her

browser to search him out, no doubt. The woman does more snooping than an NSA investigator.

"O'Toole with an 'e.' But let me save you some time: He was raised in Cork. Studied law and worked as a solicitor before he made it big. He's the oldest of three siblings and his parents are still together. In his spare time, he volunteers at the hospital. What else do you want to know?"

"You spend every day in a building full of doctors," my mom says, rubbing her eyes. "You really couldn't find anyone at work to date?"

"Trust me to know who I want to be with." I stare back at her. "Aidan's a good guy, Mom. Just give him a chance."

Exasperated, she sighs. "Don't say I didn't warn you."

It's only a matter of time until she circles back around to the question about my last appointment, so I make an excuse about studying and end the call. My blood is hot from her judging Aidan so unfairly.

No sooner have I opened my textbook when my phone vibrates. Hoping it's him, I reach for it, but do a double take at a new message from my mom. It's simply a link with the headline, "I Fall in Love All the Time: Songwriter Aidan O'Toole Talks Inspiration."

It's a clip from a radio interview from about a month ago. Aidan sits between two hosts in a studio. One is practically salivating over him. "I fall in love all the time," he tells them, going on to describe his writing process and dodge a question about who his muses are.

My mom might've meant it as a "gotcha," but I'm familiar enough with his lyrics to know that his only album has a sole muse. Each song is full of specific references to our story. He wanted to keep his inspiration private; I respect that. Besides, this interview was recorded before we got back together. He wouldn't have been in the wrong to casually date at the time.

Before I can respond, she sends another link.

A gorgeous redhead in a crochet dress fills the screen. Assuming it's an ad, I almost scroll by before I realize she's at Harvest in the Park. My eyes snag on Aidan's name in the caption.

"If you've had your eye on rising star Aidan O'Toole, it looks like *Spinsters* star Emma Kinnane has beat you to him," the post reads. The next image is a selfie together with her arm around him. "The two were spotted getting cozy backstage after the Irish singer-songwriter performed a sultry new song at a music festival in the Big Apple."

My heart drops.

"Oh, A. What have you done?" I mutter, scanning the rest of the post by an entertainment page that follows the cast of the Victorian-era drama. Apparently, this Emma Kinnane had shared the selfie with a caption of *Talent, looks, I'm in love!* Hundreds of comments pour in saying they're a cute couple and asking more about Aidan.

Only hours before these photos were taken, I'd told Aidan that I was going to tell my mom about us. She's already impossible to please. My boyfriend being the subject of gossipy speculation doesn't help. Anything I say in his defense will just sound like denial to her. Aidan is loyal, and I know when we were together before he never strayed. But on the road, there are simply too many opportunities, too many after-parties and VIPs. I'd also think someone dating a sexy singer was delusional if they insisted he's always faithful when surrounded by adoring fans.

Had Aidan changed his mind about being seen with that

actress and not told me? I can't imagine he'd expect me to go along with the world thinking he's in a relationship with another woman . . . but who knows what his label could have said to pressure him? I know how high the stakes are for his career right now.

Emma could be a genuine fan, I reassure myself. Lots of people would caption a photo with their favorite singer that way. Or it could be exactly what it looks like. No. I don't believe he'd hurt me like that, but what if fame really had changed him and I just couldn't see it? I can't help but think that maybe I should have listened to the voice inside that warned that loving him was a dangerous game to play with my heart.

A splash of water hits the screen, blurring the candid photo of the actress throwing her arms around the man I love. I put my phone face down. I can't believe I'm crying over this. It could be nothing at all. Or it could be the moment that ruins everything I've been too scared to admit I want. Somehow, Aidan got me to believe we weren't destined for failure, but I'm a scientist. All evidence points to this having been a lost cause from the start.

Determined to give him the opportunity to explain, I pull myself together and tap out a text. Good morning! Give me a call when you're up.

———

THE DAY THAT started off so productive and promising turns to shit. During my evening rotation, I mispronounce *escitalopram* in front of an attending and a couple other shadowing students who snicker at me. When a resident quizzes me on the treatment for mesenteric ischemia, I rattle off the protocol for ischemic colitis instead.

All because of those photos. Aidan hasn't said good morning to me yet. He's a night owl, and I expect he stayed up late after the performance. Briefly, I wonder if he went to bed alone. I hate thinking it about him, but I'm spiraling. Maybe he'd be better off with someone like Emma, graceful in the spotlight and used to traveling for work. Someone who wouldn't hold him back.

The man drives me to distraction, even when he's not around. And I'm beyond fatigued. It's a bad sign, considering the test results still floating around in my mind. Maybe a symptom of something much more serious than stress.

When I find a spare moment, I slip into an empty patient room and check my messages. Nothing from Aidan yet. I sigh and slump down onto a chair to alleviate my aching legs.

I'm afraid to open up my newsfeed. The photos of him and Emma Kinnane were staged, or real, or nothing but a friendly interaction with a fan . . . but I don't want to see them. Worse, I'm afraid that I won't believe his explanation when I do hear from him.

Instead, I open my email to find a message from my mom. Reminding me that I never followed up with her about the doctor's appointment.

CHAPTER 31

Aidan

I SLING AN arm around the warm body in the bed next to me, before I remember that it can't be Cielo. My eyes spring open.

"Rise and shine, princess."

"Martin!" He wasn't in my room when I fell asleep, but now he's lying fully dressed beside me on top of the duvet. With a cursory glance around, I confirm that he's the only uninvited guest. "How did you get in here?"

"I always keep an extra hotel key for my clients in case of emergency."

Dragging the covers over myself, I mutter, "Go away."

"Next time, I'll pour an ice bucket down your balls. We have twenty minutes before you need to be onstage for sound check."

Is he taking the piss? I tear the duvet off my face and study him.

"I'm here because you weren't answering the phone." Martin rises to his feet. "Now sober up and put some trousers on. I just ordered us a cab."

"I'm jet-lagged, not drunk." He knows better than that; he's the one who called me "minus craic" at the afterparty when I declined shots with an indie rock quartet.

Unwinding never comes easy after the adrenaline rush of a live set, especially one as high-pressure as Harvest in the Park. Time zones weren't much of a concern on a tour that only spanned Europe and the UK, but this was five hours' difference on top of the exhaustion of an emotional performance to such a large audience.

"Your stylist sent a few wardrobe options for tonight's show. They're already in the dressing room at the venue," Martin informs me, distracted by his mobile. "I told you to wear what they provided yesterday . . ."

Although I'd packed what they curated, I'd decided to wear my own clothes at the last minute. Martin had chewed my ear about it, but I'm more comfortable onstage when I feel like myself.

He holds his screen up triumphantly. "Look at this. Now that's the kind of publicity that gets you noticed!"

Whatever was in the write-up for the festival performance, it must be flattering. Did they like the new song? The sensual beat and personal lyrics made it the most charged piece of music in the set.

"'Irish singer-songwriter Aidan O'Toole and English rose Emma Kinnane turn up the heat backstage after his Harvest in the Park set,'" he reads aloud.

My smile drops. I snatch the device away. "Wait, what is this?"

A candid photo of Emma and I backstage fills the screen. She's on her tiptoes with her arms around my neck. And the caption says she's "in love."

Oh fuck.

My voice sharpens. "Did you do this?"

"She honestly wanted to meet you! Aidan, she's a huge fan and she's wonderful for your brand. Young women aged twenty-one to twenty-nine are her show's biggest demographic, exactly the audience that will lose their minds over you." Martin lifts his palms in placation. "But I didn't set it up. I did monitor her feed, though. When she posted about attending the festival and her selfie with you, I might've forwarded that to a few websites to give it a little boost."

"Come on. We talked about this—she seems like a lovely person, but I don't need that."

"My Google Alerts for you have been dinging all morning."

"Are they even talking about the music, though?"

"The song is fine," he says. That's not very enthusiastic for my strongest piece of work since "Come Here to Me." "It'll be a lot better if you can get Nigel on board."

Gee, thanks.

The comments on the post are a mess. Objectifying me. Comparing me to other people Emma has been romantically linked with and to the fictional love interest on her show. Asking, "Who?" Only two comments on the post mention the festival performance or my music. Shaking my head, I hand the mobile back to Martin.

"People are buzzing about you. Which is exactly what we want," he asserts. "You have the attention of Nigel Culpepper right now, just like you wanted. Do you know how many artists would kill for a chance to work with him?"

"You're messing with my personal life here. I'm in a relationship now."

"With your ex! Moving back to Galway is a bad move and you know it. You're on the brink and you need to get your head in the game."

"Where I live doesn't matter as long as I show up when I'm needed. And I'm showing up, aren't I?"

Martin raises his brows meaningfully. Okay, so maybe it's not the best reply when I'm already running late to sound check.

I shake my head. "I'm here. Even after I told you I needed time off and you signed me up for this fest without asking first anyway."

"Need I remind you that you have a matter of weeks until your second album is due?"

"This is my integrity, Martin," I argue. "I don't want to make dance music or date celebrities or be treated like a fucking Ken doll. If I don't believe in the music for the album, I won't do it."

"You're talking career suicide. Meanwhile, I'm doing everything I can to get you on the international map. You'll thank me later."

"There's a line you don't cross." Lo is going to think I changed my mind and agreed to be publicly linked with Emma Kinnane without talking to her first.

"Look, we need to be in Central Park in ten minutes," he reminds me, pushing me out the door.

In the cab, I check my phone for the first time and find a sweet "good morning" text from Lo from hours earlier, asking me to call. I scrub a hand down my face and watch the buildings pass as we approach Central Park. I've got to call her, but we're already running late and this is a conversation I'd rather not have in front of Martin and the driver.

I love her. Lo needs to know I am hers, wholly, unequivocally.

Before I lose her all over again. I fire off a text. Running late to sound check but I hope you're having a good day, babe. I have a meeting with Nigel on Monday! Can't wait to tell you everything.

What I need to say shouldn't be sent over a text message. And I don't want to bring her attention to the gossip situation before I can explain, in case she hasn't seen it yet. But I hope this message tells her that she's in my thoughts, no matter how far away I am. When I have good news, she's the first one I want to share it with.

My stomach twists as the minutes tick by without acknowledgment.

CHAPTER 32

Lo

"I KNOW WHAT it looks like, but Emma Kinnane is just a fan who wanted to say hi," Aidan insists, his face scrunched up on my phone screen. The ocean between us didn't scare me a few days ago, but after playing phone tag for the last twelve hours, I feel every mile stretching between us.

"The label wanted you to do a PR relationship with her, though." I scowl at the clock in the nourishment room as it inches toward six. I just want to go home.

I wasn't expecting to be blindsided by a rumor about Aidan and another woman less than twenty-four hours before my biopsy. Then I couldn't get ahold of him for hours and doubt festered. From the uncertainty around tomorrow's procedure to the snide comments my mom sent along with the gossip site links, I'm completely off-kilter. This will come up in every conversation with my mom that so much as mentions Aidan from now until the end of time.

"Lo, I would never humiliate you like that. All that happened was she came up after our set, said she loved the new song, and we took a photo." Aidan looks deep into my eyes through the camera. "When I say that you're mine and I'm yours, I mean it. I don't want the world thinking that I'm with anyone else."

I want so badly to trust Aidan, but am I going to ignore a massive red flag because I'm scared of losing him—and facing leukemia again on my own?

People will be interested in his love life no matter who he's with. It comes with the gig and I'd thought I was prepared for that. But how will the fans treat a regular Latina med student who dares date an Irish star? How will I manage if I'm sick and a photo of me is compared against a singer he shares a stage with or a celebrity he brushes elbows with at an event? Can he stay attracted to me if he's surrounded by beautiful fans on the road, and I'm bald and bedridden back in Galway? The stethoscope around my neck, a gift from my dad, serves as a reminder that not everyone can handle the stress of loving someone who's sick. Instead of responding to Aidan's declaration when I'm feeling so uncertain, I change the subject.

"How are you feeling about the meeting with Nigel tomorrow?"

"Shitting bricks," he answers. "After tonight's set, the band and I are going to squeeze in a last-minute demo recording. Martin found a studio willing to rent out to us on short notice."

My brows pinch. He's barely slept since arriving in New York.

"Aidan, I know this meeting is huge, but I just want you to know that you're enough on your own. Your music touches people. The more I listen to the album, the more things I find to love—"

Oisín bursts through the door of the nourishment room.

"They're doing a lateral canthotomy in room 206. We need you over there right now."

"Sorry, I have to go." I frown down at Aidan's face on my screen. How can this work when we have to steal every moment together? "You're ready for this."

If only I felt ready for what's ahead of me.

I TUCK A cake under my arm and head toward the register. Yes, a whole cake because *screw it*. After a busy shift in the A&E, I'd called Aidan again to complete our conversation but he didn't answer. We hadn't even managed to say goodbye to each other, much less *I love you*. Is that how the divide starts, being too busy to say three words? Frustrated, I dragged myself to the supermarket as the streetlamps flickered to life.

All day, my mom has been texting me about the yearly oncologist appointment. I've been ignoring her, but it must look like I'm so upset about our conversation about Aidan that I refuse to speak to her. In reality, I don't know how to truthfully answer without sending her into a complete meltdown, so I haven't answered at all.

Each message escalates from the last. Guilt needles me as I read them. First, the lecture about how important monitoring is. And then she laid into me about Aidan. How it will never work and I know it. Better to know this about him now than before I really get attached. Yeah, too late for that. Each of her texts gives a megaphone to my internal doubts. The one that sent me to Tesco in search of a comforting confection just read, He'll leave you. They always do.

A lady with an overflowing cart cuts me off and the cake slips from my grasp, the plastic clamshell packaging popping open on the floor and sending it face down onto the grocery store tile.

I stare down at the ruined dessert. I just wanted to feel sorry for myself for a few minutes, in the company of a cake, but I can't even do that.

"I'm so sorry!" the woman says, but it's too late. My chin starts to wobble right there in the checkout line next to the Cadbury. "Let me find someone who works here to clean this up—"

Mortified, she runs off and abandons her cart at the end of the line.

It's all too much: Aidan with that beautiful woman, my mom berating me for being dumb enough to date him in the first place, my bad blood test results, the dropped cake. My breath starts to come faster and my eyes fill. I'm spiraling. I need Lark, but she's on her honeymoon.

"Lo?"

Saoirse walks up, the handle of a basket tucked into the crook of her elbow. She cringes at the splatted cake at my feet, then takes a long look at me.

I take a shuddering breath to try to keep it together. "Hey."

"Are you okay?"

For the first time in weeks, I tell someone the unvarnished truth. I don't have to protect Saoirse's feelings or manage my expectations or worry about upholding a reputation. "No. I'm pretty awful at the moment, thanks for asking."

"Is it . . . Aidan?" she asks cautiously.

My chin drops to my chest. "It's a long story."

"I've got time."

Saoirse steps out of line and motions for me to follow her down an aisle. "Forget the cake. Do you mind drinking the garbage wine that comes out of a box?"

***

SAOIRSE SLIDES MY phone back across my coffee table. On the screen are Aidan and Emma Kinnane. "Maybe Emma didn't even mean for her post to start rumors, you know? She's mentioned Aidan's music in an interview before. That's probably what gave his team the PR idea in the first place."

"I believe him when he says he didn't agree to a PR stunt," I tell her. "I don't think he'd disregard my feelings like that. It still sucks, though. My mom will be forever convinced he's a cheater. She's been calling me a delusional fangirl all day."

"Oof, parents are tough."

"I'll drink to that." I take a swig and grimace at the robust notes of nail polish remover and cough syrup. My cheeks are starting to numb, but my emotions are still vivid.

"I'll tell you one thing: A guy has never said the kind of things to me that Aidan has sung about you." Saoirse sips her wine. "The last one I went out with used to come into the flower shop every week and buy a bouquet. He said they were for his mam. After four dates, I ran into him and his girlfriend at a coffee shop. With their infant twins. Turns out that all our dates were during nights she'd stayed with them in the NICU."

"If I were you, I'd rip him in half with my bare hands. Right in front of his babies."

"You terrify me," Saoirse says, laughing. "But I can't say I didn't want to. I tracked her down and sent her proof of his cheating that night. A couple months later, she emailed me an update that she'd left him and took the house and the dog."

She's strikingly beautiful, with a warm heart. It's a shame that she can't seem to find anyone worthwhile.

"Can I tell you something?" I ask, separating the purples out of a handful of Skittles. I pile them up on the coffee table. We've chewed through two bags already. Rather, I have and she's grabbed a few discarded currant-flavored ones. "I don't know if you know this, but I had leukemia in high school."

"I remember."

"I've been NED—no evidence of active disease—for a long time, but you still have to get a checkup every year. This last one was . . . scary."

She scoots closer. "It's back?"

"Maybe. Probably. I have a biopsy tomorrow afternoon to confirm."

"Will Aidan be back in time?"

I shake my head. "It's okay. It might take a few days to get my results back anyway."

Saoirse's face hardens. "He didn't want to be here for you?"

"He has his big meeting with that Nigel Culpepper—"

"Oh, screw that guy!" Tipsy Saoirse is a real girl's girl.

"This is a huge deal for him, so I didn't say anything about the appointment."

"Wait. He doesn't know? At all?"

"No one knows about the lab results but you. Until there's concrete news to share, I just want to keep it to myself."

She looks at me like that's the saddest thing she's ever heard. No doubt she means well, but I hate it. "You're going alone?"

"Yeah. It's cool. I'm an independent woman." If I'm getting sick, that's probably for the best. Relying on Aidan now will only make the heartache worse if he lets me down later. I think about the scissors inked on his arm and how much it hurt to cut him from my life before.

"I'd go to the clinic with you, but I have a baby shower to set up. Maybe I can move something around—"

"It's not a big deal. Really. And focusing on this meeting is the right choice for Aidan."

"It's not a choice if you don't let him know what's going on," she says.

"He can't do anything at the appointment anyway. It would only distract him. Between Harvest in the Park, recording the demo, and the meeting, he's got a full plate. I wish he could be here with me, but it's just horrible timing."

"Hey, it's okay to be scared. I'd be scared, too." Saoirse can see right through the final wall left standing between Aidan and me. I might as well be honest with her.

"It's not just the cancer. I mean, that's a huge part of it, but this thing between Aidan and me, I worry that it's doomed to fail. My performance during rotations is slipping. I need to put more of myself into it. Aidan will be recording and touring again soon. And if these results come back positive . . ." I wring my hands and try to focus anywhere but her eyes.

"What, you think he wouldn't be there for you in a worst-case scenario? Which, it might not be."

It sounds so simple, but it's not. She hasn't experienced it like I have. It's not something he'd consciously decide out of shallowness, but it would come between us sooner than later.

"My greatest fear is getting sick and being abandoned for it again. Having to go through it alone. My first real boyfriend cheated on me while I was hospitalized."

"Unbelievable."

Buzzed and emotional, I plow on. "My own dad couldn't stand being around me because it was too depressing."

She stares at me in disbelief. "Your dad? Wasn't he at Lark's wedding?"

"Yeah, but we haven't talked since. And he's the last person I would tell if I was sick again. It just . . . brings up lots of painful memories. Sometimes love isn't enough and people can't handle it when things get hard. Aidan might not be able to handle it."

"Look, I can't guarantee it'll work out between you two, but I do know Aidan wouldn't ditch you for having cancer or see it as some kind of flaw. You can't make him out to be a villain here when you haven't let him know what's happening."

I sigh. That's fair. I haven't given him a chance to be there for me.

"And you don't have to be this perfect ice queen all the time. You've got to be vulnerable from time to time or else you'll have a breakdown and find yourself crying in Tesco."

I give her a small smile. "Thanks for rescuing me back there."

"Don't mention it." She tosses a Skittle into her mouth. "No matter what happens, you're not going through it alone. You've got me. You've got Lark."

The boxed wine glugs as I refill my cup under the spout. "Thank you, truly, but I'm sick of talking about this. Let's talk about something else."

"Is this the part where I'm meant to lament the guy with twins? Because I already forgot his name."

"Just tell me what's new with you. Got any more weddings booked?"

Saoirse swirls her glass. "Well, the museum is having this botanical art exhibition and they want me to do the event design for their opening gala."

"Seriously? That's amazing!"

"You know, when I was setting up for Lark's wedding, this guy . . ."

I lean forward at the change in her tone and she hides her pink face behind her glass. "Oh my god, tell me."

"He was a right bollix."

"He was hot," I translate.

Saoirse laughs. "Long hair. Big brown eyes. Very . . . sturdy. Just my type, really. Until he insulted me and my work."

"Who was he? Was he a guest?"

"At first, I thought he worked for the castle, but he's an event planner. Gabriel something."

"Point me to him and I'll kick his sturdy ass."

"I think someone beat you to it. He was using crutches."

"You think I won't beat someone with their own crutches for trash-talking my friend?"

CHAPTER 33

Aidan

TODAY HAS BEEN a blur, from nearly missing sound check to the increased attention during the second night of the festival thanks to Emma Kinnane's post. At least a dozen people have asked if we're dating. I've explained that we're fans of each other's work; nothing more than that, but most of them probably just think I'm being discreet.

Lo and I haven't talked beyond that one prematurely ended conversation since that photo of me and Emma started making the rounds. I'm not sure I convinced her that there's nothing to worry about. The conversation was rushed, with Lo stealing a few minutes between patients while I was herded between festival events. Something in her tone felt distant. After she'd hung up in a hurry, I realized neither one of us had said *I love you*. I feel awful; I'll make it up to her with a special—distraction-free—date when I return to Galway on Tuesday.

Martin pulled some strings and secured us a late-night session in a recording studio in Brooklyn where the touring band and I have rehearsed and recorded three tracks for a demo to give to Nigel. It's far from perfect, but there's a rawness that lends itself well to the lyrics. At least it gives him an idea of what I'm going for with this album.

The clock above the recording booth reads two A.M. I set my mandolin down. "All right, everyone. We've got what we need. Thanks so much for all your hard work tonight. Our plane back to London leaves tomorrow night, so get some rest."

These aren't finished versions of the songs, but they're strong. Lyrically, musically, emotionally. This is on track to be a solid album and I couldn't have done it without Lo. I'll try to convince the label to let me record it—with or without Nigel's help—but now I know for certain that I can't release some inauthentic garbage in its place.

Lo had said I can't control how well the album will do, only how well I make it and how much I fight for it. She'd said that my parents wouldn't want me to perform shite music so they can retire. But if the label and I reach an impasse and I go into debt for breach of contract, we'll all be without the safety net I built and my professional reputation might be irrevocably harmed in the process. This risk feels selfish, but I don't know if I can continue to respect myself if I don't take it.

Should I send Lo files of the demo tracks? I want her to hear what we have, but I also want to be with her when she hears them for the first time. Lo's days are packed and I've been keeping strange hours, so our text responses are on a delay thanks to the time difference. It's difficult for our conversations to maintain their momentum, but I want her to share in the excitement of this moment.

Martin's been watching from the mixing board with a canned cold brew and an unimpressed scowl. "Your meeting is at noon at a place in SoHo called Garnish. You get one chance with a guy like Nigel. That means no sleeping in, no running late. If he feels disrespected, he walks."

"Nothing could stop me from being there, with bells on," I tell him. "Thanks again for setting that up."

My phone lights up with a call from Saoirse. I don't think she's ever called me; we tend to communicate through text and memes. And it's early morning back home. Excusing myself, I step into the hallway of the recording booth as the rest of the band gathers their instruments and caffeinated drinks of choice.

"Hello?"

"Aidan, d'you have a minute?" My stomach drops at the urgency in her voice.

"What is it? What's wrong?"

A beat passes and I hear her draw in a deep breath. Is Fionn in trouble? He might've asked her to bail him out, rather than get family involved.

"Saoirse, what is going on?"

"Look, you need to talk to Cielo. Today. This morning."

My internal alarms are blaring. "Is this about the rumors about me and that actress? Because it's not what it looks like," I say and internally kick myself. I sound straight out of the cheater's handbook.

"It's not just that," Saoirse answers.

Goddamn it.

"I don't want you to think that of me, either. But right now is really not a good time. Lo's already at work. I'll call after she should be home from rotations. Today I have—"

"The meeting with the producer, yeah . . . and she has a bone biopsy at four forty-five."

"I'm sorry, did you just say Cielo has a biopsy? Like on *her*, not a patient?"

She sighs. "She's gonna hate that I told you, but you need to know how serious this is. They think her cancer might be back."

It feels like the floor drops out from under me. No. No, no, no. Cielo is finally back in my life and now she might have to fight for her own?

"But she's healthy," I protest. "This must be a mistake. I just saw her. She's grand."

"Aidan, she had her bloodwork done and the results weren't great."

"She told you?" Bile creeps up my throat at the thought of losing her forever, followed by hurt that she kept this from me when I'd opened up to her about my fears. "She told you and not me?"

"Lo didn't even tell Lark. But I ran into her last night at just the right moment and we got to talking."

Cielo has been scared, needing comfort. Of course she wouldn't want to share it with me if she thought our relationship was on the rocks.

I've got to make this right.

CHAPTER 34

Lo

FUCK. MY. LIFE. A neighbor's car alarm wails, each sound of the horn ripping through my skull. Beams of light stream into my bedroom. I retreat under the covers like a nocturnal beast into a cave. Who let it be so obscenely bright at five?

Wait.

I jerk the blanket down—immediately regret it—and search my bedside table for my phone. When it doesn't awaken, I scuttle toward my kitchen. Nausea kicks me in the stomach, and I make a swift detour to the restroom.

"Tasting the rainbow" is only good on the way down. On the way up, it's an unholy, artificially colored mess that I thankfully (mostly) contained in the toilet. The porcelain tile is cold under my knees and I'm afraid of what will happen if I stand up too fast again, but I've got to find out what time it is.

The microwave proclaims it's not five. It's six.

Oh god. My heart rate surges. I'm already supposed to be starting my rotation in the A&E.

Saoirse's day at the flower shop begins early, so she didn't sleep over, but an empty box of wine and a few Skittles littering my coffee table confirm that she was in fact here and not a figment of my drunken imagination. Ugh. I never want to lay eyes on a single piece of rainbow-colored candy or cheap wine ever again. The next few minutes are a whirlwind of teeth brushing, face washing, downing a coconut water with aspirin, and giving up on my hair. In a panic, I toss my dead phone into my bag along with my stethoscope and speed to the hospital.

Today, I need to feel in control—but the universe is reminding me that I'm basically careening toward a cliff with the brakes and steering cut—I can't even have one last normal day before it all comes crashing down.

Tears wet my cheeks as I drive. For so long, I was determined to get by on my own. Now that Aidan's back in my life, I realize that's not what I want. His warmth and unwavering support have carried me through challenges before and I crave them again now. I need them now. *I need him.* Although all I want to do is lean on Aidan, I love him too much to lay my burdens on him at such a pivotal moment.

But I don't know if I can do it without him.

What kind of woman would I be if I can't even go to a clinic by myself? Maybe I really don't have what it takes to be a doctor. If I can't even handle my own thirty-minute outpatient visit when I know how dire the stakes are, how do I expect to carry the emotional weight of working with sick children day in and day out? Even in the unlikely event that the biopsy comes back clear, this might be a sign that I'm simply not cut out for this job. I think of the kids dancing to Aidan's guitar as he did a dorky dance in the rec room. Marie's shaggy hair that took forever to grow back. My chest constricts.

It's six-thirty when I arrive at the hospital, nauseated from more than just a hangover. I pull it together and soak my tears up with the sleeve of my white coat. I've already been excused for the latter half of the day for my biopsy. The last thing I need is to be late on top of it. The attending gives me a sharp look but doesn't comment on my tardiness. A small blessing.

CHAPTER 35

Aidan

"I CAN'T DO this meeting today—" I say as I enter the recording studio after the call with Saoirse. The rest of the band coils cables and tucks instruments into their cases in between yawns.

Martin slings an arm around me. "Don't lose your nerve now, mate. Get some sleep. I promise you'll feel better in the morning. You've been burning the candle at both ends all weekend, but I promise it'll all be worth it when you're back on the Billboard."

I step away. "You don't understand. Something's come up. An emergency."

"Your family?"

"Yes, it's Cielo. She needs me."

"What, she can't handle a little competition from Emma Kinnane?"

My jaw tightens. "It's not like that."

His lips purse. "I knew this would happen if you spent too much time in Galway."

I'd believed him when he told me that I needed to be in London when we started working together. Now, I wonder if part of his reasoning was isolating me from the people in my life. "I need to be there today."

"This is your career, Aidan. And I called in a lot of favors to get you this meeting."

"I know, and I appreciate it so much. You made the impossible happen. But I just can't, not right now. Nigel will either understand that or he won't."

"Don't count on it. You need to ask yourself: Is this girl worth it? She shredded your heart once before."

Heat rages through my veins, making my blood boil. Cielo Valdez is worth everything. I wouldn't even be here if it wasn't for her. For her belief in me. For the way she makes me feel. I would risk anything for her, including another broken heart, for the chance to be hers again forever. Something tells me that if she doesn't think I can show up for her today—and she already must think that, if she didn't tell me about the biopsy—then I might have already lost that chance. I've been so focused on this meeting with Nigel, and so worried about what Lo thought about that thing with the actress, that I missed what was really upsetting her. I have to show up for her today; I have to put everything on the line. The risk is terrifying, but the reward is irresistible.

"This is your only chance with Nigel. Want to be on the cover of *Rolling Stone* or on a playlist of one-hit wonders?"

It's probably shortsighted to fire my manager when I'll need help navigating my career post-label breakup, but I can't stand the sight of his face one more minute. I draw in a deep breath.

"Martin, this isn't working."

———

"YOU JUST MISSED a flight to Shannon, boarding ended ten minutes ago." The ticketing agent frowns into her monitor.

"What about Knock?" I ask through a pained smile. I'm exhausted, having gone non-stop for the past week, but I do my best to turn on the trademark Irish charm that Yanks love to go on about. "Is there anything you can do?"

"I'm sorry, the earliest flight for Knock is five-fifteen this evening." Knock is about the same distance as Shannon, both about an hour's drive from Galway.

Immediately after unceremoniously firing Martin, I'd returned to the hotel, stuffed my clothes into a suitcase, and grabbed my mandolin, heading straight to JFK airport without a wink of sleep. Desperate to hear Lo's voice, I'd tried to ring her from the cab. It went straight to her voicemail each time. Through a throat tightening with unshed tears, I left a message saying that I was coming home early. That I love her.

When I hung up, I searched for last-minute flights but came up short. Surely, I reckoned someone here should be able to help me find something that would land me in Galway before Cielo's appointment.

Maybe this is the universe telling me to stay in New York and take the lunch with Nigel. I could arrive in Galway later this evening to see Lo. But no. I need to choose her now. This is the universe testing me. Asking me to prove that I'm willing to work to be with her.

"Dublin?" There's a panicked edge to the question. Taking a train from Dublin to Galway would add hours to my travel time, but if the closer airports aren't options . . .

After a few clicks, her face brightens. "There's a flight to Dublin in an hour. Only business class seats are left."

That'll get me back in Ireland by nine—two P.M. local time. According to Saoirse, Lo's appointment is at four forty-five. I just might make it.

I shove my card toward the ticketing agent. "Sold."

While I'm waiting to board, I head to the bathroom and splash water on my face. My reflection is haggard with worry and sleep deprivation. I hardly look like myself.

Cielo's eyes lit when I'd shaved for Lark and Callum's wedding. She'd caressed my smooth cheek, admitting that she'd missed my dimples. I want her to look at me like that again. I march to the nearest convenience store in the terminal and buy myself a razor.

WHEN WE LAND five hours later and I take my mobile off airplane mode, there is still no response from Lo.

Either she received my messages and is choosing to ignore them, or something is terribly wrong. I follow the route through the terminal toward the rental cars, scrolling through my contacts. Saoirse doesn't pick up. When I try the flower shop, the lad at the register tells me she's out on a baby shower delivery. Adjusting the strap of my mandolin case around my shoulder, I send a text for her to call me back and round the corner.

Holy mother of all queues.

The line of restless travelers snakes back and forth in front of the car rental counter manned by one frazzled employee. A little girl lays on the floor, whining about the dead tablet in her hands. The man behind her loudly complains that they've been waiting an hour without moving any closer. Every self-service kiosk bears a printed sign apologizing that the system is temporarily down and redirecting them to the counter.

All right, plan B: There's bound to be a train. I jog to the ground transport section and find a schedule. The next one headed toward the Atlantic Way leaves in an hour. The earliest I'd arrive would be well after six, and that's assuming there are no delays.

I walk outside, searching for the line of yellow-topped taxis, my last option. I bend at the window of the first one. "Are you willing to give me a lift to Galway?"

"Pfft. My hole I will," the driver barks.

Okay, then.

It's a ridiculous fare, one I don't blame anyone for declining. Four, five cars down, I'm beginning to lose hope. The sixth driver gently shakes her head when I ask if she's willing to make the trip.

"Wait. You're not Aidan O'Toole, are you?" she asks to my back. Guess the mandolin strapped to it tipped her off. I turn and the driver slips her sunglasses down her nose and examines my face. "You are!"

I'm in a rush, but the delighted look on her face is sweet. "I am."

"The, erm, baby face threw me off a little." She gestures to my clean-shaved jaw. "Saw you at Vicar Street back in March. I proposed to my fiancée right after you played 'Heaven-Bound.'" I'm touched she chose that moment to make such an important memory. "She said if I'd chosen 'Never Forever,' she'd have left me on the spot."

"Congratulations and thanks for coming," I say. "Your fiancée would've been right. A 'Never Forever' proposal is a red flag." That bitter tune was written just after Cielo and I broke up. I'd been stripped of my optimism, but the sarcasm of the chorus has been lost on some fans who call it romantic.

I ask her name—Caoimhe—and express my gratitude again before I start to move on to the next taxi.

"Wait."

I turn around. "Yes?"

"You really need to get to Galway?"

"Desperately. I don't have time to wait for the next train."

"On one condition: We video call my girl and you tell her hi. She'll lose her shite."

CHAPTER 36

Lo

A DOG BITE, a fall off a ladder, a man who aggravated an old shoulder injury while hurling. Even a case of food poisoning stemming from a questionable bowl of coddle at a mother-in-law's house. Those are just the handful of cases from today's busy shift I can remember off the top of my still hungover head.

Talking to Saoirse last night helped, but my mom's harsh voice continues to echo in my mind: All the ways Aidan and I won't work in the real world when his star is rising and I have yet to finish medical school, followed by residency and fellowship. Memories of my dad hardly being able to look me in the eye during his brief visits when I was hospitalized. I can't stand the thought of Aidan turning away from me like that. He was there for Marie when she was in treatment, but it's different to see a romantic partner sick.

I slip into the nourishment room. There's a little plug hidden behind the shelves of supplies; a fellow intern let me in on the secret so that I could charge my phone without leaving it at the nurses' station. With all the activity in the accident and emergency department today, this is the first time I've come to check on it since the battery was revived. Two text messages await me, one voicemail.

> **Aidan (7:28 A.M.):** Lo, please call me. I need to talk to you right away

> **Aidan (9:16 A.M.):** I'm coming home. I'll be there today. Promise.

A little gasp escapes my lips. What? Has something gone wrong with his meeting?

Another thought pops into my mind: Did Saoirse break the sacred bond of drunken trust and say something to Aidan?

Even if it's meant well, and God knows I want Aidan by my side, I don't want him to drop everything out of a sense of obligation. This opportunity with Nigel is too important for Aidan to leave because he's distracted with my problems. I won't put my neurosis ahead of his career again. The voicemail he left hours ago is a staticky mess, cutting in and out so badly that I can't make out his words above the sound of what might be an engine. Something about the hospital. Something about Martin. Nothing else is intelligible.

When I call back, it goes directly to voicemail. My heart sinks and I hang up before saying anything. There are thirty minutes before my appointment, regretfully performed in the same building as my clinical rotations, just inviting gossip about my health and competence. I try not to think about fellow med students salivating over my possible demise. I have enough time to change my clothes, pop my earbuds in.

Heaven-Bound is the most recent search on my music app. My finger hesitates over the cover image of Aidan looking heartbreakingly handsome before I give in and click it. Choosing to listen to this album right now is a weird form of self-flagellation, but I can't help it. Aidan's ardent words begin, rich and poignant in that smooth tenor, telling the world that I'm the most precious thing to him. I want so badly to believe his lyrics are true—but how can I dare to trust in a love so devoted, when I watched sickness and distance drive a wedge through my parents' happy marriage? The odds are stacked against us already.

My bloodshot eyes drift shut as a romantic mandolin melody somehow both soothes and hollows out my heart.

CHAPTER 37

Aidan

"YOU ARE A saint," I praise Caoimhe as I thrust every crumpled euro in my wallet at her.

She taps on the cab's steering wheel as we pull around the entrance of the hospital.

"You can thank me in the liner notes of your next record. Go get her!" she shouts after me as I bound out of the car.

Cielo still hasn't returned my calls, but I'm determined to show up for her, to love her with my actions and not just my songs. My heart seizes at the thought of rejection. Maybe she doesn't want me by her side and that's the reason she hasn't answered, the reason she didn't tell me about the biopsy in the first place.

I'm more than familiar with the oncology department, and I follow the twisting halls until I reach the waiting area. Everywhere beyond this point requires a nurse to buzz you in. Saoirse couldn't tell me exactly where to go, or which doctor Lo is seeing.

A few people flip through dated magazines while eighties

pop filters in softly and a TV silently plays a daytime drama. Lo
isn't here. I turn back down the hall, looking for another waiting
room, but there isn't one.

"Excuse me." Despite the adrenaline coursing through me,
I approach the reception desk. "I'm here to meet a patient. Cielo
Valdez? Has she checked in for her appointment yet?"

The young man frowns at my desperation. He's probably not
supposed to share such details.

"I don't want her to have to do this alone," I say. "Please."

He shakes his head. "She's late."

What? Cielo is many things: empathetic, studious, competitive, independent. *Punctual.* One thing she is not, is late.

"She called to say she was running late or . . . ?"

"Never showed up."

SOMETHING'S WRONG. I thank the receptionist and stalk
through the corridors with my mobile up to my ear and head to
the A&E, hoping that Oisín knows where Cielo is, but he only
knows that she took the afternoon off. All my calls go directly
to voicemail.

I start to call Fionn to see if he can give me a lift to Lo's flat,
but something I can't explain pulls me toward the hospital's
healing garden. Hedgerows curve inward, creating a meditative
spiral out of the narrow corridor in between dense green walls.
Immediately, the peace and seclusion make it feel separate from
the clinical building. I swallow heavily as I follow the path of flat
stones to the little garden at the center of the labyrinth.

My heart squeezes. There, in the clearing, Cielo sits on a

bench, head down. Her face is buried in her arms and her feet are tucked up under her body, but my soul would recognize hers anywhere. Since I learned about the test results, I've been wondering if Lo was hiding symptoms during the wedding. I've been wracking my brain thinking about what signs I missed. Minimizing her own needs for the comfort of others isn't unheard of for Lo, but I worry that I was so caught up in wanting her, in the new material and Harvest in the Park, that I missed clues of something being wrong. She's been going through this alone, even when I was right next to her.

"Lo?" I say, willing my voice not to crack under the weight of my worry.

Her head snaps up and my knees nearly buckle when her red eyes find mine. "Aidan?"

I stride toward her, scooping her into a tight embrace. She is here and she's whole. And in my arms, she's safe. Lo presses her face against my neck and sinks into me as a sob wracks her chest.

"I'm here, babe."

Having tucked her hair gently behind her ears, I can see the tip of her nose is red and tears wet her cheeks. Every protective instinct in my body wants to build a fortress around her. Lo pulls a set of earbuds out. Faintly, I can make out the song flowing through them as she holds them in her palm. Of all the music in the world, it's an acoustic version of "Heaven-Bound."

"Wait—what are you doing here?" she asks, pulling back and searching my face. "You left a voicemail, but it was all static."

"Saoirse told me about the biopsy, Lo."

"So you're here because she guilt-tripped you?"

"Of course not," I start, but Lo steps backward out of my grasp. "No one had to talk me into—"

Her eyes widen in realization. "Please don't say you threw away an opportunity to work with your hero because of a thirty-minute outpatient procedure."

My silence says everything. Finally, I rub my hands together. "You told me I don't need him."

"How could you?!"

Indignation flashes through me and I step toward her. "How could you keep me in the dark about something this important? I'm doing everything I can to show you that I'm in it for real with you this time, but you're still not letting me in."

"This is why I didn't tell you about the appointment." Lo waves a hand as if resentful of my uninvited presence in her sanctuary. "We promised we'd never get in each other's way. I don't want to be the thing that holds you back and distracts you. I refuse to be anyone's burden."

I lower my voice so it doesn't break. "I don't understand how you've convinced yourself that you're an anchor that drags me down. You're not. You could never be that. You're the stability that keeps me from getting tossed about in a storm. When we're together I remember who I am, not just who everyone wants me to be."

Fire and pain still burn in Lo's pink-rimmed eyes.

"It was your support that made me take a career as a musician seriously, after I'd all but given up." I gesture to the earbuds in her hand, still playing my own voice. "The love I have for you is what made that album resonate with people. I owe it all to you."

"Don't pretend like it's not your talent that makes people listen," Lo says. "You're an artist, and you were an artist before we met. You've dreamed of working with Nigel since you first picked up an instrument. I didn't want you preoccupied when you were already so nervous to meet him. Besides, this appointment really isn't a huge deal—"

"Yes, it is, because you're a huge deal to me and it's fucking cancer, Lo," I shoot back. Enough of her minimizing. "You hate it when other people make decisions for me about my music, right? So don't you take away my choice to be here by not even letting me know you might be sick again. Saoirse said you knew the bloodwork was off since the wedding. Do you have any idea how much it hurts me that you didn't trust me with that?"

Guilt flashes across her face. "I was going to tell you everything after I got the results and a diagnosis. Really, I was. Even if I had the biopsy today, I wouldn't get the results back for days."

"Doesn't matter. I'm yours. And you're mine. That means I'm here when you need me."

Lo's mouth opens, but instead of arguing with me, she draws in a shaky breath. "I'm sorry for not telling you."

I try to unclench my jaw and gentle my voice. "Now that you know I want to be here, I need to know the truth: Do *you* want me here?"

"Yes." At first, Lo's cracked whisper is barely audible in her crying-roughened throat, but she repeats it with conviction. "Yes, I want you here, Aidan. Every day for the past two years, I've wanted you here with me because I never fell out of love with you. You're thoughtful and talented and you're willing to fight a wild animal for me and publicly wear the ugliest sweater in existence for your mother. Then we got another chance and this whole recurrence thing just made me terrified of losing you all over again. I'm so sorry for keeping this from you."

The affirmation of Cielo's love is the balm my anxious heart needed.

"Why didn't you show up to the procedure? The receptionist said you were a no-show."

Her chin quivers. "I couldn't do it. I left my rotation early and when I got to the check-in desk, I couldn't bring myself to take that final step. And I felt so ashamed . . ."

My heart aches at the notion of Lo going through such a life-changing appointment completely by herself.

"How did you know I'd be here in the labyrinth?" she asks quietly.

"I honestly don't know. I just felt something telling me to come outside."

A breeze stirs the hedges and gently tousles her hair. Praying that she doesn't pull away again, I extend my hand. Lo's fingers are delicate and soft entwined with mine.

"There's no place that's more important for me to be than by your side—today or any other day. Just because you're independent enough to get by on your own doesn't mean you don't deserve someone who will hold your hand when you're scared, or wipe your tears when you're sad, or cheer you on when you have to do something hard. Or—"

"Or get me candy when I'm stressed," Cielo suggests.

"That reminds me . . ."

I dig into my pocket for the bag I picked up at JFK airport when I'd bought the razor. Although sealed, the packaging is crumpled from being sat on. I hold it out on flattened palms like

I'm presenting an extravagant piece of jewelry and not a beat-up packet of sweets. Part of me knows that one day, I will be proposing to her someplace beautiful. Under much happier circumstances. Lo accepts it with an incredulous shake of her head. "And there's more where that came from if you'll let me be that person for you. Let me in. Let me love you like you deserve."

"I want to love you like you deserve, too, Aidan. No more secrets. So I have to be honest: Looking at this little rainbow right now makes me wanna gag," she says with a watery smile.

Mine drops in confusion. "What?"

"I might've . . . overindulged last night with Saoirse. In wine and candy. Vile combination, in retrospect. I passed out with a dead phone battery, but as soon as I had a chance at the end of my shift, I tried to call to wish you luck. That's when I saw your messages. You've been on my mind all day." Lo swallows heavily.

"I wanna be your emergency contact. Your support system. I know you can stand on your own feet, but I promise I won't let you fall if you lean on me." My voice is hushed, but every word is true. Cradling her jaw in my palm, I lean in. "Regardless of what is going on, if I'm on tour or anything, my family is my priority. You're my family. You're the song in my heart."

"And you're mine," Lo answers, letting herself sink into my touch. Unshed tears shine in her hazel eyes as her gaze darts back toward the hospital campus. I brush a thumb over her cheek when she finally lets the first fall in front of me. "I don't want to do this, A."

"If we could trade places, I'd do so in a heartbeat. But I'm not gonna let you do this alone. If you promise to trust me, I promise to be right here."

"I promise."

Our lips press together tenderly, but there's so much emotion in the chaste touch. I press another to her forehead and Lo lingers there. We walk hand in hand back toward the hospital entrance.

CHAPTER 38

Lo

WHEN I SAW Aidan in the labyrinth, I thought it was a trick of my bleary, tear-filled eyes, but he's the real deal.

He's also a little squeamish. It's cute how he turns away when the nurse practitioner wipes the disinfectant on my bare hip before she administers the local anesthetic. Light sedation was an option, but I weighed the risks with the benefits and decided that since Aidan is here with me, my anxiety is manageable enough without it.

I'm covered by surgical drapes, lying on my side facing Aiden, who sits in a little chair. He can't see anything from this angle, which is probably for the best. Behind me, the staff speaks quietly among themselves about the procedure. We're just waiting for my hip to numb.

Aidan goes pale as he tracks the movement of someone behind me.

"Are you okay?" I ask.

He gulps audibly. "Grand. Everything is perfect."

"Let me guess: The doctor is holding a comically huge syringe?"

"Looks like a bleedin' turkey baster, it does." Aidan squeezes my hand. His calloused touch is a lifeline. "Sorry. I'm sure that isn't very reassuring to you right now."

"It's fine, I already know what it looks like. Although for a guy covered in tattoos, you sure are freaked out about needles," I lightly tease.

"I'm not half as brave as you are. You're not even scared of Marie's dummies."

The light-hearted reminder of Aidan's ventriloquism phobia makes me smile as intended, but it soon fades from my cheeks. The thin paper covering the table crinkles under my elbow as I reposition my weight uncomfortably.

"I'm scared now," I admit for the first time, just a faint whisper. Not of the procedure. I've been through this before, and while it's far from fun, it wasn't the worst thing I've had to endure. I'm scared of what might be inside me. If something insatiable and relentless is growing within. But I'm not afraid of going through it alone anymore.

Aidan leans forward in the plastic chair and kisses me softly on the forehead. It's so tender, my bottom lip wavers. In the sweetest voice, he murmurs, "That's okay. You're still the toughest bitch I know."

Holding back a laugh is impossible. It's just what I need to break the thick tension. Aidan's smile unfurls his dimples and it's like watching the sun rise in this windowless procedure room.

"I'll be right here," he assures me. "No matter what. Okay?"

"Okay."

A FEW MINUTES after the biopsy, the nurses have taken the sample to the hematology lab. They're still monitoring me for any delayed adverse effects, coming in and out of the room, but right now we're alone.

From his seat beside the exam table, Aidan strokes my hair. Still feeling the chill of exposure, I absently rub at my arms.

"Are you cold?" Aidan asks.

"The temperature of the hospital never bothers me. I'm constantly moving during my rotations, but it's different when you're dressed in a gown with half your ass out."

He unzips his backpack and pulls out the sweater covered in guitars and mandolins that his mom made. I pull it over my head, savoring the soft knit and the subtle sandalwood of his cologne.

"It looks good on you," Aidan says.

No matter what, he'd said. Benign or malignant. Considering his family's experience, he has a grasp of what that actually means. I can't believe I'd ever doubted him.

"Do your parents know anything yet? Lark?"

"One thing at a time," I say. "They'll know when I have results to share. Before then, I can't. It would scare them too much."

"If you honestly think that's best, then I trust you. But, Lo, they want to be there for you, too. Things aren't always easy, but your parents both care. A lot. They love you, just like I do. No one wants to be kept in the dark about something this important."

"I know they do. It's just . . . Will you be there with me

when I tell them? Like come over and sit with me when we do a video chat?"

"So the conversation doesn't immediately go arseways?" Aidan surmises. "Of course."

I allow myself a modest smile. "I was going to say for moral support, but yeah, that's also true."

CHAPTER 39

Aidan

IF CIELO CAN face potential cancer while barely flinching, I can surely sever ties with my record label. I have the realization as I stare at her gorgeous face on the exam table, my heart full.

Before I became a full-time musician, I worked with some damn good solicitors—one of them should be able to help me negotiate buying out my contract without destroying my professional reputation or going destitute in the process. Paying back my advance and penalties is a certainty, though, meaning I won't be able to help my parents again for a while. But I know they'd want me to stand up and keep my integrity, just like Lo does.

My phone buzzes on the little counter next to the examination table where Lo is still resting after her procedure.

Her eyes dart to mine. "Gonna answer that?"

It's probably Martin calling to convince me I've made the biggest mistake of my career and that he's the only one who can guide me to the next step of success now. No thank you to that conversation.

When I pull my phone out, Nigel Culpepper's name is on the screen instead.

"Babe," Lo says softly when she reads it. "Pick up your phone."

"He's probably only calling to yell at me."

Noisy paper crumples under her as she takes the device from my hand and places it between us. It vibrates one more time. Getting my hopes up is terrifying—but I'd done just that with Lo and been rewarded. I brace myself.

She taps to pick up on speaker and my heart races as it clicks on.

"You canceled our meeting today," Nigel says abruptly.

No *hello,* no confirming that it's me. The pause afterward is expectant, and I wonder if he's waiting for me to profusely apologize and beg for a second chance. I won't. There's only one person worth doing that for.

Clearing my throat, I respond, "Yes. I apologize for the inconvenience. A personal emergency came up. I had to travel to Galway today on short notice."

"You don't write bullshit. And I don't produce bullshit. So don't give me bullshit."

Cielo's brows silently jump. People have warned me he's blunt. Fine. I can be, as well.

"I couldn't be there today because someone I love, the person I wrote those songs about, needed me," I explain. "You're right. You don't produce bullshit and I don't write it. The songs on the demo I sent over come from something real. A real person I couldn't abandon in her time of need."

A pause settles on the line between us. Lo doesn't move. I don't move.

"I've chosen not to work with bigger artists than you for far less."

"I understand. I won't apologize for going to the love of my life's biopsy appointment." I squeeze Lo's hand.

"It's the selfishness of this industry that makes me picky about who I interact with. My time is too precious to suffer wankers with their heads up their own asses."

Nigel misunderstands me, then. But I've said my piece, consequences be damned.

"I liked the demo," he finally adds. For the first time since our conversation began, I feel like I can suck in half a breath. "There's something special here."

Lo's eyes sparkle. She's inspired all my best work, and this is no exception. She brings out the best in me.

"When can you get here for us to start working on this album?" he asks.

An incredulous gasp leaves my chest, but I don't know what to tell him. I won't leave Lo when she needs me the most. Worry replaces that twinkle in her eye. This answer will be what decides it.

"That all depends on her test results."

Her eyes pinch closed, and she squeezes my hand back.

"Good on you," Nigel says. "How about you have your manager call me when you know?"

"Actually, Martin and I have parted ways." I look over at Lo and gather myself. This was going so well, too. "And this isn't the best time for me anymore. I'm in the early process of leaving my label."

Pride fills Lo's eyes at my words. If I didn't already know it's the right decision, that alone could have convinced me. Even if they let me record this album my way, it wouldn't be because they respect me as an artist. It would be because it's a collaboration with a hitmaker.

"May I ask what happened?"

"They care about my image more than the quality of the music. That's not the kind of artist I wish to be."

Nigel is quiet for a moment. I know what it looks like: volatile and flaky. Then he says, "The timing might be better than you think." The cryptic response makes Lo and I glance at each other. "In the next year, I'll be starting my own label and I've been looking for artists to sign."

Lo's face lights up as he and I make tentative plans to discuss more after I've hired an entertainment lawyer and figured out the label situation.

"And, Aidan?" Nigel says as the conversation winds down. "I hope it's good news for your girlfriend."

"Thank you." I repeat a softer *thank you,* and the line goes dead.

"Holy. Shit. Holy shit!" Lo shouts, then cringes when she remembers where we are. She throws her arms around my neck. "Nigel freaking Culpepper wants to sign you. That just happened."

Relief settles over me. I let myself go slack and fall back onto the hospital room's stiff side chair. Lo follows, coming to rest on my chest and curling herself into my lap.

"Nigel gets it, more than Martin does," I say. "I didn't expect that."

"You fired him? And left your label? Today?" she asks.

"I haven't spoken to the label yet, but they're trying to turn me into a douchebag. You were right, I need to keep my own creative control. As for Martin, he wouldn't listen when I told him how important it was to be here today. He tried to convince me to stay for the meeting."

"If I knew you were trying to cancel it to see me, I'd have done the same thing."

My hand smooths over her hair as she presses her face against my chest. "We've been apart too long. You can try, but you won't keep me away."

BACK IN LO'S apartment, we deposit our shoes tidily by the door and she tugs me by the hand toward the bedroom.

Early evening light streams through the window that faces the funeral home's rose garden. I draw the curtain shut as she collapses onto the bed still in my ugly jumper. Lying on her side, she avoids putting pressure on the biopsied hip. I claim the other side of the bed, lying down and facing her.

"How are you feeling?" I ask.

"Glad you're home." Lo reaches out and caresses my bare jaw. "Why'd you shave your beard again?"

"Because you're into my dimples. I don't care what the label's focus group liked."

"I like you however you feel most comfortable." She drops a finger into one of the dimples.

I turn to kiss the palm of her hand. "You like me?"

She smiles. "A little bit, yeah."

We might receive news that changes our lives soon. We might learn it was a false alarm. Either way, I'm staying by Cielo's side and she knows that now.

"Can I hold you?"

Lo turns and presses her back against my chest. I breathe in rosemary and drape an arm around her soft belly. It's so comforting, I assume she's drifting off to sleep until she nudges her backside against me with a little wiggle. Then she does it again. Subtle but unmistakable. I slide my hand from her stomach to graze her breasts and am rewarded with a short gasp.

"Are you sure?" She's still in pain from the biopsy and there is a bandaged wound to avoid. I don't want to rush it.

"I don't know if I can trust my own body right now. It feels like it's going to betray me," Lo answers softly. "But I can trust you to make me feel good."

She twists to face me, kissing me softly at first, then passionately. I bury my hands in her thick hair and suck her tongue until she's grinding back against me.

"I'll be gentle," I promise in between kisses. She wants to get out of her head, and I'll help her do that. "Tell me exactly what you need."

"Your hands."

Lo carefully removes her trousers and my jumper to reveal a bandage on her hip that I'll avoid, but I brush her hair off her collarbone and hook a finger in the strap of her bra, slowly taking it down one side at a time. Brushing my nose along her exposed neck, her jaw as I do. Some of the tension in her shoulders melts away when I unfasten her bra and the cups fall. She shivers as my hands brush her pebbled nipples.

Lying on my side behind her, my hands explore her voluptuous body, still relearning every swell and dip. I want to memorize every perfect inch of her. Lo guides my hand first to her mouth, sucking two fingers, then places my fingers beneath the waistband of her knickers. Soon she's clenching, keening, quivering under my touch. I grind against her for some relief, but this is all about her. I don't need anything else. Her pleasure—her escape, her grounding, her emotional rest—is more than enough for me.

Then she whispers, "I want you, Aidan."

"I'm here. I'm yours, babe."

"I'm yours." She hauls me closer, smothering me in a fiery kiss.

It only takes a few moments to slide on a condom that I grab from her nightstand. My hands trail up the small of her back to hold her firmly in place as I slide in from behind. Cielo moans and brings them back to circle her clit—I do so love it when she tells me what to do.

Despite the injury, she still takes me so well, eagerly rocking back till I'm deep and we form a cautious, slow rhythm. I can't help but look down, admiring the way her round arse jostles with each gentle thrust. Tension coils deep in my stomach as I try to make this last for her, but the intensity builds quickly. Her body is rigid, breath coming in short gasps. She's close, but she's holding on to control too tight to let it happen.

"Give in, Lo," I whisper in her ear and give the lobe a soft nibble. "It's okay to let go."

With a shudder and a delicious moan that I feel deep in my own body, she gives in. Climax surges through me a moment later. It's so intense that I can't even speak, I just repeat her name over and over.

I fall onto my back and Cielo curls into my side, resting her head on my chest. My heartbeat must be frantic under her ear, but I feel at peace when she brushes a lock of hair from my forehead.

Lo is the strongest person I know; she inspires me to be a braver man. We can face whatever the future holds together when the time comes, but in this moment, we're safe. We're home.

CHAPTER 40

Lo

"ARE YOU READY for this?" Aidan asks.

"As I'll ever be."

Before I turn on the laptop, I place the soy candle strategically where it will be visible in my webcam frame. Beside it rests the envelope containing my test results.

Aidan waves his hand in front of his nose. "Ugh. That thing really does smell like Fionn's football socks."

"I warned you." The first night he stayed over after my biopsy, I explained that my mom had sent the candle as a more health-conscious option. So he lit it. I told him that if he wasn't so perfect otherwise, I would have dumped him on the spot for making my entire apartment smell like his brother's gym bag. The scent still lingers despite keeping the windows open for the past three nights.

The Godzilla avatar on my mom's contact information in the chat window earns me an amused look, but Aidan doesn't comment.

It's no secret that I've avoided this conversation with my

parents, thinking that I know how it will go. But he's taught me that sometimes people surprise you, if you allow them to. He fusses with his hair in the little preview window for the video chat. It's sweet that he's nervous, but I hate that my mom makes us both feel that way. I scoot closer to him until we're both in the frame and hit the call button.

"Cielo, I've been trying to—" She cuts herself off abruptly when she realizes Aidan is sitting next to me. "Oh dear god, you're pregnant."

"No, no! It's not that. But I do need to talk to you about something important."

I glance at my phone. To save myself the stress of going through the whole process twice, I asked my dad to join us on the chat. He hasn't connected yet, and I don't blame him after I'd all but told him to leave me alone after the wedding. But Aidan says I have to give people a chance to surprise me.

I don't know if we'll ever repair things, but thanks to Aidan, I now know that sometimes, with a little work and a lot of humility, it might be possible.

Aidan lifts his hand in greeting. "Hi, Mrs. Valdez."

"Hi." There isn't any warmth in it. She narrows her eyes. "May I speak to my daughter alone, please?"

"Anything you have to say can be said in his company," I say, taking his hand in mine. "And we're waiting on one more person."

Right on cue, the video chat chimes and my dad pops up on the screen. Just seeing his face makes my chest squeeze with guilt at not having spoken to him since the day after Lark's wedding.

"Hey, Dad."

Confusion and concern are etched on his face when he realizes we have company.

"Dad, you remember Aidan from the wedding?"

"Mr. Valdez, nice to see you again, sir."

"Relax, Gus. She's not pregnant," my mom says.

He looks to me for explanation and I nod. "I'm not pregnant or eloping, let's just get that out of the way."

"I love your daughter very much. I'll give the three of you some privacy, but I needed to tell you both that myself."

I can't stop wringing my hands in my lap. "Mom, Aidan is here to stay. I know it's hard for you to see me in a relationship, but he's earned my trust."

She frowns. "I'm just trying to prevent you from getting hurt." It looks like she's glaring at my dad, but I can't be certain through the small square of the video chat.

"But, Mom, there is no way any of us can prevent that. You act like controlling every detail of my life will somehow keep anything bad from happening, and that's just impossible. I get it—but I'm trying to learn to let go a little."

Moisture pools in my eyes and Aidan wraps an arm around my shoulders in support.

"I got some scary news the other day . . ."

My mom sits up straighter. "When you moved to the other side of the world—"

"Mom, please. Let me finish."

Although it looks like it pains her, she respects my request.

"The bloodwork at my last appointment came back with some concerning results, so I had a biopsy." I explain to them the timeline between the annual visit and now, and why I felt I needed to wait for a diagnosis before I said anything. I also told them about the way Aidan surprised me by coming to my side when I needed him most—my mom's brows pinch together as we recount the story.

My dad wipes a tear away. "I didn't know—mija, I had no idea."

"I'm sorry for keeping it from you," I tell them. "The biopsy results came back today and it's negative."

Beside me, Aidan gives me a relieved smile. I'd have lost my mind with anxiety waiting for the results alone.

Worry still creases my mom's brow. "What was the problem?"

"Stress, my doctor thinks. It tanked my immune system and I'd been brushing off the symptoms of an infection because I just figured stress is a part of being a med student. I'm all right, really; she started me on a course of antibiotics."

"Do you need anything?" my dad asks. "Can you take a sabbatical? Or a semester off?"

"No, no. I'm going to be just fine. I only need your support, okay?"

This experience has inspired me to recommit myself to my well-being, including regular swims in the heated pool at the gym to manage my stress, and more open communication. Working in medicine will always involve pressure, but I won't burn myself out before I've had a chance to really change lives.

My dad nods, apparently eager to prove himself.

"And, Dad? I apologize for the way I treated you the day after Lark's wedding. I'd just been blindsided by the news and it brought up all these old feelings that have never been resolved." I focus solely on him. "You didn't deserve it and I'm sorry."

He wipes his eyes again. "Every day, I've regretted not being there for my girls when they needed me. I'm so proud of the woman you are, though I can't take credit for raising you. That was all your mother."

My mom raises a hand to cover her mouth.

"Dad, you taught me my work ethic and you provided for us so we could focus on my healing. It's not easy for me to forgive you for not being there . . . I don't hate you. I never did." I turn to my mom. "And, Mom, sometimes, I'm like you—trying to do it all on my own, all the time—but that's not healthy for any of us. You've always instilled in me the importance of self-care. That's what I'm working on: being gentler with myself. Communicating what I need. Leaning on others when I need to."

"You can," she assures me. "You can tell me. Lean on us."

"We want to be here for you," my dad adds.

Aidan swallows hard next to me, and I know I've struck a nerve. We all talk for a little while longer, and my parents get to know Aidan some more. Then my dad has to go. I make sure to tell my dad I love him before he signs off. It's something I regrettably didn't do at the wedding, and life is too short to hold a grudge. After I say goodbye to my mom, I gently close the laptop and collapse into Aidan's arms.

All the anxiety and doubt of the past few weeks is channeled into sobs against his solid, grounding chest. We were both relieved when we learned that my test result was benign, clinging to each other in the oncologist's office earlier this afternoon, but my catharsis was delayed. Now that I don't have to stay composed for the sake of my parents, the pent-up emotion is finally flowing through me.

Aidan runs his hand over my back. His eyes well with tears and I know he needed a release, too. I kiss his cheek and the tip of his freckled nose and the dimple I missed as I climb into his lap. It knocks him a little off balance and his elbow grazes the side table. The candle falls onto my sofa, wafting fetid scent as it rolls across the cushion toward us.

"Can we throw this manky thing in the bin now?" Aidan asks, snatching it up.

"Please!" I hop to the other side of the couch, putting distance between me and the soy wax.

Without another word, Aidan eyes my kitchen trash from his seat on the couch, stands, and tosses the jar. My mouth drops open as it sails toward the kitchen in a high arc. To my surprise, the candle swishes cleanly through the swinging lid and into the can with a satisfying crash of broken glass.

Laughter spills out of me like I'm the one who's been broken open.

It makes me feel alive. Aidan joins in my hysteria, wiping the mirth from his eyes. He's my ally and my solace. When I'm with him, I feel weightless. Delirious. The most talented and beautiful man I've ever known. He's mine. And I'm his.

I know, down to my soul, that what we share is real.

I won't take this life—this gorgeous, fierce love we've earned—for granted again.

Aidan

ONE YEAR LATER

THE HARE'S BREATH is so packed tonight that patrons spill out into the cobblestone street. Our hometown pub is abuzz for the launch of the first single off my upcoming album with Nigel's new indie label. We had to wait a year thanks to the non-compete clause in my previous contract, and buying myself out was eye-wateringly expensive, but it was worth the sacrifice to have control over my own creative destiny.

Hands-down, the new album is my best work to date. Irreverent and personal and aching with the yearning I'd pent up for years. Whether it's just me and my mandolin, or layered with rich analog texture and a full band. Instead of feeling daunted by the upcoming tour, I'm excited to share these new songs with fans.

My contract now guarantees a scaled-back tour that includes a month-long break scheduled between the European leg and North American dates to come home and recalibrate. No more performing myself to exhaustion. This time around, I'm also protecting my relationships from too much distance. During my recording and promotion travels for this album, Lo and I made sure to dedicate time to reconnect. Calls, video chats, plenty of goofy photos. With creativity and effort, I know that we'll be able to get through a little long distance.

"Everyone is going to love it, A." Lo curls up to my side in our favorite snug and gives me an encouraging squeeze.

"I'm not stalling," I protest. "I'm just soaking in the moment."

Callum and Lark usually avoid large crowds, but they're here to support tonight's event, sitting opposite us in the high-walled booth. Of course, Callum helped me write some of the music, along with Saoirse. She's already keen to start playing, conspicuously inspecting her fiddle by the stage, so I kick back this pint and get to it.

Out in the audience, my family cheers and whistles to goad me onstage. Mam insisted on knitting commemorative jumpers for the occasion, and outfitted Fionn, Marie, my dad, and Lo in colors that match the cover of the single. When Lo received hers, she hugged it to her chest and exclaimed that she's never taking it off.

Fine by me; she somehow makes the damn thing look sexy.

Cielo's fully let me in and we're stronger than ever. I try to join her a couple times a week for her swim. It's been a joy to watch her rediscover her passion for the water. Recent follow-up bloodwork confirmed that managing her stress has helped her bounce back after the health scare. What a relief. While her mom still keeps Lo's press stocked with all manner of supplements, their relationship has become healthier, and she's checking in regularly with her dad now, too.

I step up onto the tiny corner stage to deafening applause. Saoirse and Fionn grin sheepishly, instruments in hand, waiting for it to die down before they bother to start playing. I adjust the strap of the mandolin over my shoulder and pluck out the opening notes of "Apology Tour."

> *I humble myself to the one who I adore*
> *Our hearts beat in time*
> *When our bodies intertwine*
> *Babe, I'm yours forevermore*
> *Begging your forgiveness on the apology tour*

Cielo and I lock eyes. It's no wonder I feel inspired around such a headstrong, brilliant woman. When the music starts and we connect, the rest of the pub melts away. It's just us and the knowledge that these lyrics are more than pretty words. Just like she's so much more than a pretty face. These songs are our love story, forevermore.

ACKNOWLEDGMENTS

First off, thanks to you, reader, for picking up this book. I hope you enjoyed it and come back to Galway for Saoirse's story next.

I'd like to thank the folks who helped make this happen, especially my editor, Tara Singh Carlson, who believed in this story when my self-doubt crept in and who helped turn a convoluted mess into something halfway coherent and, I daresay, meaningful.

To my agent, Caitlin Mahony at WME, for her boundless energy and support. To my UK editor, Lara Stevenson, for help with Irish-isms. To Kristen Bianco, Regina Andreoni, and the rest of the team at Putnam for all their support to get these books in the hands of readers. Thanks to Taylor Bryon and the audiobook production team at Podium for bringing these characters to life and making the book more accessible.

No culture is a monolith, and it's always my intention to portray marginalized communities authentically and responsibly. Thanks to Lilia Choi Rodriguez, Ofelia, and Meg, the sensitivity readers who graciously gave their feedback on the Mexican-American representation in *Heart Strings*.

By the way, have you seen the freaking cover? Thanks to Mansi Vinay for the gorgeous illustration of Aidan and Cielo.

Thanks to my author friends who have swooned and commiserated with me during the writing process—particularly Andrea Andersen and Melissa Whitney (I owe you for the shaving idea). But everyone who has supported me in the last year, from conversation partners at events, to booksellers who have recommended *Morbidly Yours*, to the book clubs and content creators who keep this community fun and active. I'm so deeply grateful to every reader who has given my work a chance.

Also, thanks to my family for their patience while suffering from starvation and emotional neglect as I edited this.

Ivy Fairbanks is a shameless consumer of rom-com books, hazelnut coffee, and Hozier music. Not necessarily in that order. Living with Ehlers-Danlos Syndrome has made her a believer in the importance of representation in romance. Ivy writes steamy stories where realistic characters find love, acceptance, and their happily-ever-afters. She lives in the Tampa Bay area with her husband and son. At any given moment, she is probably trapped under a sleeping cat.

Visit Ivy Fairbanks Online

ivyfairbanksbooks.com
IvyFairbanksBooks
IvyFairbanksBooks